HAUNTED ECHOES & SOUTHERN NIGHTS

THE SANGUINE LULLABIES
BOOK TWO

PETER D. BAKER

Alyssa,
    Dean rules but
  castiel is best.

Peter D. Baker (signature)

Cover Art: Elderlemon Design

Author Photo: Stephanie Skeffington - Seattle Flashing Lights Photography

ISBN (Hardcover): 979-8-9856619-4-1

ISBN (Paperback): 979-8-9856619-5-8

ISBN (Digital): 979-8-9856619-2-7

PRAISE FOR THE SANGUINE LULLABIES

All the excitement and emotion sets *Rain City Gothic* apart from its peers. I would recommend this to anyone who loves mystery, adventure, and complex characters.

Rain City Gothic is a story that will wrap you up in its mystery and leave you so utterly engrossed that you'll be turning the pages until you reach that final, satisfying ending.

To my wife.

AUTHOR'S NOTE

I have strong opinions on the order in which a reader should read an author's works when they're part of a series. The correct way is to read them in the order they're released, unless otherwise stated, since publishing and licensing and rights can quickly become a gray quagmire the likes which can be a nightmare for lawyers and layman. Knowing how people operate, I wrote this so you can start with either this one or *Rain City Gothic* with no negative impact on your artistic experience.

With that out of the way, this story is a prequel. It takes place before *Rain City Gothic*, the first book of this series. If you read them in the proper order, you get to experience all the dramatic irony I could muster for the story of the Belascoe family so far. However, if you haven't read RCG yet, you could get away with reading it after this one.

Last, a warning. This book contains scenes of graphic sex and violence, strong language, and more mentions of former president Ronald Reagan than any book should allow. Reader discretion is advised.

PROLOGUE: RAPID CITY, SD, CHRISTMAS EVE, 2019

*B*ethany sat on the floor watching while Caroline and Meghan sifted through the boxes of the Belascoe family's memories. She looked at the collection of boxes piling up in the living room, paralyzed with indecision, not sure where to begin her look into the past. The grandfather clock ticked away in its constant meter, letting the three young women know the exact moment a quarter-hour passed when the innards rang their partial melody. In the fireplace, the flames flickered and flashed throughout the living room in a visual syncopation to the ticking clock, the crackling sometimes forming a lockstep rhythm with the passing of time.

Bethany meandered to the kitchen as the women pored through the Belascoe family archives. She poured a cup of coffee and grabbed a slice of pizza from the box on the counter, leaning onto it with her elbows. She took a bite, feeling a sliver of cheese falling onto her chin as she pulled the slice away. She held the mass of food in her mouth and stared at the coffee she'd poured. Coffee and movies were endemic to growing up with her father, and the machine sat on the counter near the sink, serving as a poignant reminder of his death. Despite the loss of her parents, the reminders weren't always without joy and love. She snapped out of her longing and focused on the pizza she'd bitten off. Her chewing matched the rhythm of the grandfather clock, and during their interplay, a guttural and cacophonic laugh added to the melody for the other room. Two pairs of padded feet scampered into the kitchen next to Bethany. Meghan's laughter subsided as Caroline showed

Bethany a class picture. "Look what we found." Three rows deep with ten children in a row, with a board in the center that read:

Knollwood Elementary

Grade 4 1998-1999

Mrs. Matsuda

Caroline looked at the picture and back to Bethany a few times. "Look at this outfit. If anyone was surprised you're a lesbian, they clearly weren't paying attention."

"The best part," Bethany said with her mouth partially full, "is that I could get away with wearing the same outfit now and I'd fit right in." She turned to the picture of her in a pair of overalls worn over a yellow shirt, complete with bangs and pigtails. "You may not believe it, but I even wore flannel when I got older."

"I don't think any of us are surprised by that. You're also the only one not smiling," Meghan said.

"I hated school pictures. Nobody made me laugh when we took them, and I wanted to be in class reading. Or doing anything else," Bethany said. "But at least Mrs. Matsuda didn't give me shit for it."

"Was she one of those teachers who didn't care about her job at all, or did she just let you do your thing because she was a good teacher?" Caroline asked.

Bethany finished her slice of pizza before washing her hands. She picked up the picture and looked at it. "Yeah, she was a great teacher. At least for me. Maybe she let me get away with keeping my own pace because I was 'gifted.'" Bethany used her free hand to do the air quotes. "Let's go see what else we can find in these boxes. Ideally, not my childhood pictures."

Once back in the living room, Bethany chose a box at random. She moved it closer to her, realizing it was heavier than the others. She opened it, revealing several stacks of books, with smaller books wedged in places where the awkwardly shaped books met with other awkward-looking books. Most of them were psychology and philosophy. There were a couple of classics, including *Rebecca*. Bethany flipped to the title pages in a few of the books, noticing the same handwriting for two different names. Rebecca Church and Rebecca Belascoe, respectively. She smiled at her mother's names as she removed books from the pile. Near the bottom of the stack, she pulled out a long, thin book with unassuming binding resembling a yearbook, but Bethany didn't notice a school name. The title read *From Buddha to Bowie: Jungian Archetypes in Popular Culture* by Rebecca Church.

Bethany sat cross-legged on the floor, thumbing through the pages while her partners looked over her shoulder. Bethany unconsciously relaxed as she read through her mother's thesis. Her father lauded his wife's intellect for as long as Bethany could remember, but nothing was like seeing it shine on its own accord. Page after page of her mother's brilliant and analytical mind made Bethany's heart burn for a glimpse of how different her and her father's life might have been. A single tear crawled down her cheek and leaped off, landing on a page of Dr. Belascoe's thesis. She dabbed the tear away, taking care not to mar the sacred pages of her mother's work before snapping it shut and setting it aside.

Caroline held up a browned and weathered set of newspaper clippings held together with a staple. "Look what I found," she said in triumph.

Meghan and Bethany looked at what Caroline held high. It was a newspaper headline from a cheaply made news rag from 1986 called *The Middlesboro Gazette*. The headline read "Bladenboro Beast is Beat!" The sub-header said, "Off-Duty Officer and Hero Solves One of North Carolina's Biggest Mysteries." Caroline thumbed through the clippings of the rest of the article. "If you look hard enough, you can find it on the internet like I did," she said, looking at Bethany. "Everything else I found was a bunch of rumors and innuendo, so I wasn't sure you actually existed."

"Let's keep up the subterfuge of my existence in case anyone else wants to cyber-stalk me or my dad," Bethany said as she started on another box.

"Any idea what happened to the other guys in the picture?" Meghan asked, skimming the paper over Caroline's shoulder.

Bethany looked at the photo and shrugged. "I dunno. I was really young, but there was a period of time when Dad was *constantly* on the phone for like a year after Mom died. He might have kept in touch with them that way." Bethany looked at Caroline. "You ever see anything about them?"

"No, but I didn't really try. They weren't the points of interest," Caroline said. She thumbed to the back of the paper where eager advertisers paid to feature their products and checked them over. "Look at this," she said, pointing to an ad featuring a small black-and-white photo of a man in a suit with his hands held high over what looked to be a congregation of people in a church. Behind him, sticking out like a rainforest in Antarctica, stood a giant crucifix. "It's a faith healer. Did people really fall for this shit?"

Meghan looked it over. "Have you been on the internet lately?"

"Yeah," Bethany said, "the message is the same, they just use a different medium. And it still works."

"And look," Meghan said, "Movie times. Back before you could find them on the internet and even see if there were any tickets left. Speaking of, based on that thesis over there, your love of movies really comes from your mom. She passed it on to your dad and then to you. She was talking about shadow archetypes and Michael Corleone in the small piece of the thesis I saw over your shoulder."

"Yeah, she was quite a woman, as far as I can remember," Bethany said. "I don't know if I can get rid of this place. It's not the memories. It's the only place where I feel like I can relax." Her gaze lolled across the living room, with special attention to the clock and the fireplace.

"Well, maybe you don't have to," Meghan said. "What if you rented it as an Airbnb?"

"You mean let strangers stay here?" Bethany asked.

"Yeah. You can control how long and who stays here," Meghan said, looking at the Black Hills in the distance. "I mean, look at it. It's a gorgeous place. It's quiet. The landscape isn't bad. If you like that desert vibe."

"Plus," Caroline said, running into the kitchen mid-thought to grab a slice of pizza, "you can keep some sort of money coming in. Those weird yoga people could rent it and run retreats here."

"You think they'd come *here*? There's nothing here." Bethany shuddered at the thought of social media superstars desecrating her family home.

"With the right positioning, you could sell it," Meghan said.

"Yeah, you could talk about connecting with nature or something like that." Caroline walked to the fireplace and looked around as if she were considering the value of an Airbnb. "If they have multiple people coming, you could charge a good price for renting. Plus, it'd still be yours."

"I do like the idea of it being in the family," Bethany said. "And a family using it."

Meghan turned, and sat on the couch, resting her arm on the boxes next to it. "How did you end up here from Savannah?" Meghan asked.

"It was pure chance. Mom got a job at the university and Dad was able to transfer to the department here. I was pretty young when it happened," Bethany mused. "Dad said Mom was excited she got a job so quickly. Before that, they lived in Savannah, and then they had me…"

CHAPTER ONE

SAVANNAH, GEORGIA, 1986

"Wait here," Shawn said before he popped open the door of the police cruiser. "This shouldn't take long."

Daniel tilted his head to the side as his partner hurried out of the car, leaving him alone. At least he could take advantage of the cooler temperature inside the car, which he did as he leaned back. He looked out the window as Shawn approached the worn suburban house behind the chain-link fence. Shawn knocked on the door and waited a moment. Not long after, two men came to the door. One stood at the threshold speaking to Shawn, while the other stood off to the side, slightly hunched over. By the looks of it, the man would've rather been doing almost anything other than what he was doing now.

The taller, blond man at the forefront spoke with apparent temerity as he stood upright with a proud chest. Daniel noticed how he seemed to oversell his actions and wondered what he was overcompensating for. He turned the volume down on the CB in the car and rolled the window down halfway as he leaned his head out to eavesdrop. Distance along with the background traffic stifled that idea. And it let the hot air in. As far as Daniel could tell, it seemed as if the blond was explaining something to Shawn as he gesticulated boisterously during his monologue. Shawn looked at the demure man standing behind his vocal counterpart and said something. The man he spoke to only nodded his head. Shawn and the blond man spoke again before the man waved bye. Shawn returned it with a nod before heading back to head back to the cruiser. On the walk back to the car, Shawn looked back one more time, before getting in the car with a slight frown.

"What was that about?" Daniel asked.

"Ah, it was just a couple of faggots squalling," Shawn said with the same scowl that always bedecked his face.

"So, what actually happened? Dispatch said it was domestic violence, right?"

"Yeah, but with them, it's just different. We handle it a little different," Shawn said. "They ain't like us. You'll catch on soon enough." New to the force, Daniel didn't have the gumption to speak up, but he wasn't sure what he would say even if he had the courage.

So, Daniel did what any sensible person in a disadvantageous power dynamic would have done. "We got about four hours left," Daniel said. "What's say we go grab some coffee and a doughnut?"

"Jesus, do you think that's all cops do, is eat doughnuts?"

"You mean y'all don't?" Daniel asked, forcing laughter to change the subject.

"No, we do. 'Specially when it's slow. Doughnut shops are open late or early, depending on how you look at it. I could go for some coffee. Don't know about the doughnuts. The wife says I'm gaining weight."

"I'll take two, in that case," Daniel said.

"Careful, Belascoe, you don't wanna end up like me," Shawn said, patting the beginning formation of his gut.

"Yeah, you're right," Daniel said. Shawn pulled into the Dunkin' Donuts drive-through.

"What do you want, Belascoe?"

"One jelly, one glazed doughnut, and a black coffee."

"Christ, Belascoe, you're gonna get diabetes," Shawn said.

"That's why I got the coffee black," Daniel said.

The remainder of their shift passed uneventfully. Being a rookie, Daniel couldn't take a cruiser home, so he climbed into his white, two-door, 1977 Chevy truck. He drove by the house he and Shawn were at earlier and parked outside, alternating stares between his steering wheel and the house. He waited, his thoughts meandering from anger and sadness to rage. Rage because he did nothing earlier when he was there, and he let his shithead partner handle the situation. He took what he thought was a sensible approach and wrote their address down on his hand. He stared out the window before driving off to Tondee's Tavern for the night.

Daniel parked on the street and made his way up to the bar in the tavern.

He perused a menu for a moment, closed it, and waited for the bartender. A woman behind the bar approached him, wiping dry a beer mug. A cigarette held onto her lips for dear life acting as a censer. She flicked her feathered hair to the side, looked at Daniel, and asked, "What'll it be, Danny?"

"Doris, you're the only one who can get away with calling me 'Danny', you know that, right?" Daniel searched his empty pockets before looking back at Doris.

"That friend of yours, Tim? Tom? He calls you Danny all the time," Doris said.

"Tom can, too, I guess. Before I order anything, I need a pen and paper."

"This ain't an office supplies store, honey," Doris said.

Daniel smiled at her. "You can put it on my tab if it makes you feel better."

She reciprocated his smile and handed him a pencil with a small pad of paper. He copied the address from his hand and made a few other notes before he ripped out the paper and shoved it into his shirt pocket. Daniel got Doris's attention and said, "I'll have a gin—neat, a burger, with onion rings instead of fries." Daniel lit a cigarette and zoned out for a few minutes while Peter Gabriel's "Sledgehammer" played in the background. Not long after, Doris set his gin beside him.

"Danny, something seems off. What's the matter?" she asked.

He took a long pull from his cigarette and thought for a second. "Can you sit for a minute?" He looked at Doris, hoping she would. "I have a question for you."

"Should I get a lawyer, darlin'?" she asked with a smirk as she sat down.

Daniel laughed, thankful for her levity. "No, I wouldn't arrest you. Just try not to murder me and we'll be fine," he said. "I just wanna eat the best onion rings I've ever had in my long life and talk to you." Daniel rested his hands on the table, while he tapped his foot on the ground.

"Cut the shit, Danny. You ain't even twenty-three yet. What's got you bothered?"

Daniel leaned through the cloud of cigarette smoke drifting through Tondee's like a blanket of tar waiting to coat everything in its path. "It's a sore subject, so if you don't wanna answer, that's fine, but it would help me out."

"All right, what is it?" She was growing nervous, too, with Daniel's stalling.

He leaned in further to make sure the background music didn't drown out anything he said. "When your husband, uh, hurt you, and you left him, where did you go?" he asked, with an overly delicate tone.

"Danny, you don't gotta dance around it. It happened and ain't nothing can change it. I went to the women's shelter near the pick-and-pull junkyard. Did you get a call about a wife beater or something?" she asked, flicking the ash of her cigarette as she took an almost matronly concern for Daniel.

"Not exactly. It was two men, and the guy needed help. His boyfriend, or partner, hurt him. I didn't talk to him, but I could tell the one guy was scared. Shawn ignored it, and we left."

"Well, I don't know if they can do anything, but it wouldn't hurt to check it out, I suppose. Shelter's by the junkyard and you wouldn't even notice it unless you were looking. Apparently, they keep it out of the way for safety reasons," she said.

"Thanks. I'll check it out."

"Hope I helped." She snubbed her cigarette in the ashtray and went to the kitchen. A few minutes later, Doris handed him his food and went to check on the other customers.

Daniel ate his burger and onion rings and watched the TV behind the bar with little thought to what was on and he made a note to find the women's shelter as soon as he could. He paid for his tab after he finished and went back to his house.

Once inside, he pulled out his notebook and made a to-do list. First, he would go to the women's shelter on the off chance they could help out. Daniel thought about Shawn, too. His next item on the list was to find out more about his partner. To help him think about how he would do that, he went for a walk.

He wandered around his normal sites, impressed by Savannah's history as if it were new to him. Along the way, he passed by the Eckerd's drugstore. He looked at the window ads and saw something that piqued his interest. He walked in and picked up the newly advertised Fujifilm disposable camera:

THE FILM THAT DOESN'T NEED A CAMERA

Daniel hoped the ten-dollar price tag was worth it as he left the drugstore. He made his way past the Colonial Park Cemetery down to the Cathedral of St. John the Baptist. Just before he intended to settle into a bar on West Congress Street, he noticed something in an alley nearby.

The alley was strewn with trash bags, the one closest to him rustling. He approached, realizing it wasn't a rat. A rat wouldn't be strong enough to move a bag that size. Whatever was there fervently plundered in the trash, unbothered by the rancid smell made worse by the Georgia heat. Daniel kneeled and inspected the bag and was surprised to see a tri-colored beagle. It was speckled with brown spots atop the white parts of its fur. The little guy was working on a piece of fried chicken. He put a hand on the dog and, with his other, snatched the chicken bone away from it and threw it down the alley.

"Come here, buddy. It's ok." Daniel held onto the dog's collar and looked for an ID tag. "Bentley. Yes, you look like a Bentley. Where's your home at, buddy? Wanna go find it?" Daniel cradled Bentley in his arms and walked over to a nearby payphone. He grabbed a quarter from his pocket and dialed the number on Bentley's tag and let it ring until he got the answering machine.

"Hi, this is Rebecca, I'm not in now. Leave a message after the beep and I'll call you back as soon as I can. Bye!"

"Hey, my name is Daniel. I got your number off of Bentley's tag. I saw him in an alley on West Congress, trying to eat a piece of chicken. He's fine, but since I didn't reach you, I'm gonna take him home for the night, so he's safe." He left his number and walked back home, Bentley cradled in his arms. When they walked in, Daniel set Bentley down and made his way to the kitchen. The dog trotted along behind him.

Bentley stood at Daniel's feet, wagging his tail and stepping on his new human friend's toes. Daniel opened the back door to let Bentley out and followed him. Despite growing up in it, Daniel never cared for the humid atmosphere and the way the murky air enveloped him like a thick cloak. As he looked up at the sky, he felt a light nudge on his foot. Bentley held a stick, looking up at his new best friend. Bentley dropped it at his feet and Daniel picked it up as he watched Bentley's full attention follow the stick. Daniel made a few false throws before he finally threw it across the yard. Bentley bounded after it only to retrieve it and bring it back to him. This time, Daniel reared back to throw it, but he bolted to the other side of the yard. Bentley's speed surprised Daniel. When they stopped, the two of them looked at each other, each one waiting for the other to move. Daniel threw it again and the dog promptly returned it. After playing for fifteen more minutes, they headed back in. When they came back inside, Daniel found some leftover rice in the fridge and, along with an egg, he gave Bentley a snack before he went to bed for the night.

CHAPTER TWO

*T*he next morning, Daniel woke up with an outstretched beagle next to him, while he was nearly falling off his bed. "How do you take up so much room?" he asked as he reached over to pet him. Bentley's only response was to walk up to his face and get nose to nose with Daniel and start sniffing him.

"You wanna go outside, little guy?" Before he could finish his question, Bentley bounded off the bed towards the back door in the kitchen. Daniel opened the door and watched as Bentley ran around outside, sniffing everything around the perimeter of his temporary dwelling while Daniel made some coffee. His phone rang just as Bentley bounded through the door.

"Hello?"

"Hi, is Daniel there?"

"This is Daniel...is this Rebecca, by chance?"

"It is. You said you have Bentley? Is he okay?" Rebecca asked.

"Yeah, he's great. I took him home for the night since I called from a payphone, and I didn't wanna leave him there in the alley scrounging for chicken scraps."

"That's so sweet of you."

"It's my pleasure, ma'am."

Rebecca laughed on the other end. "I'm twenty-seven; you have to wait until I'm at least thirty before you can call me that."

"Oh, I'm sorry, I didn't mean to offend," Daniel said.

"It's okay." She and Daniel both paused for a moment. "So when can we meet so I can grab him? I know it's early, and you probably have to get ready for work—"

"Oh, I'm off today. I just put on some coffee, and I was gonna make us some eggs. You can join if you'd like."

"I couldn't impose like that," she said.

"You're not. He's your dog, and he misses you."

"Yeah, I can head over."

Daniel gave her his address and put on a pair of blue jeans and a white shirt so he could appear somewhat presentable. He fried some bacon with an extra piece for Bentley, who weaved around Daniel's feet. After he plated the bacon, he fried five eggs, giving two to Bentley along with a slice of bacon, and set it on the floor for him. Before Daniel could sit down, the dog had almost finished the entire bowl. As he went to take a bite of his eggs, Daniel heard a knock on his door. He set his plate down in the kitchen while he and Bentley answered it.

A tall brunette woman with piercing, sable eyes stood on his front step. She'd pulled her hair back in a simple, high ponytail, and wore a red and white striped tank top to go along with her dark blue Jordache jeans. Daniel looked at her shoes, since at six feet, few people were taller than he was. On her feet were a pair of white Chucks. Right after he opened the door, Bentley rushed outside and sniffed Rebecca's feet with great interest. She kneeled, ruffled his head, and nuzzled him.

"He is definitely glad to see you. Come on in," Daniel said, holding the door open for her. "Grab a seat and I'll get you some coffee."

Daniel filled his favorite mug and grabbed the sugar and milk and brought it out to the living room. He watched as Rebecca added a few drops of milk and two heaping teaspoons of sugar. He raised his brow. "Think you got enough sugar, there?"

"I was trying to be polite and only take two scoops instead of my normal three," she said, turning her attention to Bentley. "You're just a little escape artist, aren't you?" She rubbed his head, which prompted him to jump up onto her lap to lie down and rub his head all over her.

"He's a good boy, and we had a blast. We built pillow forts and everything."

Rebecca sipped her coffee before she spoke again. "Seriously, though. Thank you. He's done this once before and I was worried last time, too. For an old dog, he's got a lot of spirit."

"He's old?" Daniel asked. "He acts just like a puppy."

"He's young at heart, and that's what counts," Rebecca said. "And he seems to like you, and he normally doesn't like anyone so soon." She downed her coffee as if she'd never had any before.

"It has to be the eggs and bacon. Nobody can turn those down."

"He loves food. But I think it's time to get him back." Rebecca stood up, grabbed Bentley, and headed for the door. Daniel stood at the threshold while they said their goodbyes and looked on as they drove off. Daniel looked down at nothing in particular and smiled for a moment as the world stopped around him. Though he was young, he hadn't been smitten in a while. And, maybe, intrepid. She was five years his senior and seemed to have her life put together, even if her dog had an independent streak.

When Rebecca was gone, Daniel went to the bathroom to shave, comb his short, black hair, and put on shoes, grabbing his camera before heading out into the world. He fired up the Chevy and drove over to the house he and Shawn were at the other day and snapped a few test photos and looked at the camera, confused. Was that all there was to it? He didn't know if the test photos would work, but despite having never used a disposable camera, it seemed pretty easy. He'd find out either way when he took the film in for development.

After he took his test photos, he stayed in the Chevy for a bit, peering at the house in front of him. After a few minutes, the demure man walked up his driveway in his bathrobe for the morning paper. Daniel got out of the Chevy and headed toward him, stopping just before the gate.

"Excuse me, sir?" he asked.

The man stopped and looked at Daniel. "Yeah? What can I do for you?"

"You got a minute?" Daniel asked.

"Not really, but I reckon it'd be rude to say no now."

"I'm Daniel," he said, extending his right hand.

"John. John Moore," the man said, taking Daniel's hand. He was older than Daniel by about ten years. He carried himself as if life had gradually gotten heavier and his shoulders were about to break under its pressure.

"I, uh, well. I was here. The other night. My partner and I got the call to come out—"

"Oh, that? It's nothing. My," John paused but not quick enough for Daniel to miss it, "roommate gets a little rowdy sometimes. Ain't nothing new. You know how it is when you get together with the guys and people get excited." John forced out an insincere laugh.

"It didn't look fine. And I know he's not your roommate. I don't care that he's not your roommate, either. The law applies to everyone, and we failed. I'm sorry. The system may not give a shit about you, but I want you to know I do. My name is Daniel Belascoe. If you ever need *anything*, look me up in the phone book and call me anytime. I'll do my best to help you."

John let his guard slip a little. "Thank you. That means a lot." John hugged Daniel, who stood there dumbfounded, before he reciprocated. Daniel wasn't sure what he'd done to earn John's confidence, but he hugged him in hopes that it offered the man something beyond what Daniel suspected his daily life consisted of. As the two men embraced, Daniel felt dampness collecting on his shirt and noticed a tear stain when John pulled his head away. "I will. He doesn't get like that often, though. But thank you." John paused like he wanted to say more and tapped while tapping his fingers on his thigh. Before long, he licked his lips. "How did you know?"

"Know what?" Daniel asked. "About the roommate thing?" He searched for careful phrasing as he looked at John. "My partner mentioned something to that effect, and it was a domestic call."

John hung his head lower and blushed. "He would," John said under his breath.

Daniel's attention perked at that addition. He paused, wondering whether or not to pursue that line of questioning, but one look at John, and Daniel thought it might be better to move on and file the information away for later. He continued, "But like I said, I don't care that you're not just roommates."

John raised his head and smiled. "Thank you." When he breathed the last word, his body visibly slackened.

"It's my pleasure," Daniel said. The two men turned away from each other and went back to their respective destinations. He drove to Dunkin' Donuts and grabbed himself another coffee for the day and a doughnut while he sat in the parking lot. About halfway through his doughnut, he decided to take a drive over to the women's shelter Doris told him about.

Upon his arrival, he walked up to the front door, coffee in hand. He went to tug on the handle of the glass door, but it didn't budge. The woman at the desk stared at him, with a confused look. He stood there, searching for the right words to say. The woman stared back at him for about thirty seconds, while Daniel's heartbeat quickened. Finally, she got up and unlocked the door, allowing a crack through which they could speak.

"May I help you?" she asked. Daniel wondered why she seemed annoyed.

"Uh, yeah. I hope so, anyway," Daniel said. "This is the women's shelter, right?"

The woman behind the glass door looked at him and said, "That depends on who's asking."

"I'm asking. I'm Officer Daniel Belascoe, with the Savannah Police Department." Daniel hoped his semblance of authority would make this easier.

"And?" she questioned.

Now, Daniel wondered if this was what it felt like to be a suspect in question. "I got a domestic violence call the other night and I think it could have been better handled. I didn't know where to go, and a friend said to come here because you helped her out."

"You'll have to get her to call the number first," the lady said, uneasy. "And then we see if we have the resources to help."

"Well," Daniel said, scratching his head, mostly to keep his hands occupied, "it's not a woman. We got called about two men. I want to give the victim some help."

The woman behind the door looked down before looking back at Daniel. "Honey," she said with a sigh, "we don't do men here."

"What do you mean you 'don't do men?' He's a victim." His discontent mounted.

"It's a *women's* shelter," she said. "We don't see men. I'm sorry." Quickly, she closed and locked the door, leaving Daniel outside with a coffee in hand and confusion stacked on top of it.

"Thanks?" Daniel said to the closed door. Daniel went back to the Chevy and sat inside smoking a cigarette, staring at the horizon and processing his defeat.

CHAPTER THREE

*O*n Thursday night the following week, Daniel and Shawn were on patrol when they got a call on the radio at around ten-thirty that night. When the call came, Daniel's stomach nearly re-gifted him the coffee and doughnuts he had a few hours earlier. It wasn't because of what he would see when he got there, but because of where the call had come from. They arrived at the house they'd gone to ten days prior, and a stillness basked in the streetlights greeted them, along with a bloodstained window. Daniel and Shawn walked up the driveway to the front door. The door was closed, and the house was quiet.

"You go in the front. I'm gonna go round back and check it out," Shawn said, drawing his gun.

Daniel drew his weapon and stepped onto the porch, peering into the bloodstained window. He couldn't fully see the layout of the bedroom, but he noticed two unmoving bodies inside that room. Still, in the interest of being thorough, he approached with caution and cleared the house, while taking care not to disturb anything. After checking the rest of the place, he went to the bedroom. The door was ajar, and he pushed it open and walked inside.

In front of the street-facing window, sprawled partly on the floor and partly leaning up against the wall, he saw the man he'd spoken to before. John's teeth were knocked out of his skull, and some of them lay on the floor nearby. Next to his body was a bloodied ball-peen hammer. John's jaw was cocked to the side, broken. His face was disfigured and dented, the malicious results of the hammer lying beside him, and his left eye was covered in blood and swollen. Daniel looked at the top of his head and noted it was caved in, and the coagulated blood mixed with John's hair as it stuck to his skin. Were it not for the bathrobe he'd seen him wearing before, he wouldn't have recognized him at all. He also noticed defensive wounds on John's hands in the appearance of broken fingers.

Something struck Daniel as odd. He looked at John's lower body and noticed his blood-soaked boxer shorts, too. Daniel grimaced as he held back the rising tide of bile welling up in his throat before he finally moved away.

When he stood up to collect himself his skin chilled, like a soft, cold wind set itself on top of him, and he shivered. Abruptly, the door softly closed, startling him. He looked at the window facing the street. Closed. Not even a crack. He looked back at the door. Seconds later, the sound of Shawn's footsteps crescendoed and waned throughout the house.

Daniel looked over at the other body lying next to the bed. With the blanket draped off the side of the bed, it looked like the other man had fallen off. He was lying on his stomach on the floor and appeared to have no blood on him. Daniel walked to the opposite side of the bed and saw an empty pill bottle of zopiclone next to a nearly empty bottle of wine. Without moving it, Daniel examined the medicine.

"Andrew Scott," Daniel mumbled to himself. He walked back over to Andrew's body and checked for a pulse. To Daniel's surprise, he found one. He reached for his radio and called for medical assistance, as well as his supervisor, and a detective. From there, he secured the crime scene. Daniel put on latex gloves before he went to the living body. At this close an angle, he also saw a small plastic bag with scant traces of an off-white powder that he set aside as evidence and administered first aid while Shawn finished blocking off the scene with yellow tape.

After ten minutes of Daniel administering first aid, he gained no ground on waking the man up. By then, the medical examiner and ambulances had arrived in complete hazmat gear.

"Move along, son. We don't want you mucking up the scene. Or getting AIDS from these guys." The examiner looked over and photographed the corpse and the ambulance hauled the likely suspect to the hospital.

Daniel's stomach protested at the sight and smell as he looked over the carnage. He looked at John's body, the result of systemic failure, and his own personal failure. "I'm gonna go talk to the neighbors. You wanna guard the entryway?" Daniel asked Shawn.

"That'll work," Shawn said.

Walking to the front door, the same cold wind followed him outside, dissipating when he walked over to the house next door on his right and knocked on the door. After a moment, he heard some rustling inside before an older woman in curlers answered the door.

"Yeah, what can I do for ya?" she asked. Her voice sounded as pleasant as someone gargling a mouthful of coarse gravel.

"Hi, Daniel Belascoe with the Savannah Police Department. Did you make the nine-one-one call earlier, Ms…"

"Buck. Edith Buck. Yeah, I did. Those two was always yellin' and screamin' about something or another. Tonight was the same, but it seemed to get real bad. It wasn't just the normal yellin' you know, they was screamin' and it was way worse. Real danger it sounded like, so I called y'all 'cause it felt like somethin' was wrong."

"Thank you. And roughly what time would you say this happened?" Daniel asked.

"I think I was in the middle of watchin' *Miami Vice* so maybe about ten, or a quarter past, somewhere 'round there," Edith said. "Never had a problem with 'em personally, though. They were loud but kept to their selves."

"Thanks for your time, Ms. Buck, and sorry to bother you so late," Daniel said. "Anything else you can remember before I go?"

"I couldn't hear a whole lot. Someone said something about another man involved or something like that. I hope I helped, officer," Edith said.

Briefly paranoid about the "other man," Daniel shot his eyes up towards Edith with a quick glance before he made his way to the house on the left of the crime scene. But when he knocked, nobody answered. As he turned to walk back to the crime scene, a broad shouldered woman with short, slicked-back hair and a simple pantsuit walked towards the gate looking in his direction. A gold and numbered detective's badge were the only adornments on the uniform.

"Detective Martin," Daniel said, nodding his head to greet her. She stood nearly a foot lower than he did, but her presence commanded no less respect because of it.

"What have we got here?" she asked.

"Looks like murder and attempted suicide. The lady next door made the call at around ten or so. Said they sounded worse than usual. The victim looks like he was beaten with a hammer, and his underwear was bloody. The other guy had a bottle of wine and an empty bottle of sleeping pills next to him," Daniel said.

"Thanks, Belascoe," Detective Martin said as she walked towards the front door.

Daniel readied himself and took a breath before he jogged back towards her and tapped the detective on the shoulder. "Before you go, Detective, can I ask you a question?" Daniel asked.

"Yeah, what can I do for you?" Detective Martin asked.

"My partner and I came out here over a week ago for a domestic violence call. He told me to wait, and we didn't do anything. I feel like we could've done something," Daniel said. "Is there anything I can do?"

Detective Martin sighed. "At this point? No." She took a step towards the door, stopped, and went back to Daniel. "Your partner. Ryerson, right?"

"Yes, ma'am," Daniel said, nodding his head.

Detective Martin leaned in out of anyone else's earshot. "Between me and you, Shawn's always been an asshole. He'll avoid doing work more often than not if he can help it. I'm honestly surprised he hasn't fucked up in a major way yet."

"Thanks," Daniel said. When they wrapped up at the crime scene, he hopped in the Chevy and headed to the Peach Tree Diner. He sat at the countertop and saw a familiar face waiting on the few customers left there.

"You have a rough night?" his server asked, her eyes on him when he walked in.

"You might say that," Daniel said. "How are you and Bentley?"

"Not bad. He hasn't escaped since I got him back from you. Meanwhile, I'm stuck here on a Friday covering for someone else," Rebecca said.

"Yeah, I know what it's like having people let you down," Daniel said.

"Still," Rebecca said as she smiled at him, "there are some good ones out there, too. By the way, what can I get for you?" Rebecca's eyes stayed on Daniel for several seconds after she spoke.

When Daniel noticed the intensity of her dark stare, he looked back down at his menu. "Oh, right, I forgot about that. A coffee and a bowl of cheese grits, please," he said.

"Coming right up." Rebecca hung the ticket for the kitchen before she poured Daniel his coffee. She turned back around and asked, "Are you a morning person and a night owl?"

"It depends on my work schedule. I thought I was a night owl. But then I started working nights. Plus, all the necessary things are open during the daytime," Daniel said.

"And you're a cop, right?" she asked, flicking her hair back and smiling at him.

"How'd you know?" he asked, blushing.

"The way you carry yourself and your haircut. I will admit, I was thrown off because you have a soft side, too. I saw that with the way you handled Bentley. You'd be the type to let him get away with anything, I bet," Rebecca said.

"Right on all counts," Daniel said, "but in my defense, who could deny his cute little droopy face?"

"I know! It took me about half his life to get there," she said. A bell rang and the cook in the back set Daniel's grits on the pass-through window separating the kitchen from the rest of the diner. Rebecca set the bowl down next to his coffee. "Enjoy."

She disappeared to the back while Daniel ate his grits to the sounds of Janet Jackson's "What Have You Done for Me Lately" playing in the background on the radio, with visions of the grisly murder scene he'd witnessed barging in on his reprieve. Once he finished his grits, he had a cigarette to go with his coffee. As he gazed into the haze he made, it seemed to form phantom shapes of John and his murderous partner.

He played and replayed a myriad of scenarios in his head. Talking to the police chief about Shawn. Talking to internal affairs about him. He thought about the women's shelter and couldn't help but wonder if he could do anything to help fix what amounted to a broken system that lets society's unwanted miscreants fall through the cracks.

When he finished his coffee, Rebecca placed his check on the table. Daniel picked it up and noticed another piece of paper behind the receipt. Rebecca left her phone number for him along with a note.

Looks like you had a bad night at work. If you wanna talk about it, call me. Otherwise, keep ignoring my obvious hints.

—Rebecca

PS I didn't want to assume you saved my number, so here it is again.

Daniel looked at the number for a minute and looked back up. He wondered how he didn't notice her coquettish demeanor, but in hindsight, it was there. He stuck the paper in between the cellophane and the box of his cigarette pack. When he arrived home, he had a glass of water before he settled in for the night. He fell asleep within minutes, despite all the coffee and melancholy flowing through him.

CHAPTER FOUR

*A*round nine, Daniel woke up and put on a pot of coffee. While it brewed, he walked outside and grabbed his newspaper. The picture beneath the headline startled him; there he was on the front page at his most recent crime scene. Alongside himself, he saw Shawn, Detective Martin, and the rest of the cast. He skimmed the article, but he didn't really care for the details since he was the one who arrived there before anyone could attach a narrative to the night. He didn't even recall any flashbulbs going off or news vans onsite at all. He set his paper down and savored his cup of coffee. When he finished, he grabbed his cigarettes and pulled Rebecca's number out of the cellophane, and looked at it again before he picked up his phone. He set the paper down on his counter and dialed. The phone rang a few times before a voice finally answered.

"Yeah?" A man answered as if a phone call were the biggest inconvenience he could face this early in the morning.

"Good morning to you too, asshole," Daniel said.

"You know how I feel about phone calls, Danny."

"Yeah, whatever. Are you ready to go train?" Daniel asked.

"Am I driving, or you?" Tom asked.

"It's your turn. But as your one and only best friend I also know how much you hate stopping off at Dunkin', so I'll do it," Daniel said.

"Ain't my fault I got good taste in doughnuts, and not that bull shit, ya know," Tom said.

"The doughnuts are my secret to kicking your ass every time," Daniel said. "I'll be there in a bit."

Daniel went and combed his dark mane of hair and put on a pair of gray sweatpants before he grabbed his gym bag. He hopped in the truck and headed to Tom's place, but only after he stopped and grabbed a coffee and two doughnuts from Dunkin' Donuts. When he got there, he pulled up in the driveway and honked his horn as he pulled out a doughnut and relaxed. By the time Daniel was over halfway done with his first doughnut, Tom strolled out to the Chevy and climbed in.

"Tom, is it every tall blonde guy's mission to try—and fail—to look like Ivan Drago?" Daniel asked. "I mean, you already failed at the 'tall' part."

"Better than a knockoff Sly, like you," Tom said.

"Before I eat it, you want this other doughnut?" Daniel asked, holding it between them.

"No, thanks. How the hell do you stay in shape eating that shit?"

"Skill. You'll learn all about that soon enough," Daniel said, his mouth stuffed with doughnut. They pulled up to the gym and went inside. Daniel grabbed two jump ropes and tossed one to Tom. "Ten minutes, then over to the heavy bag to warm up."

With what looked like no effort, Daniel seemed to dance through his warm-up as if he were playing hopscotch; Tom, however, soaked his entire shirt in sweat within those ten minutes. They met at the row of heavy bags and Tom hunched over, still breathing hard.

"Are we done yet?" Tom asked.

"My God, it's amazing you passed the academy," Daniel said. "How're things over on the east side, anyway?"

"Not as adventurous as they are for you, thankfully," Tom said. "I saw the front page today. Grisly stuff. You gonna be ok?"

Daniel took off his gloves and wiped the sweat from his forehead. "It's not even the murder itself that gets me." Daniel sighed, collecting his thoughts to form into words. "Yes, it was horrible and tragic. But it could've been prevented. It was a fucked up end to a fucked up sequence. The beginning of it wasn't even good. My partner and I went out to their place almost two weeks ago, right? Domestic violence. Shawn told me to wait in the car. He came back and called them faggots. Said things were 'different' for them. Tom, I don't give a damn who someone is. They're citizens of this country and they have rights. The law failed them. What if maybe I didn't listen to Shawn, and actually did my job? Maybe it could have been different. That's what's eating me up. Oh, and get this. I tried to go to the women's shelter for the guy. They couldn't do nothing for him."

"I don't hate gays or anything, but you think you can really make a differ-ence here in the South? The same south that fought for 'states' rights,'" Tom said, the sarcasm as heavy as his breathing.

"I don't know." Daniel set the rope down and stretched his hamstrings on a bench. "But I didn't become a cop because I wanted to do a half-ass job for the side of justice. I know we can't prevent every crime and solve them all, but we can at least act like we have standards, right? What would you have done if you and your partner got that call?" Daniel asked.

"Before this conversation? Man, I don't know. Honestly, I might have thought something was wrong with the guy, like he was a pussy or something. And to be honest, I wouldn't even think of it involving two guys," Tom said before he jumped up to a pullup bar to let his body hang.

"I didn't either until the other week," Daniel said. "And I can't believe Shawn didn't care."

"If it's any consolation, Shawn's a fucking asshole. Occasionally, they talk about him over at the east side," Tom said.

"Yeah, one of our detectives said the same thing," Daniel said. "You ready to hit the ring?"

"Yeah, I guess. You need to spar against someone better. You're getting too good," Tom said.

"You need to practice your footing more. Did I ever tell you what coach Frankie said? He taught me a bit of wrestling in high school. But this applies to boxing, too. The key is to make them lose balance. If there's space, and you're on offense, close it. If you're defending, make them work to reach you," Daniel said. "Also, ninety-second rounds."

"God dammit," Tom said.

The two men strapped on their gloves and gear and made their way to the ring. Daniel and Tom danced to the rhythmic beating they gave each other for eighteen minutes, with Daniel always the victor. When they finished, they went to the free weight section of the gym to finish their workout with some weight lifting and more jump roping.

"You do your lifting after the really hard stuff. Why is that?" Tom asked.

"If I train to do something when I'm tired, I can do it even better when I'm fresh," Daniel said.

"You're a smart guy," Tom said. "I still think you should do an amateur fight someday."

"Who knows? I might. But I've got nothing to prove,"

"What're you up to later? You up for hitting the town?" Tom asked.

"I'm working tonight. Plus, a girl gave me her number. You think I should call her?" Daniel asked.

"She pretty?"

"She's beautiful. Funny, too. She might be too good for me," Daniel said.

"Dipshit, if *she* thought that she wouldn't have given you her number at all," Tom said. "How'd you meet her?"

"I found her dog in an alley by a bar," Daniel said. "And the other night after the murder, I went to a diner, and she was working there."

"Sounds more meant-to-be than other stories I've heard before. Do it, Danny," Tom said.

"Yeah, I'll give it a shot," Daniel said. "Worst that can happen is we go out, and she hates me and never talks to me again, right?"

"Yeah. Or the best thing, you get married, have a dozen kids, and live happily ever after," Tom said.

"I don't know if I'm that ambitious," Daniel said.

"Well, get to work. And sign up for a boxing match," Tom said.

"Not against you. It'll be no contest," Daniel said, unable to keep a straight face. "Let's head out. I gotta take a nap."

When they got to the truck, Daniel stuck the keys in, but stopped, looking at Tom.

"Why do ya got that look?" Tom asked. "No. Don't tell me you got an idea."

Daniel licked his lips and let out a breath. He looked out the window for a while, pondering. Before he spoke, he shut the radio off to get rid of any distractions. "No. But what would you do about Shawn? That dick head's gonna make shit worse, and I know it," Daniel said, hoping for insight.

"Well, you can't fire someone for being an asshole. At least not cops," Tom said, thinking out loud. "What about his record? He got any dirt on him? The kind of dirt you could find if you looked hard?"

"Are you thinking what I'm thinking?" Daniel asked, grabbing the disposable camera from the glove box.

"Keep your eyes on the road, there's traffic."

Daniel looked at the few cars ahead of him and noticed all the space available on the road. "Yeah, it's really a bottleneck out there, I'm glad I got you here."

Tom chuckled. "I was gonna say you should talk to some people and see if you can get his file," Tom said. "You gonna go full private eye on him?"

"I dunno. It seems risky. Even if he's the only one who finds out, it's another thing to deal with."

"I guess don't get caught. This doesn't seem like it's in line with department ethics, though," Tom said.

"After this incident, I don't exactly know what the ethics are. But that doesn't make him being an asshole the right thing to do," Daniel said.

"I agree. But don't go getting me wrapped up in this and fired."

"No, bud, if anyone gets you fired it's the man in the mirror," Daniel said before he laughed at his own joke.

Daniel dropped Tom off and went to his house for a shower. Once he was out, he shaved the stubble off his face and patted it with aftershave. Before he went to lie down for a nap, he headed back to his kitchen. He poured a glass of water and reached for his phone and dialed Rebecca's number. The phone rang. And rang. It rang four more times before anyone picked up.

"Hello?" Rebecca answered.

"Hey, it's Daniel," he said. "The guy from the diner with your dog."

"Well, hello, officer. You act like I'd forget you. Or those hazel eyes that nearly burned a hole in my countertop the other night," Rebecca said.

"Yes! They *are* hazel. Thanks for noticing," Daniel said.

"So, did you call to ask me out?" she asked.

Daniel was silent for longer than he should've been. "Uh, yeah, I did. I'm off all day Sunday if—"

"What a coincidence, me too. Meet me at Tondee's at five," she said.

"Uh, yeah. Great, I'll be there," Daniel said.

"Then it's a date," she said before she hung up.

Daniel stood there slack-jawed. It was the easiest date ever planned. After a minute of disbelief, he hung up the phone and took a nap before he went to work for the day.

CHAPTER FIVE

Sunday came. Daniel woke up in a light sweat. Not because of the heat, or any nightmares. He was nervous to actually meet with Rebecca on equal footing, with no transactions of any kind imminent. It was eight-thirty in the morning, and he'd blocked his day off so he wouldn't be late for his date. He went to the kitchen and put on some coffee while he paced around his house. When he realized his coffee was still brewing and not much time had passed, he sat and calmed himself with a cigarette. He also reminded himself that even though he hadn't been on a date in a couple of years, much less touched a woman, it wouldn't be as bad as he was making it out to be.

His coffee was finally done, so he poured himself a cup. He let it rest on the counter and went outside for his morning paper. When he got back in, his short-lived front page fame was gone, replaced with one of the thousands of other possibilities the city offered for news. He calmed down as he thought about the world and his place in it; it was a big place, and comparatively, he was small. As he sipped his coffee, grabbed a notebook and started forming a plan. *First, see what Shawn's up to. Gather info on his comings and goings. Next, organize the data. Then? Cross the bridge when I come to it.*

When he finished his coffee, he threw on his gym clothes to go lift some weights. Reaching for the doorknob, and thinking twice, he doubled back in and grabbed a pair of binoculars.

To look his best, he worked out his entire upper body to pump his muscles up for the night, and focused on his back, chest, and arms, followed by a few miles of running around the block. He finished his workout and hopped into the Chevy. Before he went home, he made his customary stop at Dunkin' Donuts and got a coffee and doughnut to have while he made his next stop.

Fifteen minutes later, he parked across the street from Shawn's place. Shawn's house was an eyesore in an otherwise prim neighborhood. Vines snaked from the ground up on parts of the off-white side walls. The red door, marred by chipped paint, bade entry to what Daniel assumed was a house as disheveled on the inside as it was on the outside. Plants intermittently pushed their way through the narrow gravel pathway leading to the door, as if they were eager to get away from the owner of the house like any rational human would be.

Daniel looked at the house, bedecked by a shit-brown 1980 Pontiac Bonneville, waiting for something to happen. As he waited, Daniel ate his doughnut more deliberately than he normally did. He took care to keep his pastry hand free of sugar and glaze as he held the camera in the other. After he finished the doughnut, he had a cigarette to go with his coffee. The area in front of Shawn's house was silent, as was the rest of the neighborhood.

Midway through his cigarette, Daniel heard a rumbling crescendo in the distance. As the sound drew closer, a man driving a Harley with a set of ape hanger handlebars pulled up in the driveway. The man looked like Santa Claus if Santa hadn't slept in a few weeks and seldom ate anything of substance. The lanky biker put down the kickstand and stroked his beard before walking up the decrepit sidewalk to the paint-chipped door.

While he made his strides, Daniel snapped a photo of the biker, as well as his Harley. From his glove box, Daniel grabbed the binoculars and examined the bike. He saw a logo showing a hyperbolic gator with blood-stained teeth, baring them for the world to see. Twenty minutes later, the biker left Shawn's house with a small parcel in his hand. The emaciated Santa stashed it in his saddlebag before he sped off the same way he came.

Daniel cracked his window, the rumble audible above all the other noises of the day. A second later, Daniel shifted into gear and followed the biker. For someone so casually bigoted who seemed to give up on life, Shawn didn't seem like the type who would entertain guests unless someone forced him to.

As time and cigarette ashes passed, Daniel stayed several car lengths behind biker Santa as he drove on. The humidity cloaked him, and his air conditioner did nothing to ease his body heat as time went on. It didn't surprise Daniel when he followed Santa into the sparsely populated town of

Hardeeville in South Carolina. Daniel watched him turn into an old lumber mill.

To keep his distance, Daniel pulled off to the side of the road and grabbed his binoculars. The lumber mill was run down, if it were even in use at all. It wasn't the first of its kind; there would be many more lumber mills orphaned to the changing world, and more derelict relics would soon prosper before transforming into something else.

From where he sat, Daniel counted at least three other bikes in the parking lot, before he spied Santa walking in with his saddlebags. More waiting. More smoking. Half an hour later, and nothing still. Having finished his coffee shortly after crossing the state line, Daniel had to pee. He walked off the side of the road, through the soft, rain-soaked ground, the mud climbing the sides of his shoes. No sooner had he found a spot and stood with his dick in his hand, he heard a bike rev its engine, the first note of a choral arrangement conducted by gasoline. When he finished relieving himself, he went back to the track, grabbed his binoculars, and started the engine.

Six bikers turned left, heading right for him. With the close-up view the binoculars offered him, he saw other adornments on the bikes. Each one had a space on the right-hand side containing a metal gun rack and a twelve-gauge shotgun resting within the metal tubes. All the driver needed to do was reach behind a few inches and level it and the person on the other end would meet their maker.

Daniel dropped the Chevy in drive and hit the gas pedal, but the truck didn't seem to be moving as fast as it should. With the slow start not helping his cause, he floored it. When the back of the truck sank into the mood, he realized his slow start wasn't a start at all.

"Son of a bitch." He slapped the steering wheel and put it in reverse.

To its credit, the Chevy wanted to move...roughly an inch before sinking back down into the hole the tires had made. The bikers drew near as his window for escape shattered. He threw the truck in neutral before getting out and leaning against the tailgate. Digging his heels into the ground, he pushed his back against the tailgate. The only movement he got was from his heels sinking further into the mud. He fell on his ass into the soggy roadside. Moving to the toolbox, Daniel looked inside, hoping he had a board he could wedge under the tire to gain traction, but he found nothing.

From the corner of his eye, Daniel watched the bikers kill their engines. A few of them looked over toward the Chevy, squinting under the sunlight with their faces taut and devoid of mirth. Daniel's torrential sweating worsened. He looked like a mud wrestler who just got done with a wet tee shirt contest.

The emaciated Santa stepped off, along with a portly bald fellow wearing a vest with the gator insignia attached to it. Daniel saw them out of the corner of his eye and jumped at their unexpected arrival. He felt his heartbeat as he waited for them to say something.

"Hey, buddy," skinny Santa began, "you need a hand?"

Daniel looked at him, his friend, and the rest of the crew on their bikes and didn't perceive any threat. He took a breath and reminded himself that he had no reason to worry. They didn't know him. Right? "Yeah, I don't suppose you gentlemen have a board with you by chance, do you?"

The bald man next to Santa laughed. "No, but I think we can get you out by our own brute strength here. God damn, son, how the hell'd you get stuck, anyway?"

"I drank a lot of coffee and there's no bathroom nearby," Daniel said, wiping his hands on his pants.

"Allan," the bald man said, "why don't you and me push on the back here and he can push up front and turn her out onto the road."

"Works for me," Santa said. "Head on up there and control the wheel, son."

Daniel went to the driver's side and grabbed the wheel with his right hand and pushed on the dashboard with his left. Within seconds, they got the truck to move out of the muddy ruts.

"Turn it left!" the bald guy shouted. Daniel turned the wheel left as the Chevy finally made its way to the road, free of its trappings. Daniel grabbed a cigarette and fired it up as he leaned against the truck, a picture of humid filth.

"Hey, thanks for the help, guys. Daniel," he said, extending his hand.

"Allan," the unfortunate Santa clone said, shaking Daniel's hand. Daniel noted the surprising grip the guy had. "Next time, don't pull off into the mud after a rain." Allan started laughing at his joke, and Daniel blushed and laughed along at himself.

"You got it. I don't wanna keep you, though. Thanks again."

The two men got on their bikes and rode off back toward Savannah with the rest of their crew. Daniel finished his cigarette and headed back home, covered in mud. He did, however, have a name to go with the face of Shawn's friend.

WHEN HE ARRIVED BACK HOME, he looked in his closet and picked out his clothes for the night. He decided on a white button-up shirt and black slacks, along with a pair of loafers. Daniel figured it'd look nice and be cool enough to keep him from sweating too much because of the heat and his nervousness. He hung his clothes up on his closet door and took a shower and shaved. When he was finished, it was a quarter to one. Daniel retired to his room and took a much needed nap. While he napped, he also dreamed.

Daniel was back at the crime scene from before. He watched himself examine John Moore's body, and conspicuous by their absence, every living human was missing. As he surveyed the scene, he looked around. He wasn't sure what was happening, but as he walked around the room, he thought he heard footsteps following his movements, though they didn't quite match the rhythm of his own. Frightened, he turned around and saw nothing to indicate anyone was following him. Perhaps even more strange was the fact that the Daniel he was looking at didn't seem to do anything else besides checking John's body for signs of life. He fixated on it, and it played through like a looping video until he awoke back in his own bed.

Daniel's eyes shot open. Despite being under his blanket and the beaming sun shining through his window, he felt like he'd just walked outside naked on the coldest winter day. His heart thumped against the skin on his chest, and the sound permeated his entire house.

He stood from his bed and looked around. Like any reasonable person, he knew he'd just woken up just as he knew he had a dream. This particular one freaked him out more than any other he could recall. Daniel also never openly defied seniority in a police department before and by extension, never had to worry his colleagues were out to get him. So maybe the paranoia was justified. He walked across the hardwood floor into his spare bedroom and looked inside. Everything appeared as it should. From there, he walked toward the kitchen. As his bare feet hit the ground, the wooden beams on the floor groaned under his weight, mismatched by lighter protests behind him. When he stopped, they did too. He looked behind him, but of course, nothing was there. The syncopated sounds of the hardwood ceased as he continued toward the kitchen. It was a few minutes before two, according to the clock on the stove. He poured a glass of water and sat down on his couch to calm down and pass the time. He decompressed by watching *Back to the Future* on his barely used but new-to-him VCR.

The movie finished at a quarter past four, so Daniel donned his evening clothes and walked over to Tondee's. He checked in with the host and left his name so Rebecca could find him when she arrived. Daniel tapped his fingers on the table, his foot moving at a high tempo while he waited for her. He could see the door open and close from where he sat, so every time he caught it out of his peripheral vision, he looked up and hoped it was her. The fourth time it happened, she finally walked in.

Rebecca walked over in her high-waisted jeans and black halter top and sat down. "Good evening, officer, how are you?"

"I took a nap and watched a movie today, so I guess things are pretty well," Daniel said. After he spoke, a server came and took their drink orders. Daniel ordered a coffee along with a gin and Rebecca ordered an Abita lager.

"Was it a good one?" she asked.

"*Back to the Future*," Daniel said. "I really like it. Especially since time travel seems so interesting."

Rebecca just looked at him for a moment. "I hate to break it to you, but Doc is kind of hypocritical."

"What do you mean?" Daniel asked.

"All that shit about not knowing too much about your future. Then he saved himself, and he let Marty run wild, and then George hit Biff. It was a mess," she said before as the server dropped their drink order off.

"Yeah, but nothing bad happened, and Marty's family turned out fine, and then Biff got what he deserved," Daniel said.

"Yes, but that asshole sure as hell isn't a moral arbiter holding little scales of morality. He definitely shouldn't have watched that tape where he died," Rebecca said. "And I don't know that I would go this far, but you could even make the argument that Doc had become too powerful since he controlled time and could alter it. And if that fell into the wrong hands, imagine what could happen. What if Biff or his gang got the time machine?"

Across from Rebecca, Daniel sat there, stupefied. He took a sip from his gin. "Wow, how long have you been holding on to that?" he asked.

"For a while now. I'm really passionate about ethics. It's an integral part of the practice," Rebecca said.

"So, do I call you doctor…"

"Doctoral candidate," Rebecca said. "But when I nail my thesis defense, you can call me Doctor Church. Or Rebecca's fine, too."

Their server came back to take their food order. "What can I get for you this evening?" he asked.

Daniel looked at Rebecca. "I'll take a cheeseburger and onion rings," she said.

"Since you got onion rings, if I get fries, would you wanna share?" Daniel asked.

"I would love that," Rebecca said.

"Then I'll have the same thing, but with fries," Daniel said.

"Coming right up," the server said, "and can I get you two another round of drinks?"

"Yeah, I'll take another gin, please," Daniel said.

"I'm fine for now," Rebecca said.

"Thank you. I'll be back with that gin shortly," the server said.

"What about you, officer? Are you a moral arbiter like Doc Brown?" she asked.

Daniel squirmed in his seat like she was interrogating him. "I-I don't know. I'm still pretty new to the job and I already got hit pretty hard with something. It was kind of disappointing, too."

"May I ask what happened? Of course, if you're not comfortable, that's fine," Rebecca said.

"No, it's fine. It might even be right up your alley since it involves ethics," Daniel said. "The short version is I joined law enforcement to make a difference. And I couldn't. Ethically, I'm supposed to protect everyone, and I couldn't. Now, there's a dead man in my head." Daniel's voice crescendoed in a mixture of anger and self-defeat. "And I *tried* to reach out elsewhere to help the poor guy, but I couldn't."

"Why couldn't you?" Rebecca asked.

"I don't want to pass the buck, but I feel powerless. I'm a new guy in a big fucking system," he said, finishing his first gin and starting on the second. "Even the battered women's shelter couldn't help him out because he was a man."

"I don't know if it's any consolation, and I'm not trying to make anything about me. But the red tape and bureaucracy are like a blessing and a curse. It's nineteen eighty-six, and I got pushback from a lot of people and family. I'm twenty-seven, I don't have a kid, and I'm not married. Instead, I'm finishing up a doctorate and working my way through it. You'd think it was eighteen eighty-six having to deal with that nonsense. Is it disappointing? A little. But you have to look at the bigger picture. Objectively, it's not eighteen eighty-six. I can vote. I can get an abortion without going into a back alley and possibly dying. I think it was Martin Luther King who said something about the moral arc of the universe being long but bending towards justice. We can see that in American history."

"Yeah, but it feels so much more raw when it's in your face. Especially living in a place like this." Daniel looked through the gin at the bottom of his glass as the faces of justice flickered by like a slideshow. Shawn, a gilded face of justice. The woman at the shelter, a well-meaning employee enforcing the laggard standards of justice. John Moore, a victim of it all. "For all the good it can do, it leaves a lot behind," Daniel said into the glass before he finally looked back at Rebecca.

"Some places bend slower than others. I loved growing up in New York. But even there, it's not perfect. Is it better than rural Georgia? In some ways. In some ways not. But I wanted perspective, so I sought it out," she said. She was deep into her glass of beer and both of them were feeling the effects of the alcohol as one's passion melded with the other. During this pause, the server brought out their food and laid it before them.

The smell of meat, fried onions, and potatoes blended with the alcohol and sang to them. The two shared their side dishes as planned, and as far as Daniel could remember, it was the best burger he'd had in his young life. About halfway through, they started talking again.

"What's your goal, Daniel? I don't want to be pushy, but you have a few options. The big ones being to quit and go to the private sector and help those who need it, or affect change from within, if it's even possible. Which means you'll have to get promoted and stuff," Rebecca said.

Daniel hadn't thought about things like long term plans or goals in his short time as a police officer. Not to mention that his current extracurricular activities might well jeopardize any long term plans within the police department. He shifted his position and leaned back, pretending to appear relaxed. "Well, what about you? Are you gonna stay in the Ivory Tower?" Daniel asked.

"I hope not," Rebecca said. "I wanna open up my counseling practice. Still affecting change, just on an individual level. Or I could teach."

"I feel like you'd be good at both of them. Although you barely psychoanalyzed me at all, so far," Daniel said.

"That's what you think," she said, grinning in between bites of onion rings.

"Should I be worried?" Daniel asked.

"Not unless you're secretly an evil mastermind. No, you actually seem to care. Most men I've been around don't seem to think much about the big picture like you," Rebecca said. "It's always a focus on the narrow and the present. Not that I think that's a bad thing. You have to set a course now for the future."

"Well, yeah. I mean, we have goals, right?" Daniel asked.

"Ideally, yes," Rebecca said.

"What about your goals?" Daniel asked. "You start a practice and then what?"

"I don't know. I'd rather try that for a while," she said. "What if I don't like it?"

"Well, the good thing is you can always quit," Daniel said. "You can write or teach."

What if you don't enjoy being a police officer?" she countered.

"I dunno. But I'll figure it out," Daniel said. "Maybe I can see if things get better. For guys like John, and everyone else."

"I have a very important question for you," Rebecca said, her eyes looking at Daniel with an unrivaled intensity. "Can I have the last bit of your fries?"

Daniel's guttural laughter was mixed with mirth and gin, and it cut through the din of Tondee's Tavern. After a second, the noise resumed. "Of course you can," he said. She pulled the last three fries off his plate and they paid the bill. When they walked outside, daylight converged with dusk.

"Well, officer. Is this where we part ways?" Rebecca asked.

"Uh, well, um," Daniel spat out.

Rebecca giggled and said, "Daniel, you act like you haven't been on a date before."

"I kind of haven't. Not since a couple of years ago," Daniel said.

Rebecca smiled at him. "We can take it slow. Where'd you park?"

"Oh, I walked. The whole lack of distance makes it easy," Daniel said.

"Can I give you a ride home?" Rebecca asked.

"Only if you walk me to my door," he said.

"Then follow me." She grabbed him by the hand and led him along in the general direction of her car.

Daniel and Rebecca ambled along the street, passing by various alleys that connected with bars, the sounds of jubilation and music waxing and waning into different melodies as they passed a new place. At one such alley, two figures stood within. One was short with slicked back hair and a broad upper body. The other was taller, with longer, flowing dark hair, and as Daniel looked further, high heels. Daniel peered a little longer, the recognition he'd hoped for not quite coming clear as he slowed his pace.

The shorter figure finally caught his glimpse, and as the recognition came, both Daniel and the person looking his way turned abruptly, so as to not face each other. Daniel raised an eyebrow and looked at Rebecca. "You catch that?" he asked.

"Yeah. They probably got embarrassed that you caught them making out or something," she said.

"Why would they be embarrassed?" he asked. "People do that all the time."

Rebecca turned to him. "You should know. At least now, anyway. It's not always safe to be so open."

Daniel looked at her, confused for a moment before moving away from the subject with a nod of agreement.

They walked up the street a little more until they stopped at her white Oldsmobile 88. "Let me toss my books in the back for you."

"You remember where I live, right?" Daniel asked.

"How could I forget? You saved Bentley," she said.

"And he's been doing well since then?" he asked.

"Yeah, he's as happy as he can be. He hasn't gotten out either since then."

"He's just a free spirit," Daniel said as they pulled into his driveway. Rebecca even walked him to his door. They stood there and looked at each other. Daniel wasn't sure if it was his nerves or the food, but he definitely felt like he might unceremoniously vomit. Rebecca put her hand on his face.

"Don't be nervous," she said. "You're quite a guy."

Daniel's body tensed as Rebecca moved her hand to the back of Daniel's head. At first, he wasn't sure what was happening, so he stayed as still as a pillar. He gave in and his head, guided by her hand, floated closer to hers. She pressed her lips on his and kept her hand on the back of his head. He loosened up, closed his eyes, and breathed her in; the scent of lavender from her skin invaded his olfactory senses. On her lips, the traces of onion rings and beer lingered.

Daniel wrapped his arms around her waist as she hugged his shoulders and they brought each other closer together. After a while, she pulled away.

"Let's do it again, soon. Maybe I can enlighten your movie taste," she said before she walked away. "Good night," she called back from her car before she left.

Daniel walked inside and sat on his couch to let his heartbeat slow down. Once inside, he went to the bathroom and took a deep breath before he brushed his teeth and went to bed for the night.

CHAPTER SIX

$\mathcal{D}$aniel tossed and turned while he tried to sleep that night. His private talk with John Moore played on a loop in his memory and he couldn't help berating himself for not pressing the poor guy about something he'd said. Now, Daniel wouldn't get the chance to ask him in the hopes he'd get a direct answer.

As time passed and sleep eluded him, he figured he'd have to find some answers on his own since the one person who might talk no longer could, and anyone who was able to talk likely wouldn't. Daniel kicked his covers off and threw on a dark tee and some sweatpants before he ventured outside into the muggy, swampy air. Before he walked out of the door, he grabbed a handful of latex gloves from under his sink and a small flashlight, both of which he stuffed into his pockets. He made his way to the Chevy and fired it up, disrupting the silence of the night as he drove.

Not long after he got in the truck, Daniel found himself driving by the crime scene he and Shawn had witnessed. The street itself was quiet, aside from him the sound of his engine, and he slowed down in front of John Moore's house. He almost stopped, but thought better of it and went to the next street over. Daniel parked the truck and walked back to John Moore's place, cutting through the quiet backyards currently unwatched by any of the residents.

When he got to the backdoor of John's house, he reached for the handle, but stopped. He put two of the latex gloves on and grabbed the flashlight, and slowly opened the door in front of him. Deftly, he stepped around the crime scene tape marking the entrance and closed the door behind him. The back door led him into a small laundry area with a washer and dryer, with a disheveled stack of clothes on the washer and a few folded shirts on the dryer. In front of him and to the left, a refrigerator opposite some cabinets and a counter space, stood adorned with various magnets holding assorted lists.

As he walked into the kitchen, he noticed more counter space flanking the stove that led to an exit into the dining room. To the right of that was a partial wall leading into the living room and the front door from which Daniel entered the first time he'd come.

Daniel collected himself and looked around. He needed evidence to confirm his suspicion that Shawn and Andrew had encountered each other before. But where could he find it? He clicked the flashlight on and the beam of light pierced the darkness, illuminating the space in front of him in a small strip with dust particles floating within.

He took care not to shine the beam on the window to avoid any potential busybodies busying themselves in his personal, private investigation. As he stood in the kitchen, he stopped moving the light when he landed on the wall to his right, opposite the entrance to the dining room.

As if it were in its own spotlight, the rotary phone hung high, centered. Daniel walked towards it, focusing on the area to his left. Below that section of the countertop, as well as above, stood cabinets. As he opened the ones above him, nothing stood out, aside from the dust collecting on some of the dishware within them. On the counter itself, utility bills and some past due bank notices piled into the corner closest to the phone next to a bowl containing oranges and bananas in the beginning stages of rot. Aside from that, all he found were some instruction manuals for minor home repairs and useless junk mail. Daniel swept the counter with the light, frowning and second guessing whether this particular hunch was worth losing his job over if he was caught breaking and entering this house.

Finding nothing there, Daniel turned his attention back to the fridge, moving the light over it much like he would if he were reading a book. A few pictures, presumably of family members, hung from some of the magnets. Pizza delivery flyers with coupons attached. Car repair shops. Another ad for a junkyard called Cooper's Pick and Pull.

At the bottom, before the line separating the freezer and the fridge, he finally saw something that might be useful written on a single sheet of paper from a ledger pad. Phone numbers. Daniel didn't recognize any of them, so he stuck the paper into his pocket and left the kitchen, heading towards the bedroom.

The bedroom door was slightly ajar and when Daniel pushed it open to make his entrance, the room stood in stark contrast to the memory of the last time he set foot in the room. Now, the blood stains from the sheets and on the floor had been cleaned off, and the bed stripped bare. It looked more like the residents were away on a trip than anything else. Daniel flashed the light around and poked around in the drawers of the bedside tables on either side of the bed. Any trace of the sleeping pills and any other drugs was gone, leaving various knickknacks behind. Pens, notepads, and a tawdry looking paperback book lay among the remains.

After noticing something sticking out from the pages of the book, Daniel grabbed it and looked closer. On the cover, a shirtless, broad shouldered man with dark, unkempt hair fighting its way from the confines of a cowboy hat rode atop of a horse in front of a sunlit mountain landscape. On the same horse behind him, another man sat with a determined face with his arms wrapped around the rider, and beneath the picture, the title read *We Ride Together, We Ride Forever*. The author was J. F. Moore. Daniel opened the book to where the improvised book mark had been, and pulled out a single photograph. John Moore and Andrew Scott stood next to each other on River Street overlooking the Savannah River at night. The back of it had a date of 1984, and despite the two year difference, both men looked markedly younger by a decade.

Daniel thumbed through the novel to stick the picture back in, when a car door slammed shut outside. He jolted, fumbling the book in his hands, catching it before it nearly hit the ground. He looked at the curtain covering the window in the bedroom and noticed the faint interior car light peeking through the fabric, before a second door slammed, snuffing the light.

Muffled voices came through the window and he tiptoed out of the line of sight and closer to the curtains. Still, he heard nothing distinguishable. He wasn't quite scared yet, but that changed the second he heard the front door-knob turn and footsteps tap on the wooden floor. Worse, the bedroom door was wide open.

His heart sped up to a fast-paced jog as his eyes darted around the room, searching for a way out. Of course, there was nowhere to go, but he did see one door, and he slid along the wall until he reached it. He found himself inside the walk-in closet and he pulled the door closer to him as the voices spoke in whispers from the living room.

"You sure this is a good idea?" one of them asked.

"If we wanna keep the operation up, it is," the other voice said.

Daniel perked his head up when he recognized the voice of his partner.

"I already have a record, I can't get caught doing some petty breaking and entering," voice number one said.

"You'll be fine. The badge is useful for things like that," Shawn said. "I can write it off as police business, and none of these people would say a damn thing to anyone."

"You sure about that?" the other man asked.

"Mostly. *Decent* people, anyway," Shawn said.

"At the rate this city is going, won't be many decent people left."

Daniel craned his neck towards the opening to get a read on the other voice but couldn't quite place it. The footsteps drew closer to the door of the bedroom, and Daniel looked down at the beam of light shining in the cramped closet and flicked it off.

"Keep a lookout," Shawn said. "The guy said he kept all his important stuff in here."

From the closet, Daniel looked on through the sliver of opening between the closet door and its threshold. Shawn confidently strode to the left bedside table and pulled it away from the wall and started tapping the floorboards with his knuckle until he found the one he wanted. Daniel caught the glare of a metal lockbox that Shawn didn't bother to open. He replaced the board, put the table back in its place and started over to the other table.

"You done yet?" the other voice asked.

"Almost," Shawn said.

As Shawn rooted through the contents of the other table, a cold draft blew past Daniel, and threatened to carry the closet door open with it. Daniel rested his fingers on the handle and kept it still, as he watched Shawn shudder in reaction.

"You feel that?" Shawn asked, turning to the other guy.

"That cold ass wind? Yeah. Hurry up and let's get the fuck out."

"Hold on a damn minute, I ain't done yet," Shawn said to him, the way a parent scolds a child.

As if on cue, the phone in the kitchen fell, leaving the sound of its bell ringing throughout the house, and immediately after, more clanking and ringing followed, as if cookware had fallen off the rack and onto the floor.

Daniel lurched backward, and Shawn turned towards the door.

"Okay, I'm fucking leaving," the other voice said, followed by footsteps heading to the front.

Shawn glanced quickly from side to side. "Good idea," he said, and his footsteps followed.

Mere seconds later, the doors to the car outside slammed shut again and the engine came to life and faded away as they left.

Daniel waited a while to steady himself and let his heartbeat return to a reasonable pace. Cautiously, he crept out of the closet, still holding the novel in his hand. Inside the room, he remained still, listening, but heard nothing. He walked to the curtains and parted them with his fingers only enough to see outside. Like before, the street lay silent and empty.

He crept back to the kitchen; the phone lay broken on the floor, along with a few pots and pans near the stove. Daniel cocked his head to the side, looking at the fallen objects, and decided leaving sooner was a better idea than lingering.

After tiptoeing through the kitchen, and reaching the backdoor, he returned to his normal stride and left the backyard, jogging back to his truck on the other street. When he got home, he went to the kitchen and wiped the sweat from his face with a paper towel before pulling his phonebook out.

He trailed his finger down the list of last names and finally found what he was looking for. Ryerson, Shawn F. He pulled the number from his pocket that he'd taken from the fridge, and it matched the phone book listing for his partner.

CHAPTER SEVEN

*D*aniel woke up disheveled, tired, and sweaty the next morning, having barely slept the night prior. He hurried to establish his daily routine. After he managed to do so, the phone rang while he read the paper and had his coffee, throwing yet another wrench into the calculated rhythm of his consistent mornings. He marked his place in the paper and drank another sip of his coffee before he grumbled about the disruption and went to his kitchen.

"Hello?" he answered.

"Well, damn, Danny, good morning to you, too. How'd it go last night? You slide into home base?" Tom asked.

Daniel laughed, before he said, "Sorry, I just sat down before you had the nerve to call. No, but we kissed and had a great time."

"Well, shit, nice work, buddy. You working tonight?" Tom asked. "I'm off. You wanna grab a beer or something?"

"Yeah, but why don't we get lunch instead?" Daniel asked.

"I can do that," Tom said. "There's a good diner over on Abercorn. Have you been there yet?"

"No, but I'll meet you there in an hour," Daniel said.

"Sounds good, man," Tom said before he hung up.

Daniel bathed, shaved, dressed, and met Tom an hour later. The two started out with coffee while they perused the menu.

"Danny, what're you doing a week from Saturday?" Tom asked.

"I don't have any plans yet," Daniel said. "Why?"

"The Great American Bash, that's why. Dusty Rhodes versus Ric Flair. It's gonna be great," Tom said.

"Fuck yeah, I'm in. I'll let you know for sure tomorrow," Daniel said.

"Yeah, and why don't you bring your new lady friend, too?" Tom asked.

"I don't know about that," Daniel said. "A woman like that isn't gonna watch a bunch of sweaty men pretending to fight."

"It's not about the match, knucklehead. It's about spending time with her on the way there and back," Tom said.

"Good point," Daniel said. The two men placed their orders and ate.

"What'd you wind up doing about Shawn?" Tom asked.

Daniel set his fork down and went through the entire ordeal of the camera, the stakeout, and the subsequent trip to South Carolina and the lumber mill where the bikers congregated. When he got to the part about getting stuck in the mud, Tom sat there, staring at Daniel with disbelief. "And that was all before I met Rebecca for our date." Then he told him about his twilight excursion to the crime scene.

"Jesus Christ, Danny. You followed some strange biker dude you don't know on your day off? What if he's in a gang or something?" Tom shook his head and raised his hands in perplexion before he leaned closer to Daniel and whispered, "And you broke into the house after the fact?"

"That's the thing. He might be in a gang. I didn't really get to see it until I got stuck in Hardeeville, but they had a logo. It was a gator with bloody teeth. Dudes went by the name of Jim and Allan. Don't know the rest. And that was it."

"They sound like fine, law-abiding citizens," Tom said. He swallowed a bite of food in a rush, as if he had a revelation, of sorts.

"I bet those shotguns on their bike racks were all registered, too," Daniel said with a chuckle. "And Shawn was definitely there at the house after I got there."

"You're absolutely sure it was him?" Tom asked, his voice mixed with skepticism.

"I *saw* him. Heard him too," Daniel said.

Tom leaned back and stroked his chin. "You might be right about the gang part," Tom said. "That logo sounds familiar. I'm pretty sure some guys at my precinct picked up some bikers with that logo on their vests at some point. I wasn't there, but I could swear I remember hearing about it."

"Do these names ring any bells?" Daniel asked.

"Not off-hand, but I can probably find out later today and give you a ring." Tom took another heaping bite of pancakes.

"That would actually be pretty great," Daniel said. "If I didn't get stuck in South Carolina and covered in mud, I was gonna try to dig around some more."

"Jesus, you gotta be careful. You don't wanna tangle with a gang of criminals unarmed."

"Yeah, but I figured I could at least start building a case."

"Look at you talking like a lawyer. You're not even worried a little?"

"No, but that does make me think about something. What if I get caught or go to IA and the rest of the department ostracizes me?" Daniel asked.

"I dunno. But the way I feel is that it's just a job. My dad was a cop, too. He was a good guy, and it just kind of was an accepted thing that I would be one, too," Tom said.

"You mean quit?" Daniel asked.

"Yeah. If you really don't like it and can't change it, yeah," Tom said. "I ain't the smartest guy out there, but a man's gotta have principles. Somehow, I don't think quitting's an option for you, though. Is there anyone you can trust at your precinct? Give you strength in numbers kind of thing?"

"Shit," Daniel said, looking down. "That's a good idea." Daniel thought about it some more. "Off the top of my head, I don't know who to talk to. Something'll come up, especially since everyone thinks Shawn's an asshole."

"Yeah, man. When you get tired of something, it's only gonna go one of two ways. You either fix it or it fixes you," Tom said. "Might as well do what you can to fix it and make some friends. Might even help you out later."

"You're definitely smarter than Shawn looks, that's for damn sure," Daniel said. "How'd you get so conniving, anyway?"

"I think I got it from my dad. He didn't pal around with everyone in his department and go drinking after their patrols or anything. He had a couple of guys he knew well, and they stuck together. Like the way a steel chair shot sticks to your head," Tom said, which caused a cascade of laughter between the two. Daniel now had food for thought to go with food for the body.

"I wonder if Flair's gonna beat Rhodes down with one of those when we see them," Daniel said.

"They don't call him the dirtiest player in the game for no reason, Danny," Tom said.

"Woooo!" Daniel bellowed in his best Ric Flair impersonation. The two finished their lunch and walked outside and had a cigarette while they chatted. When they finished, Daniel said, "I'll let you know soon about Rebecca, me, and the Ric Flair match. Later, Tom."

"Later, Danny," Tom said.

As soon as Daniel got home, he set his keys on the counter and dialed up Rebecca.

"Hello?" she said when she answered

"Rebecca, I'm glad I got you. Listen, my friend, Tom, invited us to go to Greensboro to see Ric Flair wrestle Dusty Rhodes—"

"Hell yeah," Rebecca said, excitedly. "When?"

"Wait, you like wrestling?" Daniel asked.

"Who doesn't like the dirtiest player in the game?" she asked.

Daniel shook with laughter. "Point taken. It's a week from this Saturday. Figured we could head out early that day since it's a five-hour drive."

"Count me in. Although, if you're free sooner than that, I'd love to see you," Rebecca said.

"How about this Friday?" Daniel asked.

"Perfect. I'll be over at seven, and I'll bring a *good* movie to watch. You can take care of the food," Rebecca said.

"Uh, yeah," Daniel said, taken aback by her assertiveness. "I can do that."

"Good, I can't wait. See you then.".

"See you then," Daniel said, and the two hung up.

Shortly after his phone call, Daniel had another cup of coffee while he deliberated what he would do before his shift that night. One option was to go to the boxing gym. It was exciting and exerting. Or, he could go to the library and look at the newspaper archives to see if he could find out anything about Santa and his biker helpers. The latter idea was more appealing to him, so he made his way to the Bull Street Library to scrutinize the microfilm until he found something.

As he rolled through the archives, Daniel zoned out. He turned the dial, going backward in time via the local Savannah newspapers, looking for names or the gator logo so he could go further in his own private investigation. Headlines were wide-ranging and covered everything from The Challenger explosion to President Reagan delaying the yearly state of the Union because of it. There were writings about the Mujahideen in the Russian-Afghan war, and local news about a body found in Tremont Park. After an hour of reading, Daniel went further back and just passed into the 1984 archives. Not five minutes later, there it was. Something to quell his insatiable thirst for knowledge.

Biker Arrested on Charges of Aggravated Battery

Daniel looked at the picture accompanying the headline. The beard was almost nonexistent, and he wasn't emaciated to the extent he was when Daniel encountered him, but that was him. The same brown eyes perched without a hint of emotion in the orbitals of a man named Allan Walker.

Below the fold, Daniel looked at an inset picture captioned with the arresting officer, Shawn Ryerson. Daniel scratched his head as he took a deep breath, wondering if this was the impetus for whatever it was, they were doing now. He read the rest of the article. Apparently, Allan's crew was known as the Savannah Swamp Demons. The cartoonish gator did a terrible job at conveying that sentiment, Daniel thought. Was it performative or did their relationship begin after this? A cop with an ego and a criminal like Walker sounded like a match made in heaven. Or a swampish hell.

Daniel sat back and looked at the screen for a minute, taking his new information in and letting it simmer inside of him. As he did so, the light from the microfilm machine flickered. After a moment, it flickered again and stayed off while Daniel looked around to see if anything else was amiss. As he looked, the sparsely populated library showed no signs of anything out of the ordinary. From his perspective, anyway.

The light of the machine came back on and stayed that way. He looked at the machine, and turned his eyes back to the screen where he saw a different page from the one he'd left off at. A chill grazed him, and he shuddered as he looked. Buried inside the same paper but from a week prior, was another mugshot.

Daniel tensed and looked around again, before peering closer at the screen. The difference of two years and everything else the man in this picture had been through weren't kind to him, which was why it took Daniel a moment of staring to figure out that he was looking at Andrew Scott. The same Andrew Scott who murdered his boyfriend, John Moore.

His curiosity outweighed the dread of what he'd experienced and he kept reading. Briefly, he felt stupid because the article stated Andrew's name and he'd been staring at the picture instead, but according to this, he was arrested for petty theft along with a gang member from a defunct gang that thought it was wise to oppose the Savannah Swamp Demons.

By that point, he'd seen enough, both in terms of the case and the weirdness surrounding him as he did so. Daniel left the Bull Street Library in a hurry and returned home with more confidence and information than he had left with. Knowing that his partner had the same schedule as he did, Daniel figured it would be easier to spy on him and uncover whatever they were doing.

Once home, Daniel went to the kitchen and grabbed the phone, dialing the only person he could trust. After a few rings, he got an answer.

"Hello?"

"Tom? It's me. Can you do me a favor and look up some stuff for me?" Daniel asked. "I found out some more useful info to help you narrow the search."

"Yeah, I think I can get to work early tonight. What do you need?"

"You ever hear of a gang called the Savannah Swamp Demons?"

"No, I don't recall them. Kinda glad, too, with a dumb name like that," Tom said.

"You should see the logo. I know I told you about it, but it's hilarious to actually see it." When Daniel said that, Tom's laughter pierced his ears and Daniel held the receiver away from him until it died down. "Also, the name Allan Walker. A-L-L-A-N."

"Double L Allan Walker, Savannah Swamp Demons." The hurried sounds of scribbling came through the receiver. "How'd you find that out so quick?"

"I went to the library and looked through the newspaper archives," Daniel said.

"Damn, look at you, Detective Belascoe."

"If that's what it takes to be a detective, I don't know if I want to. I thought my eyes were gonna fall out of my head. Anyways, I gotta get ready to go in. Keep this between us. I don't want Shawn to find out."

"Of course, buddy. I'll call you back and leave a message."

"Thanks, Tom." Daniel hung up the phone and readied himself for work. Now, the rest of the day's problems revolved around the fact that he still had to go out on the streets with Shawn that night.

Daniel got to the police station earlier than usual that day and made his way to the locker room. On his way, he saw Detective Martin packing up to leave for the day, and she stopped and stared at him. Daniel noticed it, and almost kept going but she flicked her head, motioning for him to come to her desk.

"Hey, Detective Martin, how's it going?"

She ignored his greeting and sounded very much like his superior. "Belascoe, walk with me for a minute."

Daniel's stomach fluttered a bit with the same feeling he always got when an authority figure wanted him nearby but didn't give a reason. He looked at the clock on the wall. "All right," he said.

Detective Martin didn't say anything until they got to the parking lot away from their colleagues. She took a long look at Daniel. "You look like you didn't get much sleep last night. Weren't you off yesterday?" she asked.

If it weren't so hot outside, the fact he began to sweat would have been noteworthy. Hopefully, Martin couldn't hear his rising heartbeat. "Yeah," he said. "I had a date last night, we stayed out a while walking around town."

"Oh yeah?" she asked. "You guys go somewhere nice?"

"Tondee's for some food and some drinks. Then we walked around for a while," he said. "Detective, why are you so interested in what I did last night?" It was a bold question, but he could only keep his nerves at bay for so long.

Martin burned a hole through Daniel's skull with her intent gaze. "You were walking up Liberty Street last night, weren't you?" It was a question in only the strictest sense of the word. Martin lifted her hat and scratched her head.

When she did that, it dawned on him. He and Rebecca had been on Liberty Street during their date. And he saw the hairstyle and his eyes widened in recognition. "Yeah, I was getting a ride home." Then, his thoughts went to a dark place. Maybe Martin knew he was digging around for information on his colleagues. But she wasn't a fan of Shawn, so did she care? Or was she looking for info on him because she lied about Shawn when they last spoke?

"Belascoe, pay attention," she said, snapping him out of the dark path of his wandering mind.

Daniel focused on Martin again and looked at her. "Oh God," he said. He leaned in. "That was you in the alley?"

He went to say something else, but Martin cut him off. "I need you to forget you saw that," Detective Martin said, glaring at him.

Daniel relaxed and looked at her. Now he knew, at least in part, how she came to be a detective. "Forgotten," he said. "I thought you were gonna get me fired, or something."

"No, I'd rather not do that," she said. "You're a good kid. Lots of promise, with a good head on your shoulders. Keep it that way." The edge of higher ranking authority solidified itself in her voice before they parted ways.

"Of course," Daniel said. "Yes, ma'am."

"All right, Belascoe. Hope you have a good night."

Detective Martin walked away toward her car, leaving Daniel in the parking lot by himself.

* * *

WHEN THE TIME came to patrol, their first stop was for the customary coffee and doughnuts and Daniel got two of the latter to go with his coffee for the night. The muggy weather and light rainfall speckled their windshield and side windows like a humid mist. Daniel didn't say much; he stared out the window, hoping for Shawn to divulge everything he was up to so Daniel could find himself a new partner. Shawn noticed Daniel's demeanor, too.

"What's gettin' ya, Belascoe?" Shawn asked.

"What? Oh, not much. I'm just tired," Daniel said.

"You pound coffee by the pot. How the hell are you tired?" Shawn asked.

"I think at this point I'm used to it," Daniel said. "I do have a question." Daniel turned towards Shawn and noticed he had quite a set of bags under his eyes, too, and he knew why. Maybe if he could pull off some of Detective Martin's questioning techniques, he'd get an answer. "Why did we leave that gay couple's house the other night instead of handling it like we were supposed to?"

"Goddammit, Daniel. These...people...ain't natural. You can't have a baby if you do what they do."

"That's true, you can't. Tell me something, Shawn. When you go home and fuck your wife after work, are you always trying for a baby?" Daniel asked.

"No, but she can't have kids anyway," Shawn said.

"So why bother having sex?" Daniel asked.

"Christ, kid, you ever fucked a broad before?" Shawn asked. Daniel noticed the agitation rising with every question. "It feels good. Besides, we're married. What's she gonna say?"

"So, it never occurred to you they might feel the same way?" Daniel asked.

"Come on, Danny. It's a fucking exit hole," Shawn said.

"You've never fucked your wife in the ass?" Daniel asked.

"Yeah, but she's a woman, so what?" Shawn asked.

"It doesn't matter anyway," Daniel said, looking at him, surprised by the onset of temerity in his own voice.

"Fucking Christ, Belascoe," Shawn yelled as his face grew redder, "what the fuck do you care for?"

"I was thinking maybe we can do our goddamn job. Clearly, you're over-paid." Daniel's words were now a cattle prod of provocation; he wanted to piss Shawn off so he would make a mistake. Instead, Shawn gripped the wheel and kept on driving. His knuckles turned white in proportion to his red face. Daniel sat and watched as Shawn drove, his anger unabating.

Not long into their silence, they sped up until Shawn pulled into an alley. "What the hell are you doing?" Daniel asked.

"I'm pulling the car over to kick the shit out of you, Belascoe." Shawn stepped out into the alley and slammed the door behind him.

What a waste of time. Daniel got out of the car and faced Shawn. Daniel didn't take on an offensive stance, nor did he look outwardly defensive. When Shawn went in for a punch, Daniel moved his left foot back, causing Shawn to overextend himself and lose his balance. To Daniel's amusement, Shawn tried again. He missed. Again. "I'm not even trying. You fight about as well as you do police work. You know neither of us can go to the office with bruises on us."

Shawn regained his balance and straightened himself out as he looked at Daniel. From Daniel's perspective, it appeared Shawn didn't know what to do with himself; he was outwitted and outmatched in every way. Still, Shawn looked pissed.

"How about this?" Daniel asked as he moved to get back in the car. "We go back to work and I won't tell anyone about your embarrassment." The rest of the patrol was as uneventful as it was silent. Daniel, however, heard Shawn's rage and emasculation screaming and echoing through the night, long past the end of their shift.

CHAPTER EIGHT

The following morning, Daniel had a message waiting for him on his answering machine. He rewound the tape to the beginning, wondering what all Tom could've said to use up so much tape. At the beginning of the tape, he heard Tom's voice.

"Hey bud, I got something you might wanna hear. That Allan Walker guy has a rap sheet, nothing big time. Marijuana possession, armed robbery, and then there was the aggravated battery you mentioned. He didn't go to prison for that one, on account of lack of evidence. But the Savannah Swamp Demons are known for trafficking drugs, so you might wanna keep an eye on that. And I don't need to tell you, but if they're crossing state lines, it's the feds' problem. Maybe do an anonymous tip or something? Anyways, I'm gonna go to the gym around one today. Meet me there if you wanna get a lift in." Just before one, Daniel pulled up to the gym. Inside, he met Tom at the squat rack and the two started warming up. "Hundred eighty-five? Don't hurt yourself with all that weight, now," Daniel said.

"Smart ass," Tom said. "I'll out squat you one day."

"I hope so," Daniel said. "It takes more work for me because of my height, you know."

"I like to think I'm down to earth. Humble, in other words." Daniel started warming up as Tom continued. "So, what is your plan with Shawn?"

Daniel racked the weight after his set and started loading more weight. "Two twenty-five?"

"Yeah, please."

"You know what the son of a bitch did? He tried to fight me last night when we were on patrol. Pulled into an alley and everything."

"So, what happened? You don't look like you got beat up." Tom started his set while Daniel talked.

"No, he can't scrap. I dodged him. I managed to talk him down because we didn't wanna go back to work looking like we'd gotten into a fight. Especially since we didn't even do anything." After Daniel did his warm up, he continued. "The way I see it, it's not unreasonable to assume Allan is involved in the Demons' drug trafficking. He looks older than the rest, but I don't know if age means anything. We also don't have records to compare to. Maybe he got off easy and the subordinates took the fall?"

Tom leaned up against the rack, thinking. "From what I know, that's kind of how all gangs work."

"So, I wanna find out what he and Shawn are trading, and where it comes from. Once I get solid evidence, I can get Shawn and maybe put a dent in the Demons somehow. Three-fifteen?"

"Yeah. What do you do then? Go to the feds?"

"I guess. I'd have to go to Captain Wilcox, too. I'm sure he'd wanna know if his officers are dirty. Like, so dirty they can't overlook it. You need a spot on this one?"

"Not yet," Tom said, walking the bar back. He knocked out five reps before he slowed down. After he racked the weight, he looked at Daniel. "Why are you looking at me like that? You don't wanna drag me into this, do you?"

Daniel smiled. "Come on. All we gotta do is our own private stakeout this Sunday. I got the camera. I'll buy you lunch afterward."

"Absolutely not. Not for any amount of pancakes." Tom said.

"We're just gonna watch. Besides, if we take your car, it'll be inconspicuous. Nothing wrong with parking on the street, minding our own business." Daniel unracked the weight and did a set of ten.

"And you think this is a good idea?"

"Yep," Daniel said, in the middle of his set. "Maybe this time I can get Allan's license plate or something useful."

"And you think it's smart to go nosing around trying to be a detective in your off time like this? It's fucking crazy." Tom said.

"It's not like we're looking for the next Charles Manson, or anything," Daniel said. He threw 405 pounds on the bar and officially started his workout.

"We can get in trouble for it, dipshit. Or murdered by a biker gang. What would I tell your new lady friend? 'Oh, Daniel decided to go poking around in an investigation that he didn't know about and got shot in the face by a gang of biker junkies. My condolences.' That'll look real good."

Daniel finished his set. "We don't even know if there's an investigation right now. We could uncover something."

"Three sixty-five." They started reloading the bar for Tom. "This idea of yours is monumentally stupid."

"So, I take it you're not in?" Daniel asked. The two finished their workout and sparred for a bit before they took their leave from the gym. Before they went to their respective vehicles, Daniel reminded Tom about Sunday, in the event his friend changed his mind.

* * *

FRIDAY MORNING FOUND Daniel contemplating what he should cook for the night. He ran a comb through his hair and put some clothes on before heading out to the store. Before he made it there, of course, he stopped off for coffee and doughnuts.

Once at the store, he loaded the cart with chicken, breadcrumbs, pasta, cheese, sauce, and all the accouterments for chicken parmesan. He added candles for atmosphere, along with a bottle of red and white wine. Not wanting to look like an idiot, he also bought wine glasses and stared at the condoms for a while, internally debating whether to buy them or not. Would it seem expectant? Too eager? Both? Nervousness aside, he grabbed a box along with everything else. Just in case.

He rode back home and began to decorate for the evening, which mostly amounted to putting candles on his small dining room table along with plates, silverware, and wine glasses. He cleaned his entire house, which to most eyes was already clean. Nevertheless, he thought vacuuming and making his bed would be a good idea. When he finished, he made himself some more coffee and sat down for a cigarette to go with it.

Daniel looked at his clock. He still had nine hours until Rebecca arrived. Having so much time, he decided to go and read some more at the Bull Street Library.

Thinking back to 1984, the first major election he could vote in, he pondered his place in policing, along with the place policing held in the United States in conjunction with the rhetoric of "law and order" espoused by Reagan; the same type of rhetoric Nixon touted as Daniel's dad carped about what a crook Nixon was while Daniel sat on the floor of the living room in front of the TV. As he read into the Reagan presidency, he realized what many did not. Things got better for some people, like the rich, marginally better for some of the middle class, and significantly worse for the poor.

Growing up in Savannah, and now working in the city, he saw it first hand, and the rising prison population showed it. Still, he hoped he wasn't naïve in the hopes that he could do something useful for his community instead of throwing them into jail and becoming another number.

At five-thirty, Daniel put on a pair of dress pants and a white button-up shirt. He rolled his sleeves up and started to prepare the food. After he fried the chicken, he laid it all out in his baking dish, adorned it with more cheese and tomato sauce, and popped it in the oven to cook. He timed it perfectly so that it would be done when Rebecca arrived. A few minutes after that, his phone rang.

"Hello?" he answered.

"Hey, it's me. My dog sitter fell through. Is it ok if I bring Bentley?"

"Yeah, that'd be fine. Don't like leaving the little guy alone for a few hours, I take it?" Daniel asked.

"A few hours, sure. But I planned on 'accidentally' falling asleep at your place tonight and anything longer than eight hours is a lot. See you soon," she said before she hung up.

Daniel looked at the phone a minute before he hung it back up. His palms perspired at the prospect of having a woman over for an adult sleepover, and amidst all the other extracurriculars he was involved in, and despite his preparation, he didn't consider that she might actually want to have sex with him. At ten until seven, he heard a knock on his door.

He opened it to Rebecca and Bentley. "You're early. Food won't be ready for another ten minutes or so."

"I think I can manage," she said as she stooped down to unhook Bentley's leash, which apparently was the cue for him to run in and hop up on the couch.

"Well, come on in," Daniel said. "What movies did you bring?"

"You have choices," she said, reaching into her handbag and removing two tapes. "There's *Apocalypse Now* or *Gremlins*. Depending on how much you wanna introspect and think, that determines the movie."

"How do you feel about saving the deep stuff for talking and we watch the fun movie?" Daniel asked.

"*Gremlins* it is," Rebecca said.

"What's it about?" Daniel asked.

"Jesus, you're sheltered. Let's just say it's a modern Christmas classic."

"I'm not a big movie watcher." Daniel shrugged, looking at Rebecca in her short, form-fitting black skirt and low v-neck shirt. She was taller than him by an inch, with broad shoulders, and an aura of collective, erudite wisdom. After he looked at her for a moment, he led her to the dining room table and pulled out a chair for her.

"It smells delightful in here. What'd you make?" Rebecca asked.

"Chicken parmesan," he said, grabbing a bottle of wine in each hand. "Which would you prefer, red or white?"

"I'll take the red."

"Good choice," he said as he poured her a glass. He poured one for himself and left the bottle behind as he went into the kitchen to pull the food out of the oven. The instant he touched the oven, Bentley ran in, enthralled by the smell. He moved in such a way that no matter where he went, he was either in Daniel's way or close to it. Rebecca called Bentley a few times, but he wasn't leaving. He even followed Daniel to the dining room as he presented the food and lit the candles.

"So, since we last left off, you were in a moral and ethical quandary," Rebecca said. "Are there any new developments?"

Daniel relayed the information to her about how he took a stand, and in his own way, confronted his partner about his attitude.

"That's quite an emboldened stance. I like it. Ethically, you did the right thing," Rebecca said.

"Is that why it's so tough to do?"

"That's exactly why. It's easy to find fair-weather friends and people. And if there's no adversity, it's even easier to say the right thing and put on airs if there's nobody to challenge it," Rebecca said.

"So you're saying that acting brave, for lack of a better word, is often at odds with what you feel?"

"It is. And I'm not the only one to say that, either," Rebecca said. "It's common. Even in more fun movies, like *Gremlins*, you see the characters make choices, deal with the consequences, grow, and sometimes test themselves. That's part of why I like movies so much."

Daniel sipped his wine. "Because of the characters?" he asked.

"Sort of. It's less about the characters and more about the moving snapshot of time. When someone writes a book or makes a movie, where we are in the world influences the story. It's a mirror for us to look at. Horror movies are especially good because they make us face our own humanity. Not just the good parts or the contemplative parts. The grim parts, too," she said.

"Is that why you like wrestling, too?"

"Absolutely. It all comes into play when it comes to psychology. It's also getting more popular now. Guys like Hulk Hogan embody this collective—but also *very* imperfect—idea for what men in America can or should be," Rebecca said.

After he took a bite of chicken and a drink of his wine, Daniel asked, "So what should men in America strive for?"

"Depends. Have you trained, said your prayers, and taken your vitamins?" She couldn't keep a straight face as she spoke that sentence. When the laughter died, she managed to get a few more bites of her chicken. "I think Hogan's on the right track. But maybe don't harbor so many emotions revolving around anger, or revenge? Not every problem needs brute force." Rebecca paused. "Wow, I feel like I'm lecturing the Reagan administration. But don't worry. You're on the right track."

Daniel looked into Rebecca's eyes. "Is that why you hit on me?"

"I can tell you're a sweetheart, and you're not bullshitting me, or anyone else, about it. Plus, you helped this guy," she said, motioning to Bentley, who happened to be lying at her feet, "but it's everything else. You care. You care enough to seek out the truth. Found anything good yet?"

"Have *you* ever thought about getting into police work? You're extremely perceptive." Daniel wrapped some pasta around his fork as he waited for his answer.

"Hell no," she said, pouring herself more wine. "I'm still a student, and plus, I don't want to."

The two of them finished their bottle of wine and their chicken parmesan. Rebecca stood up, looking at Daniel. "You can go and get the movie ready. I'll put all the dishes away since you cooked this delicious meal yourself."

Daniel, with Bentley at his heels, went to the living room and popped the tape into the VCR. He paused at the FBI warning and went back to the kitchen to help Rebecca tidy up everything. Before they hopped on the couch together, Rebecca stopped and looked at Daniel.

"I didn't fully think this through. Do you have some spare pants I can swap out for this?" She asked, pointing at her skirt.

"Yeah, I think I have a few things lying around," Daniel said before he turned toward his room. He pulled out a pair of his gray sweatpants and a white shirt and handed them off so Rebecca could change her clothes. Daniel was sitting on his couch when she came out of the bathroom, engulfed by his oversized pants. "Wow, you look more ravishing than you did before. I'm gonna take full credit for this."

Rebecca grinned at him. "I did this to myself for not prioritizing my comfort like I normally do. It won't happen again." She sprawled out on Daniel's couch with her head on the opposite armrest and Daniel holding her feet in his lap. Bentley walked up to the couch and looked up expectedly. After a few seconds of wondering what he wanted, Daniel lifted Rebecca's legs up and Bentley filled up any remaining space. He hit play on the remote control and the two of them watched together. Out of the corner of his eye, Daniel noticed Rebecca looking at him and occasionally smiling as he reacted to the movie; Bentley was sound asleep, snoring in between her legs.

When they were watching the part where someone shoved a gremlin into a blender, Daniel was taken aback. He looked over at Rebecca, who he noticed was stifling laughter, and asked if she was sure it was a Christmas movie.

"Of course I am. Takes place *during* Christmas. It has themes of gift giving and family, with a little hint of a morality play. It's everything you could ask for in a movie."

"And you like it more than *Back to the Future*?" Daniel asked.

"Now don't go putting words in my mouth. I like *Back to the Future*. I just don't think it's as great as everyone else seems to. Like you. I also really enjoy Christmas."

"Really?" Daniel asked as he shifted in his seat to look at Rebecca.

"Yeah," she said. "It's the most wonderful time of the year. Just like the song says."

"Fair enough," Daniel said. "I still don't know if I buy this one being a *Christmas movie*, though."

"Just trust me on this."

"Fine," Daniel said. As the movie wound down, Bentley hopped off the couch and looked up at Rebecca while he sat down, his tail swiping the floor as it wagged back and forth.

"Can I help you?" she asked Bentley, pausing. "Fine, we can take you out." Bentley dashed to the back door as Rebecca and Daniel followed along. They opened the door and Bentley ran outside while Rebecca and Daniel sat on the steps leading out of the door.

"How did you like dinner?" Daniel asked.

"It was amazing. Where'd you learn to cook so well?"

"My mother," Daniel said. "After Dad died, it was just the two of us, so I mostly spent a lot of time with her."

"Are you comfortable talking about your father?" Rebecca asked him.

"I am, but I don't know if you'll be comfortable listening. My dad worked for the railroad in Waycross. You might not be familiar with it, but it's a small town about two hours southwest of here. So, in seventy-three, he had an accident while he was working on some trains and a machine decapitated him." Daniel wasn't quite aware yet, but tears streamed down his face and pooled on his shirt. Daniel sniffled as Rebecca reached up and wiped a tear away with her thumb. Daniel tried to protest, but Rebecca held him steady.

"It's okay to cry," she said.

"I don't recall saying that out loud. At least not recently." He ruffled his collar and used it to wipe the salty remnants from his eyes as Rebecca drew him closer and hugged him. Daniel looked to his left and saw Bentley sitting there, without a care in the world. He couldn't help but laugh. Rebecca looked at her dog and laughed along with Daniel.

"Mood killer," she said to Bentley. "Let's get you inside so you can sleep like a good boy." The trio walked in, and Rebecca and Daniel cleaned the kitchen, did the dishes, and tidied up the living room. Bentley alternated standing at the feet of whoever made the most noise at a given time. Or maybe it was because he thought one of them had food for him to scrounge. Afterward, Daniel went to brush his teeth and put on his night clothes.

He walked back out to his living room, shirtless, wearing a light pair of pajama bottoms. When he noticed Rebecca sitting on the couch, she looked back at him and her eyes briefly widened in surprise at Daniel's physique. "I can sleep on the couch if you two wanna take the bed," he said.

"Daniel, we're not twelve. We can all sleep in the bed," she said.

"I'm just trying to be respectful," he said as he started walking back towards his room. "It's back this way."

As they walked down his short hallway, Bentley's clacking footfalls abruptly stopped, and he stood in the middle of the hall, staring. His gaze was intent and purposeful. He lowered his nose to the ground and started sniffing. Daniel looked where Bentley looked; after a moment, he looked back at the dog. Daniel then looked at Rebecca, who wore a mask of confusion. Daniel thought about the strange dreams he had and the noises he heard before he said anything.

"I think your dog's broken," Daniel said.

"Either that or you have ground beef hidden in your floorboards. Or a body, like in that Edgar Allan Poe story," Rebecca said, crossing over to Bentley before scooping him up in her arms. "All right, you. It's time for you to stop being weird and go to bed."

Daniel slowed his pace and looked back before he followed Rebecca into his room, where they instantly fell asleep as soon as they lay down.

CHAPTER NINE

*W*hen the sun rose the next morning, Daniel woke up with Bentley's back legs kicked out and jammed into his left side; Bentley's head rested on Rebecca's stomach. Daniel was the only one who seemed uncomfortable, but at least his anxiety quelled since his erection wasn't poking Rebecca or the dog. Bentley snored while he slept, and it matched the tempo of the rise and fall of Rebecca's chest as she breathed. Daniel looked at her broad shoulders at the point where they began to slope upwards to her neck and admired the shape of her body through the covers. Not only that, he admired the fact that the three of them managed to fit on his bed, his own discomfort notwithstanding.

He slithered out of bed and left the two to sleep longer and went to the kitchen to prepare coffee and breakfast for the morning. He pulled some eggs out of the fridge and started beating them while his stove heated up. He poured most of the eggs into the frying pan and let them sit as he sliced off some cheese and chopped an onion. Not long after, he had a nice, if not massive, omelet ready to plate. He set it aside and cooked the rest of his eggs, which he placed in a bowl. He then made three slices of toast, one of which he tore into pieces and placed onto the smaller portion of eggs. He set the bowl down at the edge of the kitchen and the moment the bowl hit the wood floor, he heard dog paws clacking.

Bentley bounded to the food bowl and within seconds, ate his eggs and toast before he looked up at Daniel and asked to be let out. When Daniel opened the door, Bentley sped into the yard and ran from one end to the other.

"I hope you like omelets," Daniel said as he turned around to face Rebecca.

"How'd you know I was here?"

"Really? I may be young, but I *am* observant and a cop," Daniel said.

"Tell me something else then, Sherlock," she teased.

"You use a soap that smells like vanilla bean," Daniel said. "And bed head suits you."

"Fine, you are good," Rebecca said, smiling as she ran her fingers through her hair.

"You ready to eat?"

"Absolutely," she said as she walked over to the door to call for Bentley. Daniel grabbed the food, and as he turned toward the table, Rebecca slid herself between his arms, wrapping her hands around him and pulling him close. Daniel moved forward, pushed Rebecca closer to the table and set the plates on top of it so he could grab her hips and hold her close. With his hands full, he couldn't do much when she took his face in her hands and their lips met halfway. "Thank you. Keep this up, you'll be house-husband material in no time." Daniel's eyes widened in synchronicity with her smirk. "Not anytime soon, don't worry. What's the plan for the Great American Bash?"

The pair sat down and Daniel served the omelets and coffee. When he finally situated himself, he took a sip and proceeded to lay out the plan. "Well, it takes about five hours to get to Greensboro from here. I figured since Tom's bringing his girlfriend, you and I could ride in my truck, and they could ride in Tom's car."

"I was thinking about you and me, specifically," Rebecca said. "Do you think you can leave Thursday and we can spend some time together? And make it a slow trip where we have fun?"

"I think I can make that happen," Daniel said. "What about Bentley? Will you be able to find someone to watch him for that long?"

"Yeah, I'll ask Nacha and give her a few bucks. Getting out of work at the diner's easy, too. They're surprisingly supportive of my schoolwork, and with my potential graduation this winter, they know I'm gonna need to be more flexible."

"Nacha? Who is that? And how did you get into wrestling?" Daniel asked.

"That's easy. I was doing homework about a year ago, and I had TBS on in the background one Saturday. I kept working and then wrestling came on. At some point, I stopped doing homework, and I ate half a bag of potato chips and kept watching. I even caught a few matches Jim Crockett put on here in

Georgia since then. Nacha is a friend. She got really into *Indiana Jones* and wanted to be a biblical archeologist. Her real name is Mariana. We got close when we were undergrads. Took some classes together, too."

"Everything you said made me even more excited to go to Greensboro next week to see Ric Flair with you," Daniel said as he finished his food.

"I would hope so. It's gonna be a good test to see if we can handle each other for long periods of time, too."

"As long as we get Dunkin on the way there, I think I'll be all right," Daniel said.

"You have good taste," Rebecca said, clearing her plate. She stood up and grabbed Daniel's plate and put it in the sink for him. Daniel stood up and tidied the table as Rebecca came back to join him. "Thanks for a wonderful night." Rebecca pulled Daniel close, and he returned her gaze for a lifetime in those five seconds. They both leaned toward each other and kissed goodbye.

"I'll call you soon and we can hash out the details of the Great American Bash," Daniel said.

"Sounds good," she said before she picked up Bentley and left.

Daniel poured another cup of coffee and called Tom on the phone to coordinate their boxing and lifting plans for the day. Tom picked up after two rings. "You up for a workout?" Daniel asked.

"You ready to get your ass kicked in the ring? I'm feeling good today," Tom said.

"Wow, you must have had a good night last night to be this bold. We'll see what you got."

"I look forward to it," Tom said. "Hey, do you mind if Christina comes too? She wants to get a workout in, plus it might be good for you guys to meet since we're going to go on a trip and all."

"Yeah, you know I don't mind. The more the merrier. I don't know Christina's skill level, but maybe she'll be closer to an even match for you. You'll still lose, of course, but not as bad."

"Yeah, yeah. We'll see you soon," Tom said.

About thirty minutes later, Daniel walked into the gym and met Tom and Christina at the pull-up bar. "Don't wear yourself out too much before we get into the ring, now," Daniel said, smiling.

"You're pretty jolly today. You go out with that lady again last night?" Tom asked.

"Yeah, I made her dinner, and she stayed the night." Daniel grabbed the bar and hung from it while he stretched.

"Oh *really?*" Tom raised his eyebrows.

"Not like that," Daniel said. "We slept together. But we actually slept." He hopped down from the bar.

"Well, someone has to be respectable out of the two of you," Christina said, holding her hand out. "I'm Christina."

Daniel looked at the woman before him, in a neon leotard that highlighted all the striations on her musculature, which was part of one of the best physiques he'd ever seen in his life at that point. "I'm Daniel," he said, grabbing her hand. "Are you a bodybuilder?"

"Not yet, but I plan on it," she said. "Thanks for noticing. Upper or lower today?"

"Upper," Tom said. "Mostly back work and some benching."

"I guess we're starting with pull-ups?" Daniel asked as he grabbed a belt to load with a forty-five-pound plate before he did a set.

"You got it. Listen, you and your girl—Rebecca, right? How do you wanna coordinate the trip to the Bash?" Tom asked before starting his set.

"We talked about going on Thursday and making it a mini-vacation," Daniel said. "Five-hour drive to Greensboro. We can make a few days out of it."

"Our plan was to hang around Charlotte for a little while beforehand and leave on Friday," Christina said before she did her pull-ups.

"We could all meet the day of the match and grab lunch and wander around Greensboro before the match starts," Tom said.

"I think that's a good idea. Make sure to find some good places to eat. We'll wanna get something afterwards, too," Daniel said. "Let me know where you're staying so we can keep in touch along the way."

"Works for me. I'll grab the hotel number for you later," Tom said.

Shortly before they finished the bulk of their workout, Christina motioned towards the smaller pre-loaded barbells. "Think you guys can handle some twenty-ones?"

"Twenty-ones? That's when you curl the weight seven times in the lower portion, the higher portion, and then the full range of motion for a set, right?" Daniel asked.

"Yeah," Christina said, "but we're gonna do it for three sets."

The three of them did their biceps work in succession, resting only when the other two were lifting. By the end of it, Christina had the easiest time, and her final reps were still a struggle; Daniel felt his biceps pulsating, like they were going to pop out of his skin.

"That's the last time I let you give me an arm workout," Tom said.

Christina laughed. "You'll get used to it."

They all finished their workouts and sparring, then decided to go out for burgers.

"Tom, I don't know how to tell you this, but you didn't meet your sparring goal today," Daniel said.

"Don't remind me. I still think you should do a fight," Tom said while he loaded his burger up with mustard. "You find anything out about the Swamp Demons this week?"

"No, we got into it a little, though, but other than that it was uneventful," Daniel said, taking a bite from his burger.

"The *Savannah* Swamp Demons?" Christina asked.

Daniel and Tom turned to her, surprised. "Yeah, you've heard of them?" Tom asked. Daniel looked at her, rapt, waiting for her answer.

"Yeah. Real bad crew. My uncle Al rides with them. Mom always felt bad for him and invited him over for Christmas. They love drugs and hookers." Tom looked over at Christina and was about to speak before Daniel kicked him in the shin, hoping he was subtle enough to impart the message to be quiet to him. "But he's gotten so deep into that life, he's not really welcome at the family gatherings anymore, and I don't mind it at all. He always creeped me out with the way he looked at me."

"Out of curiosity, what kind of drugs?" Daniel asked.

"Now? Mostly crank, as far as I know. Tom, are you out arresting these guys?"

"Not me. Danny here was the curious one," Tom said as a glob of mayonnaise splattered onto his plate.

Daniel shoved as many fries into his mouth as his thumb, index, and middle fingers could hold before he spoke again. "You don't like the gang and their cause. Did I hear that right?"

"Can't stand them," Christina said.

"Good. So let's keep this between us. I think my partner is doing something with them. I saw him pass off something to one of their guys and followed that same guy to Hardeeville, in South Carolina. After figuring out who the guy was, I suspect it's some sort of drug deal or something. This guy looked like a skinny Santa."

Daniel watched the look of recognition come over Christina's face. "Sounds like Uncle Al," she said. "I wouldn't put it past him to put the squeeze on a cop. Or work with a willing one to help out their dumb fuck cause."

"If you're not comfortable, you don't have to tell me anything. You know that, right?" Daniel lowered his burger and bore into her with his serious gaze.

"Fine with me. I haven't committed any crimes."

"Yet!" Tom said. "I got the special cuffs ready for when you do act up." She laughed as he leaned in and kissed her on the cheek.

Daniel laughed along with them before cracking a joke. "Like you can do anything about it. Especially after your go at me in the ring today."

"But that's about all I know," Christina said.

"So if anything, finding out more about the crank is a good step?" Daniel asked.

"I'm not a cop, but probably," she said.

"Good to know," Daniel said.

"So, are you and Rebecca getting serious? You haven't even told us what she looks like." Tom started to work on his pile of French fries.

"Well, she's an inch or two taller than I am." Daniel watched both their eyes widen in surprise. "She's getting a Ph.D. in psychology and writing a thesis and has the most beautiful head of hair I've ever seen. Dark brown with eyes to match. And she likes wrestling, too. She's really smart."

"You sound..." Christina began, "Almost like you met your match? That's not the best word, but hopefully, you know what I mean."

"Well, she's older, too. I feel like she's got her life together more than I do. Plus, with how brainy she is, I guess it's a little intimidating, you know? Like it's too good to be true." Daniel was pensive as he formed his thoughts about Rebecca.

"I mean, she fell for you. She can't be *that* bright," Tom joked.

"Very funny, smart ass. I dunno, I just don't wanna screw it up," Daniel said.

"I have to give you two some credit. I'm a nurse at St. Joseph's and the amount of bull shit I get, from patients even, is crazy. Apparently, I am not only a man, but I'm an idiot based on how I look. I think it says something about you that you even care about something more than the size of her chest," Christina said.

"That reminds me," Daniel said. "How did Tom act when you met? I imagine you scared the shit out of him with his tiny calves."

"Nobody pays attention to calves, Danny," Tom said in the quick space between the end of Daniel's sentence and the beginning of Christina's.

"We go to different gyms and Tom popped into mine one day for a workout a few months ago. He said he tries not to bother anyone when they're working out, but he broke that promise when he saw me, I guess," she smiled at Tom, "and I didn't care. I came up after a set of bench and we started talking for a bit. I figured I'd ask for a phone number."

"And I wanted to get some workout tips to pass along for you." Tom looked at Daniel and smirked.

"He was really sweet. He didn't care that my biceps have a better peak than his," Christina said, squeezing Tom close to her.

Daniel smiled as he finished his fries. "You guys ready to get out of here?"

"Yeah, I could go for a nap. Among other things," Tom said, his gaze shifting over to his girlfriend.

"It was nice to meet you," Christina said. "I'm looking forward to Greensboro."

"Likewise," Daniel said before he turned to Tom. "See you tomorrow."

After that, Daniel went back home and got ready for his Sunday scouting mission.

CHAPTER TEN

That night, while he was lying in bed, Daniel couldn't sleep. He spent most of the night looking up at his popcorn ceiling, barely visible among the brown-tinted hue of the street lights cavorting with the moon. Around three in the morning, he heard the slow creak of his floorboards, followed by what sounded like light footfalls. He waited. When the noises ceased, he threw his covers off of him and opened his bedroom window, allowing a cloak of light fog and humidity to hug his nearly naked body.

Outside, the muggy drapery clung to the silence of the street and his yard. When he was sure everything inside and out was quiet, he tiptoed to his door, and carefully crept into his hallway, stepping on the boards he knew to be noiseless. At the opening of the hall, he looked to his right into his living room. The coffee table sat, untouched and unspoiled, as it often did; the day's newspaper garnishing it in the lower right corner in front of his favorite reading spot. To his left, his dining room was just as still. The sight of the dinner table synced up with the poignant rumbling of his stomach, and he slinked towards his kitchen. Nothing was amiss, so he opened his fridge to pull out a big container of Country Crock margarine. He grabbed a fork from his silverware drawer and opened up the container and reached in.

He pierced a slice of chicken along with a floret of broccoli and brought it to his lips as he ate over the sink. When he bit into it, he frowned. Setting the tub down, he grabbed the glass salt shaker from his counter and looked at the chicken, broccoli, and rice in the margarine container, and liberally sprinkled the salt over his food. Shaker in hand, Daniel looked out of his window, and the reflection there made him shriek.

Behind him, he saw the dented, toothless face covered in a mask of crimson looking at him, accusatory in its silence. John Moore's visage was silent and ominous.

Daniel dropped the salt shaker and as it fell, it hit the edge of the counter, shattering into a glassy explosion all over his floor. He jumped back and looked back into the kitchen window, but the figure was gone.

Daniel spun quickly, only to find the space behind him bereft of anyone. He checked the window again. Nothing. The veins in his neck noted their fright, and he waited for it to subside before taking a few more bites of his food and cleaning up the mess. Before going back to bed, he went to the bathroom and splashed some warm water on his face to calm down, hoping he'd sleep. He did another check to see if any specters remained; upon finding none, he went back to bed for the night.

The next morning, Daniel gathered his camera along with pen and paper, while he made coffee before he left to spy on his partner. The kitchen window was less grim in the daylight, with no ghostly reminders of his personal failures. As the percolator sounded, the phone rang.

"Jesus Christ, what's with all the damn phone calls?" He grabbed the receiver. "Hello?"

"Good, you haven't left yet," Tom said on the other end.

"No, it's too early to go yet. I haven't had any coffee."

"You're still gonna go through with it, then?"

Daniel yawned and stretched before he talked again. "Yeah, of course I am. Why wouldn't I?"

"I dunno, maybe because you realized it's a braindead idea."

"Did you call to remind me you think I'm a fucking idiot for doing this?" Daniel asked, his impatience mounting.

Tom sighed on the other end. "No, but it is a dumb idea. Listen, I'm gonna go with you today."

"What's with the change of heart?"

"Well, I thought about it. And Christina gave me some perspective. Her uncle and the other guys will wanna keep this matter off the books, but it's to rein you in just in case you decide to do something too crazy."

Daniel smiled. "Well, I'm glad to see you changed your mind."

"Don't think too much about it. I don't wanna be out there all day. We get some information, we get the hell outta there."

"Yeah, that's all I wanted. Thanks, Tom."

"See you soon."

Daniel hung up the phone, delighted by the news, and poured his coffee while he sat on the couch and waited for his friend.

After his first cup of coffee, Daniel heard Tom pull up in his blue Chevy Nova Super Sport, adding to the harmony of the morning sounds, so he grabbed another coffee mug from the pantry.

Without so much as a knock, Tom walked in. "Good morning, sunshine. You ready?" Tom looked at Daniel for a moment as he kept his place by the door.

"Good morning to you, too," Daniel said, taking the hint. He poured his coffee and made way to the door.

"Let's be quick and not do anything stupid like getting us caught," Tom said.

"That's why we're taking the Nova. He doesn't know what it looks like," Daniel said with a smirk as they pulled away from Daniel's place.

"Did you sleep last night? You look like shit." Tom looked over at him while they stopped.

"Do you believe in ghosts?"

"I was hoping you'd tell me you were having a 'slumber party' with your girl. You mean like in *Ghostbusters*? I dunno. I've never seen one, I know that. Do you?"

"Maybe. I woke up last night, and I saw the guy from that domestic violence call. Scared the hell out of me. Spilled the salt, and he was gone when I looked up," Daniel said.

"You sound serious. I dunno if there're ghosts, but I did date this woman a while back, and her Italian grandma believed some weird stuff. Throwing salt over the shoulder, sometimes having it blessed. They burned sage, too."

"Sage?" Daniel asked.

"Yeah, she said it was to protect against evil in the house or something like that."

"Did it work?" Daniel asked.

"I mean, I don't go over there anymore, so maybe." The two men laughed at Tom's joke. "Those Catholics, man. They believe in some pretty crazy stuff. Crazier than normal religion, even."

"Shit, maybe it's all in my head. It's the first time I have seen something like that. I mean *really* saw it, not just pictures or rumors."

"Maybe ask your girl if it's in your head. She's into psychology, right?" Tom asked.

"I might do that."

Just like before, they pulled up to the end of Shawn's street and watched. The Bonneville sat in the driveway, motionless. Heat wavered off the asphalt and even with the windows down, the men started perspiring.

"It's fucking hot out here." Tom complained. I hope whatever happens, it happens soon."

"You're not even wearing your gear, you'll be fine," Daniel said. After some back and forth about the heat for a few more minutes, Tom got his wish. "Shh," Daniel said, holding up a hand. The sound of a Harley closed in on them as the ape hanger handlebars came into view. "There's Uncle Al." Like last time, Allan walked inside, and sometime later, he walked out with a bigger bag in hand than before. All the while, Daniel snapped photos on his disposable camera. "When he leaves, follow him."

"You want me to follow him? This biker, my car, off duty?" Tom asked incredulously.

"Absolutely," Daniel said. "I wanna see where he goes."

"You're nuts."

"Different car than when I ran into him last, and he won't recognize you. He probably won't even remember me."

"Danny, nobody forgets you. You're as tall as a basketball player without the skills," Tom said.

Daniel watched as Allan loaded his saddlebags with more illicit contraband; he looked at Tom, waiting. Tom looked at Allan, as sweat slowly collected on his temples and rolled down. Allan started his bike with a raucous revving of the gas and pulled out of Shawn's driveway. "Fuck it," Tom said, putting the Nova in drive in pursuit of Allan.

Somewhere before the South Carolina border, Allan pulled into a gas station, and parked at a pump. Tom slowed down.

"Pull in," Daniel said. "When he goes to pay, go in and distract him."

"How the fuck do I do that?" Tom asked as anxiety leaked from his words.

"Shit, I dunno. Buy a lotto ticket. That always holds up the line. I wanna get in those bags," Daniel said.

The gas pumps stood in view of the entrance to the store, with parking spaces in between and on the side of the building. Tom pulled the Nova up to one of the side spots, furthest away from the pumps. "Jesus Christ. When I get out, count to thirty, then go do whatever you need to do, and hurry."

"Relax, I got this," Daniel said as Tom left. He began his count. In those thirty seconds, he grabbed a pen and his camera before he speed-walked to Allan's bike and crouched between the gas pump and the Harley. He peered over the bike and saw Tom and Allan laughing together. Daniel got to work and turned to the back of the motorcycle and wrote the license plate number on his arm and followed that up by snapping more photos of the bike up close.

He stole a glance back inside just as Allan moved towards the cash register. Daniel haphazardly opened the saddle bag near him and saw the bag Allan got from Shawn, along with another large bag that looked and smelled like marijuana. Daniel purloined the bag of powder but did have the courtesy to leave the weed. He closed the bag, but in his haste, he wasn't careful when he latched the straps closed; oblivious to how motorcycles worked, Daniel didn't know that Allan kept it in neutral when he parked it here, and as such, he didn't expect the bike to roll forward, undoing the kickstand. Even more flustered, he tried to stand the bike up on its own again, his hands full with his camera and Allan's parcel, and tipped it the opposite way, where it landed with a crash. A crash that unfortunately drew the attention of both Allan and Tom.

Tom mouthed something resembling, *Oh fuck.* Allan's face contorted into a rage-filled scowl, and as he jogged towards the door, Daniel made a break for the Nova. As he ran, he tripped, and the camera clattered to the ground, causing Daniel to backtrack and grab it, hoping the asphalt collision didn't damage it.

Allan was closer than he would've liked, and Tom was gaining on him. As he turned to run back to the Nova, he felt hands push him forward. The camera flew out of Daniel's hands and fell to the ground, and he followed. He managed to tuck and roll to avoid any scrapes and quickly regained his footing. Tom restrained Allan as Daniel went towards them. Daniel planted his feet. "Let him go."

Tom raised his eyebrows in question, and Daniel nodded his assurance. Tom pushed Allan forward, at which point *his* forward momentum and the forward momentum of Daniel's fist met in the middle. Specifically, Allan's face met Daniel's fist. Allan dropped to a knee as Daniel and Tom ran to the Nova, with Daniel grabbing the items on the way. Daniel watched Allan work through his daze as the pair peeled out from the parking lot and back to the road.

"That wasn't exactly smooth going," Tom said, with no trace of his usual mirth.

"You're fucking telling me. You're the one who told me to hurry. It's okay to bow out if you want to," Daniel said.

"Yeah, I said to hurry, not wreck the goddamn bike. It's too late now," Tom said. "The fact that we got Shawn and who knows who else rolling with that strung-out Santa Claus means we have to stop them. What the hell is in those bags, anyway?"

Daniel opened the brown wrapping, revealing a compact brick of off-white powder wrapped tightly in plastic. "We've already fucked up enough. I don't wanna destroy this evidence. You think it's the crank Christina mentioned at lunch the other day?"

Tom looked over at the brick while he kept his periphery on the road. "From what I can tell, yes. Who runs the evidence lockup at your precinct?"

"I'm not sure. Shawn handled all that," Daniel said. "It looks like the same stuff that was in the small bag at the crime scene we were at, too."

"You gotta find out if it's making its way into the evidence room. Having access to that much to sell isn't gonna look good for him. Or whoever aided him in getting it," Tom said.

"Am I fucked because this will get shoved over to the feds? Will they even do anything?"

"I dunno," Tom said. "I still can't believe I let you talk me into that. Where are we going, anyway?"

"No clue, but away from The Demons. And Shawn, for now. Let's find a Waffle House somewhere out of the way."

"I like where your head is," Tom said.

When they arrived at the Waffle House, they sat in a booth away from everyone else while they cooled off in the air conditioning. Daniel pulled out the disposal camera and examined it. The lens and viewfinder both had cracks on it and the plastic of the camera was dangerously close to breaking in half and exposing the insides to the world. "You can't put film in sunlight, right?" Daniel asked.

"No," Tom said, "it ruins all the pictures. Maybe you can take it to a one-hour photo place and see what they can do."

"You think they can do the disposable camera?"

"Worth a try," Tom said. "We can check on the way back to your place."

"Let's see if we even have any of those places." Daniel motioned for the server. "Sorry to bother you, ma'am, but could I trouble y'all for a phonebook?"

A spritely young woman walked their way, her voluminous, dark brown teased hair bouncing along with her footsteps. "I don't know if we got a phone book, but I can check in the back for ya, hun. Give me a few minutes," she said.

"Even with the photos, we need a plan to take him down. Someone has to be working with him. Even if they just gave him the key to the evidence room and didn't ask questions," Daniel said, pulling a cigarette from his pack that he rapidly tapped on the table before he finally lit it.

"You gotta be careful poking around like that. These guys can get pretty defensive really quick. Especially the old-timers. Those mother fuckers love 'tradition' and that doesn't leave room for asking questions. *Especially* questions about dirty cops."

Daniel stared at the cigarette smoke as it rose in a stream, thinking about his options, given what he knew about his partner so far. "Maybe I'll talk to Detective Martin about it. She seems on the level. She can't stand Shawn, either."

"That might be a good idea," Tom said. "You think she'll be honest with you? Do you think you can trust her?"

"So far she has. It won't hurt to ask about any motorcycle gang cases at any rate." Daniel thumped his cigarette on the side of the ashtray, revealing the brightly smoking ember behind as the server walked towards them, phonebook in hand.

She placed the phonebook on the table, along with a pen. "Can I get y'all started with some coffee or sweet tea?"

Tom and Daniel looked at each other and nodded. "Let's get two coffees, darlin'," Daniel said.

"Coming right up." She turned from the table back towards the kitchen.

Tom leaned closer, lowering his voice. "What's with the 'darlin'' shit, Danny?"

"I was watching TV a long time ago, and they said to talk like people talk to make them like you, or something like that." Daniel stuck his cigarette in the ashtray as the server delivered them their coffee.

"My name's Nikki. Let me know if I can get ya anything else."

Daniel nodded to her and opened the phonebook, looking for any one-hour photo shop and coming up with nothing. "Looks like I might just have to take it to Eckerd and hope to get them back sometime soon. Before we go to Greensboro, ideally."

"Let's finish these and we can head out, then."

"You don't have to go along with this anymore if you don't want to. I don't want your name getting dragged into it too if we can help it."

"I appreciate that," Tom said before he drained his coffee. "I can probably still do some digging over at the east side if you need it, though."

"Thanks, Tom." Daniel finished his coffee and set four dollars on the table before the two made their return to Daniel's.

Tom parked his Nova in the driveway behind Daniel's truck. "Despite that massive mistake of letting that guy see you, that was," Tom paused, reluctant to finish, "fun. We don't have to make a habit of it, but it was fun."

Daniel laughed. "Well, when I see you again, it'll be relaxing. We'll have a good time. See you later." Daniel grabbed his camera along with the biker drugs before he stepped out from the Nova.

Once he got inside, Daniel pulled his notepad out and paged through the phone numbers before landing on Detective Martin. He dialed, and it rang several times before he got an answer.

"Martin residence, Holly speaking."

"Hey, Detective, it's Officer Belascoe." Daniel paused a second before adding, "From work."

Her voice came through the receiver, with a touch of confusion. "Hey, Daniel. I know who you are. What can I do for you?"

"I'd prefer to talk in person, as soon as possible, if you can."

"Is everything all right?"

"Yeah, everything is fine, I think. I just need some help, and it's urgent."

Detective Martin let her breath out. "Give me an hour, and head over."

"Thanks, Detective. See you soon." Daniel hung up, hopped in the shower, and grabbed the drugs and his camera, and all the information he'd written so far.

CHAPTER ELEVEN

*D*aniel hopped into the Chevy and made his way to Detective Holly Martin's residence. He pulled up to a well-kept red brick house on the opposite side of town. The house itself reflected her station in life. She was ten years Daniel's senior, stern and neutral when she spoke, and rarely opened up to anyone unless she trusted them. Daniel figured she'd only done so to him because she got caught, and he figured that information might be useful in getting her to lend a hand in his personal quest.

He parked on the street where he gathered all of his evidence against his partner so far before he walked up to the detective's door and, with his free hand, rapped the plate beneath the door knocker three times.

The door opened, and it wasn't Detective Martin standing there, but a shorter woman with ochre-tinted skin and dark brown hair.

"Hi, is Detec—I mean Holly Martin in?" Daniel asked.

"She's just getting out of the shower, but you're welcome to come in. Daniel, right?"

"Yes, that's me." He crossed the threshold and extended his hand as he slid his shoes off at the door.

"I'm Holly's partner, Sofía." She smiled as she shook Daniel's hand. "Have a seat on the couch. She shouldn't be much longer. Can I get you some sweet tea or water?"

"I would love some sweet tea, thank you."

Sofía went to the kitchen for the tea and grabbed three glasses from the cupboard as Daniel saw Detective Martin walk down the stairs with her hair wrapped in a towel and wearing an off-white tank top and a pair of men's jeans.

Daniel looked at her, confused. "What's with the manly outfit, Detective?"

Holly started to speak, but Sofía's laughter cut her off before she could finish a word. Holly looked at her partner and smirked. "That's a conversation for another day." She turned her attention to the items in Daniel's possession. "This better be good, Belascoe. What do you have for me?" She sat on the couch opposite Daniel, looking at him as Sofía served the tea. "Thank you, baby." Holly kissed Sofía on the cheek when she leaned over to set the tea down.

"I wrote what I know so far. And I have this." Daniel plopped the brick of drugs onto the coffee table next to the tea and the decorative roses.

Detective Martin looked at the drugs. Then at Daniel. Then the drugs again. "A brick of what looks to be crank. And how did you come to acquire this?"

"Are you familiar with a group called the Savannah Swamp Demons?" Daniel asked.

"Belascoe, I didn't start with the police department yesterday and become a detective today. I have worked some cases involving the Demons. You think this," she gestured towards the drugs, "is related to The Demons somehow?"

Daniel tried to take just a sip to cure his dry mouth and steady his nerves but wound up draining half the glass before he could speak. "I think," he began before clearing his throat, "I think Shawn and a few of them have some sort of business going on. This camera, if I can get the film developed, has pictures of one Demon entering and leaving Shawn's place with the drugs. Only lasted a few minutes. A few years ago, Shawn arrested him for aggravated battery."

Detective Martin leaned towards Daniel, her interest apparently piqued. "What tipped you off?"

Holly and Daniel looked at each other. Daniel was acutely aware of the power dynamic at hand and where he stood, but he couldn't read Detective Martin. "Can I be honest with you?"

"Are you asking me that professionally? Because the reason you're here now isn't part of the job. At all. If you're asking if you can trust me, I invite you to think about where you are. Nobody else knows about Sofía and me. You can figure out why I allowed you here. And, I guess there's something else. You have sort of an innate sense of..." Holly looked up, searching for the right word. "Justice. That's the word. And then I saw how you handled the

John Moore case. But doing your job well doesn't mean you're not an asshole. You didn't treat them like they were less for who they are. You wanted the right outcome. It's a gamble, but I think I can trust you being here and that you won't tell the rest of them about Sofía. You know who's on the right side of history. Even if you're too idealistic."

Daniel sat there stunned, holding his iced tea. "Uh," he said nervously, "Thank you. As to what tipped me off, that's pretty simple. I saw his behavior, and it pissed me off. So, I went looking to see what he was up to. I didn't expect to find anything like this. And I found a little bag at the crime scene that appears to match what's in this brick." Daniel added, "I have a suspicion it didn't make it into evidence."

She eyed him for a while. "Does he know what you're up to?" Holly asked.

Daniel paused unreasonably long.

"Jesus. He knows?" Holly asked in exasperation.

"Maybe not yet," Daniel said. "A buddy and I might have met up with someone in the gang on my excursion earlier today. A guy by the name of Allan Walker. The same guy I saw leaving Shawn's place."

She rested her head in her hands, looking down. "Jesus Christ, Belascoe, what happened?"

Daniel relayed the incident with Allan and the drug theft with Tom. He left out the breaking and entering portion of his investigation.

"Here's what we're gonna do. You leave the drugs with me. Take those pictures and get them developed and hope that something comes from it. If you have a typewriter, write a report. Bring that along with any pictures back. I'll get them to where they need to go as far as federal investigators go. We don't wanna step on anyone's toes because they can be dicks about it. We also don't wanna fuck up any investigations they have going on. Questions?"

Daniel looked pensively at the mountain of contraband he handed over before he decided it was safe to leave the only sure, physical evidence he had with Detective Martin. Coupled with the disapproval she had for Shawn, along with everyone else's disapproval of him, Daniel judged that her relationship meant more to her than fucking over a low-level cop. "Not that I can think of. I'll make a report as soon as I get home."

"Good. Drop it off here, not at the station. And leave out the incident from today."

"Got it. Thank you, Detective." Daniel finished his tea and stood up as Detective Martin did the same.

"I suppose I should thank you and your spite, Belascoe. To reiterate, Sofía and I are nobody's business at the precinct."

"Your secret's safe with me." Daniel and Holly shook hands before he hugged Sofía goodbye.

Daniel stopped at a drugstore to drop his camera off on the way back to his house. The clerk behind the photo counter said they'd be ready on Wednesday, but she changed his mind when Daniel handed her fifteen dollars and told him to come back tomorrow morning. At home, he got the type-writer out, made some coffee, and drafted his police report.

CHAPTER TWELVE

$\mathcal{T}$he next morning, in an unusual deviation from the norm, Daniel threw on his sweatpants, and without missing a beat, left to retrieve his pictures from the disposable camera. When he arrived back home, he made his coffee and sat down at his kitchen table. Only then did he notice he put his pants on backwards. Ordinarily, that would've bothered him, but he was more eager to see if his amateur photography paid off.

Daniel ripped open the packaging and his stomach fell to the floor in opposition to his rising nausea. All the work it took to snap the photos he thought would help was in vain. When he dropped the camera, it ruined everything. One by one, he pulled out discolored and badly developed pictures, showing nothing resembling what he shot.

After paging through them, he finally found something. In a single photo, Allan Walker walked toward his bike, drugs in hand, with a view of Shawn's car, as well as his neighbor's vehicle, in the background. Seeing that it was the only one that came out, Daniel had to use it. He placed the one passable photo with his report. When he left for his workout, he took a rather out-of-the-way detour to Detective Martin's house and folded the report around the photo before he slid it through the mail slot in her door.

That night, work was uneventful. Shawn didn't appear suspicious, nor did he act unbecoming when they went on patrol together. The sameness unnerved Daniel more than any obvious tell would have done. Monday passed, as did Tuesday and Wednesday, without incident. Without incident, beyond Daniel's uneasiness.

* * *

TWO PEANUT BUTTER and jelly sandwiches adorned Daniel's countertop, along with two cans of Diet Coke. Daniel packed his suitcase the night before and had it sitting next to his dining room table. His only job now was to wait for Rebecca before they set off on the drive to Greensboro. Not long after he made the sandwiches, he got a call from Detective Martin.

"Belascoe, I know you mentioned you're busy, but I got your delivery. I'll make sure it gets where it's needed."

"Thanks, Detective Martin. I'll see you when I get back."

After Daniel hung up the phone, Rebecca let herself in, suitcase in hand. She wore a backless, orchid-printed sundress along with a pair of sunglasses and asked, "Are you ready to go?"

"Two things before we go," Daniel said, walking back to the kitchen. "One, I still think we should take the Chevy, but I know you don't want to. And two, I made us sandwiches to eat."

She crossed over and hugged Daniel, and in so doing, grabbed her sandwich off the counter and ate. "You really are one of the most considerate people I've ever met. Thank you," she said in between bites. "But the Oldsmobile has more legroom."

"You don't *need* legroom when you have the power of a Chevy," Daniel said through his laughter.

"We don't need power when we're going on a leisurely trip," Rebecca said.

"Yeah, you're probably right. I hope you got some tapes so we don't have to listen to religion radio while we drive through the Carolinas."

"Religion radio?" Rebecca asked.

"Yeah, the hellfire and brimstone preachers have radio shows. The smaller the town, the better their signal comes in. And even more exciting, there's nothing else to listen to."

"Lucky for us, I got a few tapes lying around. Prince, Dire Straits, Tears for Fears, Wham! There are a few others, too. If you don't have good taste like I do, then I can't help you," Rebecca said.

They ate their sandwiches in the kitchen, with Daniel barely taking the time to chew his food properly because of his excitement. He leaned back against the counter as Rebecca finished her sandwich, and watched as she washed her hands. His eyes traveled down as they stood in silence, watching the pink orchids on her dress cling to her thighs as she leaned over the sink. They wandered past her butt, teasing its exit from the dress's hemline, and landed on her back. Rebecca's muscles contracted as she moved her hands back and forth, lathering the soap on her hands. When he didn't see a sign of a bra, his heart beat like a timpani at a double forte. He stood, paralyzed, long enough for Rebecca to turn around and catch him looking.

"Can I help you?" she asked before she bit her lower lip.

"Maybe. I'm watching your dress wrap around your legs and I like it." Daniel thought using words might be more prudent instead of physicality. Not to mention he still couldn't move, and even speaking was a noteworthy achievement for him right now.

"Yeah?" Rebecca stepped in front of him, trapping him between her and the counter when she placed her hands beside him, creating a barrier he couldn't free himself from. She leaned her face close to his. "What else do you like?"

Not much doubt remained regarding their congruent intentions and before he could answer, their lips met in a torrent of passion and lust. Their serpentine arms crawled around each other, leaving Daniel doubtless about her feelings as he moved his lips to her collarbone and kissed it.

Rebecca let out a deep breath when Daniel's lips grazed her clavicle. He pressed his lips harder and slid his hands down her back, stopping at the hem of her dress. He raised his hands and lifted it over her head then tossed it back to the living room where it landed in a clump of pink orchids and white fabric. Rebecca stood before him in a light beige pair of bikini underwear and her exposed breasts. She returned the favor and stripped Daniel of his shirt, tossing it near her dress.

He ran his hands down the muscles of her back feeling the cold sweat of her body before peeling the underwear off her, leaving her fully exposed in his kitchen with nothing but a perfectly trimmed rectangle of hair on her pubic mound directing his gaze to her vulva.

Rebecca grabbed a handful of Daniel's hair, moved her lips to his ear, and whispered, "Put me on the counter and help yourself to dessert."

With her directive, lifted her off the ground and sat her on the counter, before he kneeled down on the floor to obey her. With her legs loosely draped over his back, his tongue traversed the line between her southern lips upward, stopping just shy of her clit and repeated the process. Every small moan that escaped Rebecca's lips stoked Daniel's fervor, his pressure increasing with every movement. He quickened his pace as he felt her body respond to him. When she tensed her body, he backed off and repeated the process until her breathing escalated into a rhythmic cadence with pools of his saliva and her come dripping on the countertop.

As he traveled upward again, he stopped at her clit and wrapped his lips around it and sucked on it as Rebecca's bodily tension grew. The more her tension grew, the more she squirmed in ecstatic throes until her heels pressed into his back as her legs squeezed his head tight at the peak of her ecstasy. Daniel kept going and seconds later Rebecca let out a long, deep moan and relaxed her entire body on the countertop, letting her hands hold her limp body upright. She leaned into him as the two embraced each other and Daniel noticed red splotches on her flushed body.

"Do you wanna keep going?" He asked before he tasted her cold lips in a kiss.

She nodded her head as she unbuckled his pants and got down from the counter. Now they both stood naked in the kitchen and Rebecca kicked his pants away before she turned around and placed her hands on the counter.

Daniel placed a hand around her hips and held firm while the fingers of his free hand swam through her body's cream. He moved his finger in a circle around Rebecca's clit while his cock let out a few drops of pre-come. He slid his middle two fingers into her pussy, coating them in her wetness before he stroked himself. His dick stood aroused, aching to be taken. Daniel licked his fingers to taste her again before he grabbed Rebecca by the folds of her hips. A string of come dripped from her pussy onto the floor, and Daniel accepted the invite and slid into her.

Rebecca looked back at him, and a low moan escaped from her. The sound of it pulled Daniel close to climax, and he slowed himself, reaching down between her legs to finger her in rhythm to his thrusting. As he slowed, Rebecca's body contracted her pelvic muscles, gripping him as he went back and forth. As her muscles contracted more, her legs shook, and Daniel used the strength of his free hand to keep her steady. She rocked back forcefully into Daniel, growing weak-kneed and relying on his support to keep her legs straight to keep the symphony of skin and perspiration going. The clapping echoes reverberated all through the kitchen.

With every squeeze of her pussy around Daniel, he was closer to climax. Sweat dripped from his forehead into a small pool at the small of her glistening back. As Daniel thrusted and worked his fingers, Rebecca's legs trembled, and her knees nearly buckled until she gripped the countertop. From her mouth came a prolonged, high-pitched whimper as her body tensed and released in her orgasm. She moved Daniel's hand away as he kept going.

"Are you close?" she asked him.

He grunted something resembling an affirmative answer.

"Come on me, not in me," Rebecca said.

With her permission now, Daniel picked up his pace, until he pulled out to stroke himself to completion. He grabbed his shaft with a sweat-polished forearm, sliding up and down until his come shot out, streaking Rebecca's back twice before the remnants mixed with their sweat collecting in the small of her back. Daniel slumped over her, not caring about the mess they were making, and hugged her closely. When he lifted his head, he was stunned. The gasp he let out was a little louder than he'd hoped.

"What happened?" Rebecca turned her head to look at him, her face shiny and her skin flushed.

Daniel paused awkwardly, deliberating how he would say what he needed to. He went for the direct option. "I accidentally got come in your hair."

Rebecca smiled and stood up, facing him. "It probably won't be the last time it happens," she shrugged her shoulders and ran a finger along his chest before licking it clean.

"Let me get a towel. Stay right there." He speed-walked to the linen closet and grabbed a towel. He wiped Rebecca clean. "I think we should take a shower before we go."

"That's a good idea. I don't feel like digging my shampoo out, so I hope you have some."

Daniel smirked. "I do. I suppose I can let you use it."

She punched him playfully on the arm before they hopped in the shower.

* * *

"WHO'S DRIVING FIRST?"

"You can," Rebecca said. "Just take care of the Olds."

"What do I look like, a bad driver?"

"No comment," she said, smiling.

"You're gonna find out." Daniel picked up his suitcase, locked the door, and the pair headed to the Oldsmobile. Along the way, he stopped to make sure he locked the Chevy, and they sat as Daniel pulled out a map and a pencil. He looked at the route, folded the map, and made some notes about the directions. When he was finished, he handed Rebecca the map and drove.

Less than ten minutes later, they pulled into Dunkin' Donuts and Daniel ordered two coffees and a half dozen doughnuts.

"Coffee, Diet Coke, and Doughnuts? It's not even eleven, and we just had sandwiches, too," Rebecca said.

"Well, the doughnuts are for later, and the caffeine is for now."

"So, is the cop and doughnut stereotype true?"

Daniel looked ahead as he pulled onto the highway. The roads, as well as the sky, were clear. "Apparently it is true. I've always liked them. But the hours of doughnut shops make it more convenient and cheaper because police work odd hours."

"Wouldn't a healthier option be a better idea? Like maybe apples or something?" Rebecca asked.

"You can't dunk apples in coffee," Daniel said.

"Not with that attitude you can't."

"By the way, we covered my father's grisly death, but we never talked about your upbringing. Spill it, soon-to-be Dr. Church."

"I will. But then you have to tell me about your mom."

Daniel grabbed a doughnut from the box before he said anything and took a bite.

"Growing up in New York should've been more fun than it was. Big city like that, with so many places, and they thought being strict was a good idea," Rebecca said, looking out the window.

"Was it a religion thing?" Daniel asked.

"No. That would've at least made some sense. Still would've been ridiculous, but at least there would've been a reason." Rebecca paused for a moment. "I think it was just because it was a big blue-collar city, and they didn't want me to die. They wouldn't let me take a bus or a train until I was about halfway through high school."

"How'd you end up there?"

Rebecca turned to Daniel and put her feet up on the dashboard. "You ever see one of those fancy mirrors, with the woodcarving around the glass?"

Daniel nodded. "Yeah, the carving that doesn't really serve a purpose."

"Yeah, those are the ones. We lived upstate, and he was a craftsman. He made those mirrors by hand. He figured he'd try opening his own shop in the city. So, after the war, he and my mom moved to Manhattan when they had enough money to open up his shop. And to his credit, he did well. I'll show you a mirror when you come over."

"I'd enjoy that. You also don't seem so," he paused with the word he wanted on the tip of his tongue. "Sheltered. You don't seem sheltered."

"I read a lot. And books have lots of ideas, and you can go down the threads for a long time. I read lots of good books at the library, since we lived near one and I could go."

Daniel thumped his fingers on the steering wheel, saying nothing.

"What's the matter?" Rebecca asked. "Your fingers are drumming a mile a minute."

"I—" Daniel started, before he took a breath. "Oh, the heck with it. If I can eat you out on my counter, I should be able to say it." He took another breath. "I don't read much, and I think I'm afraid you'll think I'm dumb."

Rebecca put her elbow on the door where it met the window, and rested her head on her palm, looking at Daniel. "I don't think you're dumb at all. Besides, if you wanna read books, I can always lend you mine. Or give you recommendations."

"Oh, yeah?" he asked.

"Of course. People who like to learn are sexy," Rebecca said. "I'll give you a copy of *Their Eyes Were Watching God*, when we get back."

"I'd like that. Don't tell me anything about it. I want to go in blind."

"Consider it done." She smiled at him and shifted in her seat.

"This talk was sort of a sad reminder of how small my family really is. But my mom is actually still alive and living in Savannah."

"Do you see her often?"

Daniel paused and shifted his body as he drove. He stuffed the last half of the doughnut in his mouth and finished it. "Not as often as she'd like. Or as often as I should," he said with more solemnity than he'd intended.

"Why?"

"I don't really know. It's hard. She was always there for me after my dad died, but it's like she just stopped moving. She never really 'got' me, if that makes sense. But I don't think she's a bad mom. Even though she calls me at the worst times. You're not Freuding me, are you? Wasn't he obsessed with people being obsessed with their mothers?"

Rebecca stifled a laugh, "He totally was. But we don't really revere him as much as they did twenty years ago. Did you ever see *Psycho*?"

"Not that I recall," Daniel said.

"At least you've seen *Gremlins*. Anyways, there's a scene at the end where the shrink psychoanalyzes Norman Bates and it's pretty Freudian. It's not necessarily bad, but it's definitely a product of the time. And for his time, Freud was pretty remarkable. He also did a lot of cocaine and wrote about it. But the good thing about pioneers of their time is they give way to pioneers of the future."

Daniel looked to the side and smiled in delight as he saw Rebecca's legitimate excitement over the things for which she was passionate. "So it's like improving on technology? But with ideas and not necessarily things?" he asked.

"Sort of," she said. "It's adaptive and it's intentional, because in science, you're trying to prove yourself wrong, and then you can think of new hypotheses."

"So, what are you doing your thesis on?"

"Jung and pop culture," she said.

"That's the archetype guy, right?"

"He is. And they play out in some of our movies and books today if you buy into them."

"When do I get to read it?" Daniel looked at her with admiration.

"Maybe when it's done, if I allow it."

Daniel grinned at her as they continued their northward trek to Greensboro.

CHAPTER THIRTEEN

"You smell that?" Daniel asked, sniffing.

"Smell what?" Rebecca looked at him and sniffed, following his lead.

"Smoke and burning rubber. I'm gonna pull off and see what's going on." Daniel veered off the next exit and, according to the sign, a town called Middlesboro was two miles ahead, with a population of fifteen hundred.

"I smell it. It's overheating. Look at the temperature gauge," Rebecca said, pointing out the gauge as it jogged towards the right.

"Shit. Roll the windows down. I'm gonna turn the heater on until we can check it out." Daniel turned the heater on. With the heat outside of the car mixing with the heat inside, he and Rebecca were dripping sweat within minutes to where Rebecca contorted herself to roll the back windows down, too.

After five more minutes of riding along the desolate back road of Middlesboro, they came upon a gas station with a garage attached to it. As they pulled in, they realized it was open, despite the lack of activity they saw from the road. The two-car-wide service area housed two vehicles on lifts in the middle of repair, with no attendants to be found. Daniel stopped next to a pump and once he shut the car off, smoke billowed out from the small openings on the side of the hood. Once he opened the hood, a large plume escaped skyward.

"Well, that's not good." Rebecca stood next to him, with her hands on her hips.

Daniel moved to look beneath the car before he stood back up. "There's a leak somewhere, too," he said. "Told you we should've taken the Chevy."

Rebecca gave him a playful slap on the arm. "Well. At least we're here." She gestured at the expanse of nothing that lay before them. "Wherever 'here' is. They should be able to fix it. Wouldn't be so bad if it weren't so damn hot." As she stood there, she started pulling the sweaty fabric of her dress away from her skin.

"I hope so. They don't seem too busy." Daniel closed the hood, and they both went inside the store.

Once inside, Daniel grabbed two bottles of water for them while Rebecca used the bathroom. As Daniel wandered the small store, the faint sounds of the AM radio played in the background, talking about a second missing person likely to have gotten lost in the woods in the past week. The unfortunate victim this time was a congressman's son. Behind the counter, a middle-aged clerk dozed off in a chair with a fan pointing directly at his sun-kissed face. The sound of the blade mingled with the light snoring while Daniel waited as Rebecca returned to join him. He rang the bell, startling the clerk awake.

The clerk's eyes shot awake. "Dammit, this heat'll take it outta ya. What can I do for y'all?" The man's eyes widened when he saw the giants by comparison standing in front of the counter.

"Sorry to wake you up like that. Wanted to grab these and see if you got anyone who can look at that Oldsmobile outside. Looks like something might be wrong with the radiator," Daniel said, sliding the water bottles forward.

"Be a dollar for the waters, my friend. I got two guys on the way back right now. They'll be able to take a look at the car and see what they can do for you. I'd offer you to wait here in the cooler air, but I think it's hotter in here than out there. Choice is yours."

Daniel chuckled. "I appreciate that. We'll be around."

"Name's Bruce." The clerk and Daniel shook hands. "Gimmie a holler if y'all need anything. Shouldn't be much longer until they're back."

Rebecca and Daniel went back outside and sat under the overhangs near the entrance to get some reprieve from the sun while they waited for the repairmen to return.

"Look at this," Daniel said as he held his arms open to the wooded landscape of Middlesboro.

"I see some trees on the other side of the road," Rebecca said.

"*This* is a great American bash. Right in the heart of small-town America." Daniel couldn't keep a straight face and shortly, Rebecca joined him in his laughter.

"This reminds me of the gas station in *The Texas Chainsaw Massacre*," she said when the laughter subsided.

"What, it was a small town, and a chainsaw-wielding monster ransacks it?"

"More like a family of cannibals rendered jobless, living in the same town as an abandoned slaughterhouse. They butcher and eat the tourists."

"I love lighthearted fare like that," Daniel quipped.

"We'll watch it sometime. That way, I can broaden your cinematic horizons some more." She smiled and rested her head on Daniel's shoulder as they waited.

A while later, a tow truck pulled into the service station, with "Jim's Gas and Go Garage" on the doors. Once parked off to the side, a man with long, light brown, sweat-covered hair pulled back into a ponytail stepped out. A cigarette dangled from his lips and the smoke snaked its way through his two-day-old stubble. From the passenger side, a woman, nearly as tall as Rebecca, stepped out. Her dark hair was matted by perspiration on her head and face.

"You waiting around for us?" the lady asked as she and the other guy walked towards Daniel and Rebecca.

Daniel noticed the jumpsuits with patches bearing the same logo emblazoned on the truck. "If you are the mechanics, yes. Something's going on with the radiator in that Oldsmobile over there." He and Rebecca stood up and shook hands with the mechanics.

"I'm Lisa, this is Little Jim, Jim's son. Damn thing overheat on you?" she asked.

"Yeah, a few miles back on the highway. We pulled off here and found this place," Rebecca said.

"Well, that's usually the way of it. We get a lot of that." She looked over as Little Jim started poking around in the hood and under the car. "Hopefully we can take a look and get you out of here quick."

Little Jim joined the group and had a prognosis. "Looks like you got a crack in the radiator. Short term, y'oughtta be okay. We might be able to put some epoxy on it and it'll hold for a while."

"We need to let it cool, and that'll take a few hours," Lisa said, "but we can hopefully get it road-ready today."

As she spoke, a police officer rolled into the gas pump behind the Oldsmobile. A strapping man in his mid-thirties stepped out of the car and filled up his tank. Daniel noticed a menacing bee with an overly phallic stinger holding an anchor tattooed on the officer's forearm. His sunglasses obscured half his face but couldn't hide the stern, chiseled jawline or expressionless face. Nor could they hide his short and tight fade of a haircut or his perfectly tailored uniform.

As the mechanics moved the car out of the way, Rebecca leaned into Daniel and whispered to him. "You're not getting jealous of your distant colleague now, are you?"

Daniel did look at the officer. "Only because his tailor's bill is probably lower since he can find a decent inseam without much work. I'm thinking maybe he can give us a ride somewhere if he's got the time. Maybe somewhere with air conditioning."

"Yeah, that'd be nice. I'm dying out here. I'm gonna go grab a doughnut from the car."

Daniel looked at the fabric of her sundress and the way it stuck to her hips and outlined her curves before he introduced himself to the officer. He noticed the officer's head watching Rebecca walking away, too.

"Hot damn, son," the officer said, sliding his sunglasses up to get a better look. "That woman of yours has a rack that would make a damn grown moose cry." The officer continued to look until Rebecca made it inside and he finally lowered his sunglasses.

Daniel ignored the rude remark and offered his hand out. "Hey, Daniel Belascoe, Savannah Police."

The officer removed his sunglasses and took Daniel's hand. "Deputy Kevin Hall, Middlesboro Police Department. What can I do for you?"

Daniel squeezed Deputy Hall's hand a little tighter than he normally did before moving it away. "We got stranded here and we're having them check out the car to see if they can get us up and running again later today."

"Well, Lisa over there is the best mechanic I've ever seen, if anyone can do it, she can," Hall said.

"Excellent. I was wondering if you could give us a ride over to the station or anywhere where it's cool while we wait for them to check out the car." Daniel looked at Deputy Hall to see if he could discern anything else about his character beyond the off-color remark he made to Rebecca, but any perceptions were as illegible as a novel handwritten by a three-year-old.

"Yeah, that won't be a problem. Let me go to the can real quick and I can take you and your lady over there. I'll give Sheriff Sutherland a call and let him know." Deputy Hall headed inside the store as Rebecca walked toward Daniel.

"Wanna hear something neat I just learned from the deputy?" Daniel asked as he wrapped his arm around Rebecca's waist.

"Let's hear it." She handed him a doughnut.

"Apparently, you have 'a rack that would make a damn grown moose cry.' His words, not mine."

Rebecca looked down at her chest. "Well, they *are* great. I bet all the women love him, too."

"He's also gonna give us a ride to the police station so we can wait for them to look at the car." Daniel took out half the doughnut in his hand in one bite as Hall came back out and led them to his cruiser.

CHAPTER FOURTEEN

Ten minutes later, they pulled up to a nondescript building. If they were driving on their own, they might have missed it entirely; the only indication it was the police station was the faded lettering above the entrance that marked it as the Middlesboro Police Department. The lone building was distant from any businesses or residents. The pine scent of the woods permeated Daniel's olfactory senses as they all walked inside.

Beyond the glass door, there wasn't much to look at. Two desks, one for Hall and the other for the Sheriff, were in the main lobby, along with a bench for visitors. Deputy Hall showed them around, and besides the hallway, there was an area in the back with an overnight holding cell, a small, solitary locker room next to another room sparsely populated with evidence and a few case files. The only other rooms were closed, opposite each other. Daniel assumed they might be interrogation rooms and wondered how often the officers in this town had to interrogate anyone. When they got back to the main lobby, another police car pulled into the parking lot and out stepped the town's only other working officer, as far as Daniel could tell.

The cop looked to be a man in his mid-fifties. He placed a hat atop his full head of alabaster hair and smoothed his shirt, thus completing his immaculate uniform. As he walked towards the door, Daniel wondered if every move this guy made was as intentional as they appeared. He looked like the type who wouldn't even let a five o'clock shadow grow on his day off, and his broad shoulders and thick forearms belied the type of strength that came out on rare occasions. The same type of strength allowed blue-collar men to go from calm to a state where they could rip the engine out of a car and heave it across a garage in one clean action.

"Y'all the ones Hall radioed me about?" he asked the couple once he crossed the threshold inside.

"Unless another couple got stranded between now and then, I think we are." Daniel held his hand out. "Daniel Belascoe." The man shook Daniel's hand with an iron-forged grip.

"Nice to meet you, Daniel." He looked at Rebecca and tipped his hat. "And you, Miss…"

"Church. Rebecca Church." She stepped forward and shook his hand.

"I'm Sheriff Sutherland. Call me Wayne, if you'd like." Sheriff Sutherland sat at his desk and continued. "Kevin here tells me he ran into you at Jim's when your car died on you, is that right?"

"Yes, sir," Daniel said. "We were headed up to Greensboro to see The Great American Bash, and the thing started smoking."

"Great American Bash, huh? I hope Rhodes kicks that son of a bitch Flair all over that arena."

"You watch wrestling, too?" Rebecca asked.

"Me and the wife like to catch the Crockett shows when we get the chance. Can't get Hall over there to watch, though."

"Even if I wanted to, you think my wife would let me put that nonsense on the TV?" Hall asked.

"Just remind her whose TV it is. Whenever you get better taste, of course."

"Anyways, I'm gonna head back out and make my rounds. I'll keep you posted if I hear anything." Hall made his exit.

"Is it just you and Deputy Hall for this whole town?" Daniel asked as he and Rebecca sat on the waiting bench.

"Yeah, just the two of us. Mostly kids being knuckleheads, and people who know better acting like petty thieves." He spoke as he opened a file on his desk and pulled out some papers.

"Any news on the missing person?" Daniel asked.

Sheriff Sutherland stopped shuffling and writing and looked up at Daniel. "How'd you hear about that?"

"The radio at Jim's said something about it," Daniel said. He looked at the sheriff, worried he'd overstepped by asking.

"Well, it's been some days, but nothing came up yet." Once amiable, the sheriff's responses now bordered on laconic.

"And no suspects or bodies or anything?" Daniel asked.

"You always ask a lot of questions like this?" Sheriff Sutherland looked hard at Daniel.

Daniel wondered if he could bring the sheriff back to a friendlier cadence. "Not as often as before I joined the force down in Savannah." Daniel watched Sutherland's shoulders loosen when he mentioned his employment.

"Apologies for being brusque." He set his hand down and stood up, leaning on his desk as he looked out the window. "Sometimes nosey types like to cut in and meddle with the work. You're young, so you might not have dealt with it, but if you've been around as long as I have, you'll see it."

"No need to apologize, sir. It's your jurisdiction and I'm just a curious out-of-towner." Daniel lit a cigarette.

"Hall's a decent deputy. Hell, that's why I hired him, but he's a damned lecher if there ever was one. He didn't tell me you were with SPD on account of him practically drooling about your girl there. Could practically hear it hit the ground when he was radioing me."

Rebecca rolled her eyes and chuckled.

Sutherland continued, "I imagine one stern look from you, miss, will put him in his place."

"It usually does," she said. "At least he didn't ask me how the weather was up here."

"Sometimes I wonder how that boy managed to find a wife. Even still, stay married to her for ten years. Anyways. We've been a bit quiet on this one. The missing boy was a politician's kid. State politician, and in a small town, but those news rags'll latch onto it if they could. Especially since not much happens here."

The phone rang and cut off Daniel's reply. The sheriff promptly answered it and motioned to Rebecca to grab the phone.

She shifted the receiver to her right ear and tilted her head to clamp it on her shoulder. "Hello, Rebecca speaking."

Daniel watched her play with the phone cord as she responded to questions from the unseen caller. Shortly after answering, she hung up.

"Was that Jim's calling back?" he asked while he jammed his cigarette in the ashtray.

"Yeah. The crack in the radiator is too big and they need to replace it. Looking at a day or two to fix." Rebecca stretched before she took her seat next to Daniel. "Or whenever a new radiator comes."

Daniel scratched his head and looked down for a moment. Finally, he looked up. "What if we stayed at a motel and went to a junkyard and see if they have one?"

"Hate to deliver bad news your way," the sheriff interrupted, "but the only motel burned down years ago and nobody built it back. The wife and I got an extra room and you're welcome to it, though."

"That's sweet of you, but we couldn't impose on you like that," Rebecca said.

Daniel looked at her and wondered why they couldn't.

"If it was an imposition, I wouldn't have offered," the sheriff said. "Room ain't doing anybody any good just sitting there. I'll call my wife and let her know to get some extra food."

* * *

DANIEL, Rebecca, and Sutherland pulled up to his family's house near the woods on the edge of town. The old paint had faded into an off-white color in the hundred-plus years since it had been built, but the Sutherlands main-tained it well. Inside, the deep-stained hardwood floor gleaned a dark brown hue that didn't fade or falter as Daniel and Rebecca toured the interior. Rows of family pictures lined the walls upstairs.

Sheriff Sutherland's family, in particular, came from a long line of enlisted men. Four pictures of individual men caught Daniel's eye with the earliest black-and-white photo depicting a man who looked young in his physicality and battle-hardened in his visage. *John W. Sutherland, 1845 - 1918.* The next one was a better quality photo, with an updated military uniform. *Lewis T. Sutherland, 1885 - 1961.* The next, another black and white showing their host, years before he became the sheriff. *Wayne G. Sutherland, 1930.* And there was a final photo, more updated and in color, but nearly identical to the one before it. *James G. Sutherland, 1954.*

"Korea?" Daniel looked at the next to the last photo and then at his host.

"That's right. Before that, the First World War, and back to the Civil War. The damn Confederacy made my granddaddy fight, and I guess it's in the blood since my dad and me wound up doing the same." Sheriff Sutherland looked at the pictures, his eyes lingering on his grandfather's in particular. "James didn't get drafted, but he wanted to go, anyway. I told him to think about doing something else with his life, but kids these days are stubborn. Think they know it all. At least he's not over in Iraq, I guess, getting tied up with whatever that idiot in office is doing."

"Not a fan of Reagan, I take it?" Rebecca asked as they walked down the hall toward a room at the end.

"Heck no. Granddaddy worked out a deal with some Union officers to help their side and turn the tide of the war towards something better. Reagan and Nixon? Those prejudiced crooks wouldn't be friends with my granddad if they met right now."

They passed more portraits filled with the enormous families the Sutherlands belonged to before arriving at the guest room.

"You two can stay here," Wayne said. "We sleep downstairs if you need anything. We even had some upgrades done to this old place, so you got a bathroom in there, too. I'm gonna head back downstairs and help my wife finish up the cooking. We'll give you a knock when it's ready."

Daniel judged that this room was once James's room. A poster of The Rolling Stones decorated the door to the closet. When they closed the bedroom door, they found Julie Newmar in a swimsuit and high heels staring back at them. Next to the bed, there stood a wooden nightstand adorned with a tie-dye cover, complete with a lava lamp.

Rebecca looked back at the Julie Newmar poster. "Lava lamp aside, he's got good taste in women."

"Is that a famous movie star or something?" Daniel asked as he sat down on the bed.

"You don't know Julie Newmar? She was Catwoman twenty years ago." Rebecca started unpacking her bags and retrieved her toothbrush.

"I was a Raquel Welch guy myself," Daniel said. "And Audrey Hepburn."

"I see you're a man of tradition," Rebecca said as she started removing her clothes.

Daniel tilted his head to the side and looked at her.

"You're keeping to your tradition of good-looking brunettes." Rebecca went to the attached bathroom and splashed water over her face.

"I find that consistency works well for me," Daniel said. He got up and removed his shirt. "You think this shower will fit the two of us, much less one of us?"

"I think if we crouched down a little bit, we could make it happen." She spoke with a mouthful of toothpaste before spitting it out. "Ready to find out?"

* * *

"I don't know if I'm ready to experience that again. Frankly, I'm surprised we both made it out of there alive," Daniel said as he slowly slid his thick leg through the resistant fabric of his jeans.

"Come on, it didn't leave a mark at all." Rebecca, despite having jeans just as tight as Daniel's, didn't have the same difficulty getting her legs in the pants.

"Yeah, it's fine. You only might have dislocated my jaw." He moved his jaw in every direction and rubbed it before Rebecca stood before him and grabbed his chin. She looked at his jaw and touched it in a few places.

"Any of that making it hurt worse?" she asked as she examined him.

"No, it'll be fine. Tom got a lucky shot on me there at the gym one day, and it feels about the same. His was on purpose though. Imagine what you could do if you *meant* to headbutt me there."

She kissed his jaw. "Hopefully that helps. You're gonna need it later."

Daniel smirked. "At least yours is intact and pain-free." Daniel smiled and pulled Rebecca closer, returning her kiss. "It also smells really good down there."

When they went downstairs to the dining room, the scent of hot food wafted towards them. An invisible cloud of oil and spices permeated through the old southern home, and the warmth from it all added to the southern heat lingering in the air. Daniel's stomach jumped forward, eager for whatever it was that lay beyond the door in the kitchen.

"Hope ya like fried chicken," Wayne said when he entered the dining room. "Got some roasted carrots, mashed potatoes and gravy, and succotash. Now, if you'll excuse me, I'm gonna go put some more fitting supper clothes on. Have a seat at the table and we'll join you soon."

Daniel and Rebecca sat at the side of the dining room table and helped themselves to the water already laid out along with the plates. Shortly after they sat, a sinewy, lanky woman with a two-tone gray and dirty blonde head of hair came out to greet the guests. She wore a long yellow dress with white frills beneath an apron covered in food that didn't make it to the meal.

"Evening, y'all. I'm Dorothy Sutherland. I know Wayne said it, but it don't hurt none to hear it again, but make yourselves at home." She shook their hands as a door closing echoed in the background. Wayne, now dressed in loose-fitting overalls, made his way into the kitchen. Dorothy removed the apron and hung it on the kitchen door.

One by one, Wayne started bringing out casserole dishes. First, the roasted carrots, followed by the succotash. Then, a generous pot of mashed potatoes accompanied by a gravy boat, and on an ornate serving plate, ten pieces of assorted fried chicken with steam rising off the golden brown cornmeal and flour breading.

Daniel, in his haste, went to dish out the food until he felt a blunt kick right in his shin. Rebecca looked to him and then the Sutherlands, who were in the process of joining hands for prayer. Daniel immediately turned his focus on the prayer and joined hands with Rebecca and the Sutherlands.

Wayne prayed, "Father God, we offer thanks for this meal before us and the blessings we have and get to share with our neighbors Miss Church and Mister Belascoe, in the name of Christ. We hope their travels go as smoothly as they can, and we ask that you keep watch over our boy while he carries out his oath to his country. Amen."

"Amen," the rest of them echoed.

Now they passed around the dishes and served themselves. Between the four of them, the chicken was divided in a matter of moments, and the heaping side portions seemed infinite in quantity. The taste remained perfect, no matter how much Daniel ate.

Rebecca finished a chicken leg, removing every visible section of spare meat from the bone before setting it down. "This is the best chicken I've had. Which one of you wants to share the recipe with me? I won't cook it, but he will." She cocked her head in Daniel's direction.

"I don't know if I could match this," Daniel said, his voice pouring with admiration.

"That would be my mama's recipe. I learned it when I was a boy, watching her." Wayne smiled, full of pride. "But Dorothy here made it her own."

"It's a team effort," Dorothy said. "We both love to cook. Wayne maybe a little more than me."

"One of these days, I dream of opening a restaurant. Nothing fancy, just feel-good food. The type that gets you feeling right after a long day of work or being on the road," he said. "I could do it sooner if I could convince Hall to take over for me."

"I thought you said he was the best?" Daniel asked.

"He is. And to his credit, he is good, but his heart isn't in being the Sheriff, I don't think. Plus, it's a small town, and the worst candidates are...well, they don't come close to Hall's skill, let's just put it that way. Hall and his wife want to get into a bigger city, at some point. Can't imagine why, the job here ain't too bad. But he could make an honest living anywhere, even if he isn't polic-ing. He's good with his hands."

"If it makes a difference, I hope you get to live out your dream. I'd tell everyone I know to visit," Rebecca said.

"What about you, Miss Church?" Dorothy asked. "What do you do?"

"I'm getting a doctorate in psychology down in Savannah. Should be done with it in the winter if all goes well."

"Well, that's a mighty fine achievement. One of my nephews did something like that. He has his own office with a chair for people to lie down in and everything. Are you gonna have your own office, too?" Dorothy asked.

"I'm not sure. It's one route I could go. I could also teach and do research, which I also like the idea of." Rebecca finished her glass of sweet iced tea and helped herself to another one right as the phone rang.

Wayne stood up before Dorothy. "I got it, honey. You do enough around here as it is. At least they let us eat in peace before they called."

Five minutes later, Wayne walked back into the dining room, looking down as his fingers stroked his chin.

"Wayne, who was it?" Dorothy looked concerned.

"It was Hall. They found that missing boy's body, and it sounds bad. I gotta get over there. Daniel, you're welcome to come along. We haven't had anything this serious go down in Middlesboro in a damn long time and an extra set of eyes—or muscle, if it comes down to it—never hurt."

Daniel looked at Wayne, thinking. Then he turned his head towards Rebecca.

"I don't mind. More rest for me," she said.

"We can manage here just fine," Dorothy said.

CHAPTER FIFTEEN

*D*aniel and Wayne took a silent drive down a dark road near the woods outside of town. The light from the ornate waning moon barely pierced the humid fog, smothering everything it touched like a heavy, damp blanket. They stopped on the side of the road near an entrance to a farm, settled on a few acres of land, stepped out of the car and waited. Daniel smoked and spied a barn in the distance. Closer to him a single house stood in view.

After Daniel finished his cigarette, a stout man walked from the house to join the two officers. The man was shorter than the two, and sturdy, with a hefty layer of body fat covering the muscle. He looked as if he could effortlessly heave bales of hay from one end of a barn to the other with one hand.

"Evening, Ed. Good to see ya, though I wish it were under better circumstances." Wayne tipped his hat to Ed. Daniel noticed the sheriff's southern accent was more prominent.

"Thanks, Sheriff." Ed was short of breath when he spoke and his face was absent of any color. "Who's this fella? Did Hall take an early retirement between now and when I saw him a while ago?" Ed looked at Wayne with his thumbs stuck in the thick pockets of his jeans while he waited.

"No." Wayne chuckled. "He should be up here any minute. This is Mr. Belascoe, with the Savannah Police. Since this is big news for the town, I figured an extra set of eyes wouldn't do no harm. Plus, him and his lady had car troubles and got stranded here."

"Well, we're glad to have you, sir." Ed stuck his hand out and Daniel accepted it.

"Please, you can call me Daniel."

Another car pulled up and joined the trio. Hall stepped out of the same car Daniel saw him in earlier, still wearing his uniform, and his face that looked like a granite frown. "Gentlemen," he said when he joined them. He gave a curious glance towards Daniel before turning his attention to the sheriff.

"Ed, why don't you walk us through what happened? To the best of your recollection." Wayne crossed his arms, his expression dour.

"There was a noise out there in the woods. I walked out of the house with my rifle to see what the hell it was. I started walking over here." As he talked, Ed led them through the main gate to his property, to the back of his home, and to a smaller gate that opened to a wooded area.

Daniel noticed how dark it was in Middlesboro compared to Savannah, with its city lights providing light on the darkest of nights. Here, all he had to rely on were the lights of Ed's property.

"It sounded like a coyote howling," Ed said, "and I didn't want them messing with the chickens over yonder since I had to patch up the fencing before on account of them."

Even the noises differed. Every crack of a twig or chirp of an insect contrasted boldly with the silence of the country. They sounded sharply through the trees, and Daniel heard them all. His heart beat increased and his palms started sweating. He wiped them on his pants as they wandered further into the woods until they found the beginning of a clearing.

"I guess whatever did this left because when I got here, I saw the boy." Ed slowed down and avoided looking at the clearing they had set out for. His breath grew shallow.

When they got into the clearing, Daniel looked on the ground a few feet ahead of him and saw the body. The moment they all laid eyes on it, everyone looked away just as quickly. Ed outdid everyone and ran a few yards away to vomit. The three officers slowly looked back at the scene. Viscera spilled out of the open abdominal cavity. Inhuman amounts of blood staining the earth. As Daniel scanned the body, there wasn't much of a neck to speak of, as the throat and sinew had been torn out, and parts of each flecked the ground nearby. Blood, dirt, and maggots covered what remained of the clothing. For several long minutes, nobody said anything, and the three men stood there, stunned. For as big as he was, right now, Daniel felt small and insignificant.

He finally broke the silence. "How long ago did the politician's son go missing? And the other kid. Boy or girl?"

"Johnson's boy went missing on Monday. The other, Max Reavill Junior, yesterday," Wayne said in a low, somber voice.

Hall stepped next to Daniel with his arms crossed and the first formations of a scowl, shaking in anger. "This is goddamn sick. How in the hell can this kinda thing happen?" The deputy paused, looking at the carnage before them. "Boys. Both of 'em. Not even teenagers yet."

Ed rejoined them, standing a few feet away with Wayne. The sheriff wrote some information on a notepad before he spoke again. "Ed, I'd hate to burden you at a time like this, but the night ain't gonna get any shorter. You think you can go and brew us a mess of coffee?"

"Be glad to Sheriff, you just let me know how I can help," Ed said, ready to look at anything else.

"Thanks, Ed. We might need your phone, too." Wayne scratched his head before he turned to look at the devastation.

"Door's open as long as you need." Ed made his way back to his house

"What do we do?" Daniel puzzled over the next steps since Middlesboro didn't have the same number of resources or personnel that Savannah afforded their investigative efforts. There were no teams of medics or detectives ready to deploy. Sheriff Sutherland and Deputy Hall *were* the police department here.

"Pray that we can figure it out on our own before it gets worse," Wayne said under his breath, belying the cracking of his stern demeanor. "Hall, go inside Ed's place. He's making coffee. Have a cup and compose yourself. Make sure he's all right, too. Then, I want you to call Doctors Burton and Ward, tell them to get over here as quick as they can."

"Ward?" Hall tilted his head as he looked at Sheriff Sutherland. "The dentist?"

"Might be that's the only way we figure out which boy this is since there ain't much else to go by. Get the paperwork in order to acquire the dental records of the two missing boys."

"Yes, sir." Hall went to his cruiser to grab some stationery before making his way to Ed's.

"You don't have a coroner here?" Daniel asked, still fixating on the scene in front of them.

"Sure, we do. Doctor Burton. It's not his job title, but he knows his medical stuff and he's been doing it for us for about two dozen years. If he can't figure it out, we call someone in Oakwood or Robinvale. Atlanta, if need be, but I hope it doesn't come to that."

Daniel gazed at the wounds on the child and thought back to the murderous aftermath he witnessed in the prior weeks. How could anyone go back to work after witnessing this type of massacre? How could *Daniel* go back to work, year in and year out and make a career out of this sort of thing as if it were another day at the office? Not even six months on the force and he stumbled across one grisly murder, and here he was, hoping to have fun, but somehow in the middle of another maelstrom. Maybe it was the will to prevent it from happening that kept his colleagues there for so long. At least he would convince himself of that right now so that he could help stop whatever it was. He couldn't imagine a human being capable of what was in front of him, given the heightened severity compared to John Moore's murder, and an animal culprit *seemed* reasonable. Reasonable enough for him to do the job, anyway. Sheriff Sutherland startled Daniel from his thoughts when he handed him a pair of latex gloves.

"Might as well get it over with and take a look," Sheriff Sutherland said as he led the way to the body.

Daniel followed Wayne's lead as he kneeled by the remains of the child's skull. They looked at the bone fragments along with the bits of flesh that stuck to some of them. Daniel thought back to the murder scene and how fresh everything was in comparison. Here, the blood had dried, but the smell wasn't as awful as it could've been since the open air helped spread it out. Still, the humid trappings of summer held on to the smells of copper and decay more than Daniel cared to think about.

"Sheriff, look at this." Daniel pointed his latex-covered finger at a skull fragment with the end portion broken into smaller pieces. His point of focus was the faint smear of blood on the bigger fragment. "It looks like the blood might have been wiped or smeared away."

"Good eye." Sheriff Sutherland moved his attention to the torso. "And look here." Scattered next to the torso were the trace remnants of the body's viscera. "Whatever did this didn't do so good. Brute strength, no finesse."

"What if it wasn't a coyote?" Daniel watched as Wayne studied the scene further.

Wayne stood up and let out a deep sigh. "That crossed my mind, too. Damn thing has to be big as a horse to damage somebody like this."

"What's our next step?"

"I'm gonna take some crime scene pictures. You can grab the crime scene tape and I'll get the camera. Then we wait for the doctors to get here."

* * *

THE HUMID NIGHT air was thick as it passed through the screened door in the kitchen and mingled with the steam from Daniel, Wayne, Ed, and Deputy Hall's coffee mugs. They were silent, though there wasn't much to say, as it was. They'd all seen the devastation. Wayne checked his watch intermittently. Hall tapped his foot. Daniel formed elaborate scenarios about what could have happened to the boy and wondered at the cruel fate that allowed him to witness the aftermath of two bloody deaths within the same month. As the scenarios compounded inside of him, the men turned in unison at the sound of knuckles sharply rapping on the front door.

Wayne eagerly answered the door, revealing an unlikely pair before the threshold. A portly man in his early sixties with a bad comb-over and glasses stood to the left of a brown-haired woman roughly Rebecca's age who looked like she could hit a home run in a softball game with little effort.

Daniel and Wayne extended their hands, and once Hall scrutinized the woman's legs up to her chest, he did, too.

"I'm Leslie Ward," she said.

The doctor offered his hand as well. "Randall Burton." They all shook hands and went for coffee in the kitchen as Dr. Burton continued. "Wayne, you don't normally call this late at night, so I assume it's urgent. What can we do for you?"

"You know those two missing boys? It looks like we found one. I need y'all to help identify him and give him an official cause of death." The pall crept over Wayne's stoic demeanor as he stared at his coffee during the conversation. Daniel had no indication things were going to get better.

"I'm happy to assist," Dr. Ward said, her genteel, southern voice a sharp contrast to the dour mood cloaking everyone.

"I suppose we might as well head out there," Hall said as he pushed his mug away from him and stood up.

"Yeah. Ed," Wayne said, "I think you can turn in for the night. I already got your statement, and I can talk to you tomorrow if I need to."

"Don't you hesitate." Ed clapped Wayne on the back as the rest of them made their way outside.

The walk to the crime scene was solemn and silent, and the incoming shroud of fog made it feel worse outside. Once they arrived at the scene, Daniel and the other two police officers stayed outside of the perimeter and looked on as the doctors examined the body of the missing boy. Deputy Hall stared at the scene, his body as rigid as a piece of rebar supporting the weight of his scowl as opposed to concrete.

Wayne gave Daniel a light tap on the arm before he motioned for him to step back a few steps. He leaned into Daniel's ear. "Hall's got himself a real personal vendetta when kids die. He'll be fine. He just needs a bit of time."

"So, do we search for the other kid in the meantime?" Daniel whispered back.

"Uh-huh. We'll wait a few more minutes here, head back, round up a search party, and start tomorrow." Wayne wiped the sweat off his forehead with the back of his hand as the doctors walked through the yellow tape. The officers looked at them, waiting.

"It's Representative Johnson's boy," Dr. Ward said as she looked down, holding back her tears. "I just cleaned his teeth two weeks ago."

"I trust Dr. Ward. We'll confirm it for you, and I'll write up an official report," Dr. Burton said, shaking his head. "It's a damn shame."

"Thank you, both. If you're free tomorrow, do you think y'all can help in a search party for the other missing boy?"

"I can't stay all day, but I'll be there," Dr. Ward said.

"With school starting back and the kids getting their shots and whatnot, I'm booked solid. But I'll get that report to you early tomorrow. And if anyone cancels on me later in the day, I might make it out."

"Thanks, Leslie. Randall, let's say we meet here about six tomorrow morning."

"I'll be there."

Wayne called for an ambulance and waited for the paramedics to retrieve the body so that Dr. Burton could perform the autopsy and write his report. When the rest of them cleared the scene, Daniel, Hall, and Wayne were the only ones left.

"I'll see if Amanda can come along and help the search party," Hall said. "You can bring your lady, too. The more eyes we have, the better."

"He's right, we gotta find Max's boy before we have another death on our hands," Wayne said. "Kevin, why don't you head back home, talk to your wife about it, and we'll see you back here tomorrow?"

"You got it, boss."

Daniel studied Wayne's face for a moment. "You look like you got a lot more on your mind than you're letting on."

"Good observation. We gotta make a little stop on the way back," Wayne said as he turned toward his car.

"Where to?" Daniel asked, following him.

"To do one of the hardest things I've ever done in my life; notifying the parents their son is dead. And not that you asked, but this might help you out in the future.

Any time you are directly responsible for someone, or a lot of people, you carry that cross the entire path. The hard times, the good times, and everything in between." He shut the door after he and Daniel entered the car before he went on. "Even before I became an officer in Korea, that whole telegram business didn't sit right with me. Takes away the humanity of it. Least I could do was personally tell my guys' family that they died for something they'll never know paid off or not."

For Daniel, this was the most heroic thing he'd witnessed in his short life, and his admiration for Sheriff Wayne Sutherland grew steadily as they rode to Representative Johnson's house.

"It might be best to stay in the car for this," Wayne said when they reached the driveway. "Can't imagine they'd want an outsider there to hear this for a lot of reasons."

"You got it," Daniel said.

Daniel watched Wayne Sutherland walk up the driveway and the few steps leading to the porch. A gentle wind blew, rocking the swing that hung several feet to the left of the door, carrying with it the sounds of crickets chirping and the occasional hoot of an owl.

Peering through the windshield, Daniel observed the delivery of the untimely news to Representative Johnson and Mrs. Johnson. Wayne knocked on the door, and when the Johnsons answered, he took his hat off, holding it over his heart, yet still commanding respect from the Johnsons despite the gravity of the news. Wayne gestured a little, his movements subdued. Mrs. Johnson covered her eyes, and her face contorted with grief, giving way to tears, as she rested her head on her husband's shoulder.

Representative Johnson turned to his wife, and hugged her, his face unmoved. Wayne was in no hurry to make the announcement, but he was emphatic in his belief that taking responsibility for your leadership in the worst of times was one sign of stalwart character.

Daniel was an outsider, but despite that, he felt for the Johnsons, as well as Max Reavill. He was only a few years into adulthood himself, but he'd been on the other side of the situation before, having lost his father at a young age. The big difference was you expect to outlive your parents, not your own children.

"How many times have you had to deliver news like that?" he asked Wayne when he got back into the car.

"Too damn many," Wayne said.

"Does it get easier?"

"Not in the last thirty years," the elder replied.

Maybe that's why Sheriff Wayne Sutherland excelled at the job. They made it back to the Sutherland home before midnight that night.

* * *

IN THE GUEST room they shared, Daniel cozied up to Rebecca as he relayed the events from earlier.

"What do you think happened?" Rebecca said.

Daniel sat up on the bed and leaned back against the wall, running his hands down his face. Before long, he turned to Rebecca. "I dunno. Wayne seemed concerned. More concerned than I think anyone else would be. Maybe he thinks there'll be more to it? I asked him if it gets easier to make calls like this, and he said it never does." Daniel managed a small smile. "It gives me *a lot* to look forward to, that's for sure."

"Maybe there is more to it," Rebecca said. "Or maybe the idea of getting another law enforcement agency involved isn't high on his fun list. I can tell the sheriff has a good heart, though. He cares about what's at stake and knows how to work to solve the problem."

"Maybe. I guess we'll find out soon. By the way, you're invited to be in the search party for the other kid. At six in the morning." Daniel held her hand and looked at her.

"You mean we have to get up at six?" She leaned her head back with the flair of a stage actor and expressed her hyperbolic shock.

"No. We have to *be there* at six in the morning. So we leave around twenty minutes before that."

"Well, it's not like we can leave when we want to," she lamented.

"Shit, I almost forgot about the wrestling match."

"Yeah, but you found a new role model." Rebecca smiled at him, and the low light of the lamp heightened the contrast of her hair and eyes to her sun-tinted skin.

"Oh, stop," Daniel said blushing. "He probably didn't take Hall to deliver the news because Hall would stare at the congressman's wife the whole time."

Rebecca leaned onto Daniel's shoulder, "True, but it's like he's taking you under his wing. He might see potential in you."

"Do you see the good in everyone, or are you biased because it's me?"

"I do try to see the good in everyone, but sometimes it's not easy to find. With you, it's not like it's hiding." She reached up and ran her hand through his hair. "It's a shame we have to wake up early, otherwise I could see your potential in me," she said before she kissed him on the mouth.

"Yeah, I'm pretty tired myself. Even though we didn't really do anything besides drink coffee and talk about the scene."

"Physical exertion isn't the only thing that leaves you tired. You've seen a lot of horrifying stuff in the last couple of weeks. Plus, the heat, and the car troubles. It all adds up."

When they got into their bedclothes, Daniel decided to be the little spoon, and he grabbed Rebecca's arm and draped it over his waist. She went to sleep before he did, and the soft snoring sounds pulled Daniel into slumber shortly after.

CHAPTER SIXTEEN

*R*ebecca, Daniel, Wayne, and Dorothy pulled up to Ed's farm at ten of six. The red maple trees that hadn't reached their scarlet hue blocked the sun on the horizon. The heat from it pressed through the green leaves, and Daniel knew it would be a scorching day. In an even more surprising turn of events, Dr. Ward was already waiting for them. Everyone piled out of Wayne's cruiser and met up with Dr. Ward and made their introductions while Hall's car appeared in the distance.

"This isn't the entire search party, is it?" Daniel asked, looking at Wayne.

"It might well be. The crew at Big Jim's'll be working on that Oldsmobile. I'd be surprised if Max wanted to look. Wouldn't blame him myself, after last night. But we'll give it a few minutes before we head out."

As Hall's car drew closer, Ed lumbered out of his house beyond the gate, met the search team, and introduced himself to Rebecca. When Hall stopped next to Wayne's cruiser, three doors opened. From the passenger side, a woman with shoulder-length reddish-colored hair stepped out wearing overalls and plaid. She'd tucked the cuffs of the legs into her ranch boots and despite her demurity, she looked ready to get dirty. She looked around and when she saw Rebecca standing near Daniel, she went towards them.

"Hi," she said, introducing herself to Rebecca, "Amanda Hall. Mrs. Hall, if you wanna be formal." She and Rebecca greeted each other before Amanda turned to Daniel.

"Daniel Belascoe," he said, extending his hand.

She looked up at Daniel and grabbed his hand, surprising him when. Her dry, calloused-hardened hands gripped his, nearly matching his strength.

Hall's crisp, immaculate uniform was his symbol of readiness. From the rear passenger side, a lanky man near Daniel's height, with dark, gray-streaked hair stepped out. A sour expression darkened his face and Daniel assumed it to be Max.

Wayne leaned towards Daniel and spoke in a whisper. Confirming the man's identity. "That's Max Reavill. You can tell he's expecting the worst. I want you to fill him in; I doubt Hall would've done it yet."

"Me?" The volume of his voice startled Daniel, and cascading on that, he wondered why Wayne would give him that job. "Why me?"

"Because you're young and you care. One thing you have to remember, son: *you* serve *them*. It ain't the other way around. The sooner young officers learn that, the better they will be."

"But I don't even know him." Daniel's incredulity bled through his words.

"You won't know a lot of the people you encounter at first," Wayne said. "Get to know him."

Daniel sighed before steadying his breathing as he walked towards Max. "Mr. Reavill, you got a minute?"

Max tilted his head in curiosity as he looked at Daniel. "Who are you?"

When Daniel heard him speak those three words, his palms grew wet, and he could feel the telltale beat of his heart that always accompanied any anxiety he felt. Max looked like he'd rather be anywhere, and the only thing bringing him there was a sliver of hope. "I'm Daniel Belascoe with the Savannah Police Department. My girlfriend and I are guests of Mr. and Mrs. Sutherland." Daniel extended his hand.

Max brusquely shook Daniel's hand. "Well, get to whatever you're gonna tell me. I know it ain't gonna be good."

Daniel averted eye contact and glanced down before looking back at Max. "I'm not gonna lie to you, sir. It's not the best news. It's not the worst either. Last night we found Representative Johnson's boy dead in the woods. That's why we got the search party today. We don't want another death in this town. I can't promise anything other than doing everything we can to find him, but we wanna be realistic about it." In the background, everyone convened around the hood of Wayne's cruiser and talked about the plan for the search.

"So, you're telling me Max Junior might turn up dead like little Matt?"

"It's possible," Daniel said, measuring his next words with tact. "But we don't have enough evidence to say, so we proceed as if he's alive."

"I'm glad his mama ain't alive to see this." Max left, shaking his head and Daniel followed him to the rest of the search team.

Wayne's words about it not getting any easier made more sense now. When Daniel and Max arrived at the car, a map was spread across the hood with three red lines plotting out the search route leading to the border of the neighboring towns to the North, West, and East.

Wayne led his finger over each of the lines as he explained the plan. "Daniel, Max, and Rebecca, y'all go north through woods starting at Wilkinson Drive. Ed, myself, and my wife will start here; we found something here before, that might be worth expanding our search even further. Doctor Ward, Amanda, and Deputy Hall, y'all take the east starting at Turkey Creek Road. Ed, your place is gonna be our ending point, too.

"Now, Daniel, you're gonna take my car to your starting point. Deputy Hall, you drive to yours. If the three of us need to get somewhere, Ed has wheels, and he's got a radio, and Deputy Hall and I have our portable radios. We got an extra for Daniel, who I am officially deputizing. So if any of you find anything, you'll be able to let us know on the radio. Any questions before we go?"

Nobody spoke up.

"All right," Wayne said as he folded the map and popped the trunk. "If we don't find anything, we meet back here at dusk. Mrs. Hall also graciously offered to provide us all with a nice supper after we're finished. Let's hope for the best and hope for it soon. Ed, before we break, why don't you lead everyone inside to grab some water and anything else we can think of? It could be a long day. Me and Daniel will be right behind you."

Rebecca gave Daniel a quizzical glance, to which Daniel shrugged his shoulders as he and Wayne waited for everyone to depart.

"I don't have a handgun for you, so I'm gonna let you patrol the woods with this." Wayne opened the trunk all the way and pulled out a mint-condition Mossberg 500. "How'd you do with your twelve-gauge practice in the academy?"

Daniel made sure the weapon was clear before he examined it. "This is a good gun. I think I might have done better with this than the Winchesters we had to use."

"A man after my own heart," Wayne said, handing Daniel a box of buckshot to go with the weapon. "I doubt you'll need it, but you can't be too careful. Not after last night."

"You don't think we're gonna find Junior, do you?" Daniel asked plainly.

Wayne looked at him and shook his head. "No. No, I don't. Something about it seems…off. But I don't know what. No damn coyote killed Matt Johnson. I can tell you that much."

"If I recall, aren't red wolves around here? You think it might have been one of them?" Daniel asked.

Wayne started walking towards Ed's place as he spoke. "It'd be more likely, but still. You remember how big the marks were? The wolves are bigger than the coyotes, and more likely to bite someone. Coyotes don't normally go after humans. We scare them more often than not. But chickens and small animals, yeah, they'll go after them."

They all convened in Ed's brown-tinted kitchen and helped themselves to coffee and water, barely tasting any of it as they rushed to leave. Rebecca stood next to Daniel, the pair holding hands. He shifted his eyes her way, hoping they'd never be in this situation, and finished his coffee.

The three groups gathered near their respective cars and Daniel stopped with a final question before they each headed towards their destination.

"Max, what's your boy look like? What was he last wearing, if you can remember?"

"He's pretty short, even for a kid his age; red hair, blue eyes. Lots of freck-les. If I remember right, he was wearing a blue and white striped shirt, some blue dungarees, and a pair of black shoes that day." Everyone acknowledged his statement before they split up.

Daniel drove Wayne's cruiser to the tree line at Turkey Creek Road so the trio could start their search for Max Junior. Along the way, Daniel and Max spoke about his son.

"If we find any houses along the way, we can ask anyone there if they've seen him, too. Maybe get some help if we need it," Daniel said.

The three slowed to a stop. They piled out, and Daniel, armed with his loaner Mossberg, gave the directions to the other two. He had them walk fifty feet on either side of him before they made their way into the woods. Rebecca was to his left, and Max to his right. Aside from lots of shrubbery getting in the way in their initial run, nothing momentous occurred during the first hour of their trek. Rebecca seemed to have a tough time navigating the woods between the thorny branches and the lack of a footpath. Daniel constantly ducked under the branches and shoved them out of his way while Max Senior trudged his way through the woods, letting nothing stop him on his life-and-death search for his son. After an hour and change of nothing, the two men looked to their left when Rebecca whistled and held a hand to stop.

They walked over to her section of the wooded area, and Daniel noticed what made her stop. Broken and folded sticks and branches, along with trodden leaves and dirt, kicked about.

"Look at this. Any native animals have fur this color?" she asked, looking towards Max, who was familiar with the locality better than they were.

"Well," Max said, "it looks like a big son of a bitch, whatever it was. Look at that toe print. See it?" He pointed his finger down below, where a tuft of fur attached itself to some thorns on a branch on Rebecca's side of the trail.

"That right there?" Daniel crept closer and looked to see what Max was referring to. After some hard gazing, he finally found it. "Looks like a cat print. A big cat," he said.

"I think so, too," Max said. "Bigger than your run-of-the-mill panther or cougar, that's for damn sure."

"What about the fur?" Daniel asked. "Red and gray mixed?"

"Honey, I don't think the red is part of the fur," Rebecca said as she leaned in closer to inspect it. "Look at it. It looks like it might be blood with the way it's stuck together like that."

"She's right. A bigger cat than usual, leaving traces of itself behind." Max sounded more hopeful than he had been until this point as he stood in the presence of the first clue. And it wasn't a clue that had nearly the same ramifications as what Daniel and the others had found the previous night.

"It looks like we can see roughly where it went," Daniel said. "What do you say we veer off and see where the paths take us?"

"Sure. And if we don't find anything, we can always come back to this spot and keep going as we were. You wanna look for more stuff like this. Footprints, loose fur, blood, and what have you," Max said.

The three of them veered off their initial path and followed the disorder of the woods. More broken and disturbed fauna filled their sights as they made their way. Despite all that, there was no sign of Max Junior yet. As the three of them trudged onward, they drew closer to the border of Middlesboro, where the woods cleared. Daniel slowed his pace and Rebecca and Max followed suit. He took in the edge of the woods with deliberate sweeping looks.

Daniel allowed Rebecca and Max Senior to take the lead, while he stopped. Looking to the left at the tangled brush, Daniel walked forward and squatted down. "Max!" he called.

Max and Rebecca stopped looking and joined Daniel.

"Blue and white striped shirt, you said? This look like it might be it?" Daniel grabbed a piece of fabric from the ground, stiff from bits of hardened blood. It bore jagged edges with one clean edge still intact at the hemline.

Max eyed the fabric until the faucet turned on. Tears streamed down his face, and he said nothing. He stepped forward towards Daniel, embracing him, sobbing on his shoulder. His rapid, shallow breaths shook him, reverberating through Daniel.

Stunned, Daniel raised his hands in trepidation, as he looked at Rebecca, who was fighting her own emotional battle at the same time. She turned from the two of them, but Daniel heard the low, whispered cries coming from her. Daniel pulled Max Senior close, returning the hug, and let him cry. He knew nothing he could say would bring Max comfort, so he instead looked beyond the woods and noticed a steeple in the distance a few hundred yards ahead of them.

Minutes later, Max Senior's well dried, and he stepped back, wiping his sadness away with the back of his forearms. "What now?"

Daniel directed their attention to the church in the next town.

CHAPTER SEVENTEEN

The trio crossed an imaginary border into the new town. The differences, compared to Middlesboro, were negligible. One big difference was this town had textile mills nearby, along with other markers of early American industry. The dilapidated building ahead of them, however, sparked Daniel's interest. It looked as old as the country itself, complete with chipped white paint, aged wood that likely needed treating again, and a starkly contrasting red door upon the steps. The big standout compared to the rundown church was the steeple. A large, white glossy crucifix shone into the world, greeting them as they strode forth. The marquis noted that it was The First Holy Tabernacle Baptist Church of St. Paul. Daniel, Rebecca, and Max Senior walked up the rickety steps, each one complaining under the increasing weight as each member of the team walked upon them.

At the door, Daniel knocked three times, hoping someone would answer their call. He waited a few seconds before he tried again. On the third try, the door slipped open enough to let out a droopy-eared, big-jowled basset hound. It immediately sniffed everyone in sight and invaded their personal spaces.

Rebecca kneeled to greet her new canine friend, tussling his hair and petting his droopy ears. "Hey, buddy! I bet you're Bentley's cousin, aren't you? He's got ears like yours, but they're not quite as big. You're a good boy."

Shortly after Rebecca greeted the dog, an elderly black man with white hair wearing a plaid shirt stepped out. "Well, hello," he said. "I'm Reverend

Raymond. I see you already met Jasper, my hound. What can we do for you today?"

"Hello, sir—"

Reverend Raymond immediately cut Daniel off. "Please, call me Ray. Reverend Ray, if you wanna be a little more formal."

"Reverend Ray, I'm Daniel Belascoe, with the Savannah Police Department, and I'm helping out the folks in Middlesboro. We're looking for a boy and hoping maybe somebody here has seen him." Daniel held the shirt fabric with the blood on it out in front of him, showing it to the preacher. "He'd have been wearing this, if it helps."

Reverend Ray stroked his beardless chin, the mirth leaving his expression. "Why don't y'all come in for a spell and get some water? Looks like you could use it."

Daniel glanced at Max who stared forward, expecting the worst. Rebecca's face showed more cheer than it did before they arrived at the church. "All right," Daniel said, following the preacher inside. Jasper loped around their feet, making sure he didn't miss a single smell.

Contrary to the outside of the building, the interior of the church was immaculate. The hardwood floors comprised well-treated wood, with matching pews. On the stage stood a single podium with an opened book resting on it. At stage right, a modest, upright piano sat, just as pristine as the floors and seating. It didn't have much, but it was flawless, and Daniel looked around in admiration.

"Wondering why the inside don't match the outside, I take it?" Reverend Ray looked at Daniel as they walked.

"Was I that obvious?" Daniel asked.

"Yes, but that's not uncommon. Jasper, go lie down." The hound trotted away towards a nest of small blankets adorning the bottom edge of the pulpit on stage. Reverend Ray led the group to a door on the side nearest the piano and back into a kitchen, where he filled up three glasses of water for the guests. "I built this church to be a sanctuary for the downtrodden, derelict, and destitute, Mr. Belascoe. Those who need it the most will look past the exterior and see the beauty within. At least that's my hope. First Peter, chapter three, verses three and four say it best; 'Your beauty should not come from outward adornment, such as elaborate hairstyles and the wearing of gold jewelry or fine clothes. Rather, it should be that of your inner self, the unfading beauty of a gentle and quiet spirit, which is of great worth in God's sight.' This church is more than a building. It's about people and community and I want those who enter to feel welcome."

Daniel noticed the tension as everyone waited on the news of Max's son. Daniel looked at Reverend Ray expectantly.

"I don't like giving bad news when people are already distressed, so forgive me for keeping you waiting," the preacher said, "but the news isn't all bad. Your boy is alive, and last I heard, his condition is hopeful."

Max looked at Reverend Ray. "Hopeful? What in the world does that mean? What happened? Can I see him?" Max shook as he tried to control his emotions. Reverend Ray looked at Max before he continued. "I ain't a doctor, so my words might not be as good as theirs. But your boy got his bell rung pretty good. My wife and I were in the church the other night practicing my sermon for this Sunday. We heard some noises outside in the woods and went out to look. And he was in awful shape. Looks like he got attacked by a wolf or a cougar or something like that. His head was all swollen up and he couldn't really talk straight. Couldn't tell me his address, who his parents were, or even what day it was. So we knew we had to do something right away, so we got him to a hospital. The short, his head was so banged up they had to put him in a coma when we took him to the hospital. He's in the ICU."

Max started bawling as he leaned against the fridge. Rebecca grabbed Daniel's hand, and the couple looked at each other, hopeful for more promising news. Reverend Ray went up and put his hand on Max's shoulder to soothe him before he pulled Max in for a hug and continued to let him emote.

"The hospital's a few minutes away and my wife's over there now checking on him, like she did the other day. She's been keeping an eye on him as best she could, but we had no way of figuring out how to notify you or where he was even from. Police over here seem to be taking their time. If you want, we can go there now." Reverend Ray said as he looked at Daniel, "or whatever you think is best, Mr. Belascoe."

Daniel looked at the two men hugging and back at Rebecca before he finally spoke again. "I think we will do just that. Before we go, I need to call up the others and let them know what's going on." He filled Reverend Ray in on the search party and the other missing child and let him know all the surrounding details of that. "I'm gonna go outside and have a cigarette and radio the other two officers from Middlesboro and we can reconvene soon."

Daniel made his way outside and stood with his back to the big red door of the church before he notified Wayne and Hall of his whereabouts. The two men said they would head up to his location as soon as possible and to wait for them. Daniel pulled out a cigarette and leaned up against the door, relaxing for a moment with the good news. He looked around the town, wondering the name, and was curious about the kindness of everyone else who lived here. Above all, he was thankful that Reverend Ray and his wife had a good heart and looked after Max Junior.

Daniel rejoined Rebecca at the table as Max and Reverend Ray sat back down to join them. "The other officers and the town's doctor are coming up now. Then we can all go to the hospital together." Daniel turned his attention to the preacher. "Reverend Ray, when the sheriff gets here, he'll wanna ask you some questions. Your wife, too. We're determined to get to the bottom of what happened and the more answers we get, the better the chances are of us doing so."

"It's no problem at all. In the meantime, make yourselves comfortable. Max, you've had quite a mental battle. What can I do to help you?"

Max looked at him with the tears fading from his eyes raw cheeks. "I think all I can do is wait, now. You can say a prayer if you'd like. I don't know how I can thank y'all for saving my boy."

"It's the right thing to do. Let's go back to the main area and we can pray together." Reverend Ray grabbed Max's hand and led him into the main church area, leaving Rebecca and Daniel in the kitchen by themselves.

Rebecca leaned back in the chair, slumping and heaving a sigh out into the world. "I hope the car is done today. I'm glad we found the child, but this trip has been nonstop hell."

"And it's only been a day," Daniel said. "Hopefully, the others show up quickly and we can head back over to Big Jim's and get the Oldsmobile back. I need to call Tom, too. He's probably wondering where we are and what's going on."

"Do you know which hotel they're at?" Rebecca asked.

"Yeah, he let me know before we all left. If memory serves, they're in Charlotte today, and planning to head to Greensboro tomorrow to make it to the match." Daniel wiped the sweat out of his eyes and finished his water before returning the glass to the sink.

"Good. I think we should book a really nice hotel. I wanna take a bath."

"You can fit in a bathtub?" Daniel asked with a smile forming on his lips.

"Just as well as you can," she replied, love-tapping him on the leg. "Honestly, I am pretty glad we got to do this, even if we didn't plan on it."

"Yeah?" Daniel asked. "Why's that? The intense heat? The southern hospitality?"

"In some ways, yes. But it gave us time to spend with each other. It gave me a look at the man you are, deep down. And it happened quickly, so I didn't have to wait." Rebecca leaned towards him and smiled as she looked into his eyes.

"I take it you like what you've seen?" Daniel gazed back at her, mirroring the warmth she gave to him.

"There's room for improvement. But that's for everyone. Imagine what you'll be like when you get to be *my* age," she said, pointing out herself with an exaggerated flourish.

"Oh, that's *so* far away, though. You're practically a crone." Daniel could hardly finish his sentence without laughing at how absurd his joke was.

"Careful, I might get a bunch of cats and cast some spells on you, mister."

"Make sure they're good ones, preferably in a slightly cooler climate and with no missing children. I think I will be all set then."

Reverend Ray and Max rejoined them in the kitchen and as they bustled around cleaning up, they heard a knock at the door of the church. Reverend Ray answered and returned to the kitchen with Dr. Burton, Kevin, Wayne, and Mrs. Hall. With the party together, Daniel told them everything that had happened until that point and, as he had predicted, Reverend Ray and Wayne went off privately so the latter could ask him some more questions. When they finished, they set forth towards the hospital so Max could see his son.

* * *

HALF AN HOUR LATER, they all arrived at Max Junior's room. A woman who looked to be about Reverend Ray's age stood vigil near the bed. She had longer two-toned gray and black hair, with skin a hue lighter than Reverend Ray's. She looked their way as they walked through the door.

The monitors surrounding Max Junior beeped in rhythm, keeping his body working as it was supposed to. Despite the abrasions and bruises, he looked peaceful sleeping on the hospital bed. The woman embraced Reverend Ray, who said, "I'd like you all to meet my wife, Mrs. Coretta Smith."

Coretta walked over to Max and hugged him for a while before shaking hands with everyone in the room. "He's sure gonna be glad to see you when he wakes up, I expect," she said to Max Senior. "We couldn't figure out anything he was trying to say, other than that he missed his father. The doctor will know more, but I think they're going to wake him up soon since the swelling in his head has gone down."

Max nodded at her. "I can't thank you two enough for what you've done for my son."

"It was the right thing to do," Coretta said.

Wayne stepped forward and took on the mantle of leadership. "Mrs. Smith, do you mind if you and I talk a minute, along with The Reverend? Everyone else, why don't y'all go get some coffee while the three of us talk?"

Everyone nodded in agreement, knowing Wayne had to do his job. When they all left to go to the lobby of the hospital, Daniel made his way towards Kevin.

"Did you find anything when you were in your neck of the woods?" Daniel asked.

"Nothing too important. But our search was slow going; they ain't used to going out and putting in work like that in these woods, you know?" Kevin said, motioning to the other two members of his search party, his wife and Dr. Burton. "So we didn't see much, but something didn't seem right about it. I don't think the animal that did this is from around here."

"Did Wayne tell you that?" Daniel was surprised that Kevin would also come up with a similar conclusion as Wayne; maybe he misjudged this officer's abilities.

"He didn't mention it, but the animals here can be pretty wild. Gators, and whatnot, everyone knows about that. Hell, y'all got wild animals in Savannah, too, you're no stranger. But we aren't near water, and coyotes don't go around eating people." Kevin peered over his shoulder at Junior's room then back at Daniel and lowered his voice. "We still got most of the day left. Let's you and I talk later."

Daniel furrowed his eyebrows, considering Kevin. The deputy rubbed him the wrong way, especially after the comparison he made of Rebecca's breasts to a pair of antlers. That, and his general lechery. "With or without the sheriff?" Daniel asked, stuffing down any overt skepticism that might show through.

"Without." Kevin paused, maintaining strict eye contact with him. "It's not that I wanna hide anything from him. I just don't want him to think I'm a damn loon. We got our differences, Wayne and me, but they don't get in the way of the trust we have. If one of us loses trust in the other, we can't do the job the way it needs to be done."

"Why don't we meet somewhere around here in about an hour?" Daniel asked him.

Kevin ran his hand through his hair, staring at the floor as he thought about his response. After a moment, he nodded his head. "Yeah. Let's do that. I'll deal with the sheriff, so we get the time together. As far as everyone's concerned, I'll be driving you around and going over the details of my search while he does some paperwork. I'll get him to drop the girls off and every-thing, so we don't have to worry about that."

Daniel's nerves kicked in and he had to stop the shaking that came with it. He had no idea where his conversation with Kevin would start, much less end. "All right. We'll finish up here and head out."

CHAPTER EIGHTEEN

$\mathcal{N}$orth of the hospital, Kevin and Daniel stopped at the Waffle House, with cups of coffee appearing almost instantly as they sat down and ordered their food.

"Now, I know lots of people and places around here are really into Jesus," Kevin said between sips of coffee. "I believe in Jesus, just like the next guy. But I don't go for all that fire and brimstone fear tactics some of these preachers do."

"What's that got to do with the missing kids?" Daniel asked, annoyed that he fell for Kevin's weird brand of proselytizing when they had work to do.

"I'm saying I never bought into the whole 'hell' business. At least not the way some of these types describe it. But when I was with my search party looking for Max Junior, I think you could've convinced me."

Daniel raised his eyebrows and waited.

"When we were walking out in the woods, we didn't see anything like you did, but something was there. It rustled up the woods, left a mess of things. Damn thing was big, whatever it was. Bigger than coyotes and wolves and cougars and what have you." As he spoke, Kevin gestured with less reserve than Daniel had seen him exercise before. His eyes were wider, too. "But that's not even the most important part. Maybe it *was* a big coyote or something. Like Andre the Giant. You get normal sized people, a couple every now and again grow up like you and your girl. Big, but not massive. Occasionally, you get a giant. Birth defect, act of God, Nephilim, whatever." He breathed deeply as if needing to collect himself before finishing, "But it was the smell."

Daniel set his coffee down. Finally, Kevin piqued his curiosity with an interesting detail. "What'd it smell like?" He paused before he went on. "It wasn't sage, was it?"

"Sage?" Kevin scoffed. "Christ, nobody's cooking out in the woods. No. It smelled like sulfur. Brimstone. I was the only one who smelled it, I think. My wife said she couldn't smell anything, and the dentist didn't have too good of a sense of smell to begin with."

"What does sulfur have to do with anything?" All of Daniel's worries and nervousness eroded as Kevin went further into this non sequitur that brought them out here. Still, it was enough for him to meet outside the prying eyes of his boss and his wife.

"Don't you get it?" Kevin grew exasperated as the waitress filled his mug up to the top again. He lowered his voice. "It's a goddamn demon, man. Didn't you see what happened last night?"

Daniel went on the defensive and played Devil's Advocate. "Yeah, but that could have been an animal. A really vicious predator, right?"

"It could be. But I can't think of one that would maul up anything like that. And predators usually eat their prey. Last night looked malicious."

Daniel drained the remnants of his coffee and signaled for another one. Once the server topped it off, he paused. John Moore's ghostly image scaring Daniel as he made breakfast the other day flashed in his mind. He tried to counteract Kevin's theory with more skepticism. "Well…let's say that's true. I didn't smell sulfur when we found Matt Johnson. And how did Junior get away and live?"

"I'm glad you asked," Kevin said with a look of triumph. "We didn't smell sulfur last night, but you know what we did smell?"

"Besides death?" Daniel asked.

"Exactly. The death smell was stronger than anything else. It always is. Even if there was sulfur there, we would've mostly smelled the dead body."

"Okay, then how did Max Junior get away?"

"He was in the presence of an enemy. The preacher man's wife found him and they were near the church. I don't think demons go poking their noses on holy grounds, and if the wife found him, she probably made it flee, on account of being a woman of God." Kevin sat back in the booth, his expression smug, and waited for Daniel to say something.

Daniel wasn't sure how many more peculiar things could be for him, with the specter of John Moore fresh in his mind and Kevin talking about demons. As dubious as both were, the ghost certainly seemed real. Real enough to ask Tom about ghosts. Never mind the tangible and real threat of his partner and the coincidentally named Savannah Swamp Demons waiting for him back home. Daniel made a mental note to give Detective Martin a call after he got ahold of Tom. "All right. Why don't we take a look at what you found?"

The two men finished their coffees before they got back in Kevin's cruiser to check out the area his search party covered. Kevin drove as close as he could to the spot before they had to travel by foot. Sure enough, the area was ravaged like a small cyclone went through it, localized to that specific spot.

Daniel squatted, noticing the broken branches and stray tree bark at the scene. He picked up a piece of bark and sniffed it, recognizing the scent of sulfur. Just like Kevin had said—it was there, and it was strong. "I smell the sulfur, all right. How do you know it isn't just in the water here like it is in some other places?"

"In this one spot? Nowhere else in the town?" Kevin looked at Daniel incredulously.

"I'm just trying to cover all our bases here. I think you should talk to the sheriff, though." Daniel looked around at the scene before him a little more, scrutinizing the shrubbery and the ground.

"Why's that? He will think it's nuts." Kevin stood behind Daniel, peering through the trees as if worried he was being watched.

"He doesn't buy the whole coyote business, either. Thinks it's strange, too. I assume that's why we haven't called the wildlife department yet, right?"

"Well, that, and we wanna be sure we need them before we waste any resources."

"I think we should both talk to Wayne later. Maybe after supper, at your place?"

Kevin stroked his chin as he thought for a moment. "Yeah. I think we can do that."

"Good. I think we'll find something out. In the meantime, I won't go talking about demons or anything out of the ordinary like that."

"Yeah, let's keep that between us at the moment," Kevin agreed.

"Now, can you give me a lift back to the sheriff's place? I wanna call about our car, among other things."

The pair drove back to Wayne's house, as Daniel thought about the clearing. The visit had done nothing to abate his concerns. If anything, he was less skeptical than he was before, since nothing else seemed to make sense. Half an hour later, they pulled up to Wayne's and Daniel got out.

"We'll be seeing you around six or seven, I believe," Kevin said as Daniel exited the car.

"Excellent. And remember, you, me, and the sheriff have to talk afterwards, too."

The house was silent when he got inside. Nobody stirred in the kitchen, or anywhere downstairs. There was nothing but the creaks of an old house settling. He made his way upstairs to the guest room, treading lightly on the rickety staircase. He quietly opened the door and saw Rebecca's tall frame curled in a ball, in dreamland. Daniel splashed some water on his face, kissed Rebecca's forehead, and went back downstairs in search of Dorothy. He found her rummaging in the refrigerator.

"Hey, Dorothy?" Daniel asked from the kitchen doorway.

"What can I do for you?" she asked, looking in the fridge.

"I gotta make some calls back home and to Charlotte to let our company know we got delayed. They might be worried. I know it's long distance, but I can leave some money with y'all before I go."

"Like I would make you leave any money. You're a guest." She pulled out some meat and bread and started making a sandwich on the counter. "Would you like a sandwich? I got turkey and ham, you pick."

Daniel thought for a moment and the rumblings of his stomach indicated that a sandwich would be a good idea. "Yeah, how about both, if possible? Thank you."

"In the meantime, go make your phone calls. If Wayne says anything about the long distance charges, I'll remind him he had extra help for work yesterday and today."

Daniel chuckled before he went to the phone. He looked at the receiver and started dialing Martin's home phone but thought it over again and dialed the number to her office at the police station.

"Detective Martin, what can I do for you?"

"Detective, it's Daniel. I wanted to ask how everything went." He kept the wording vague enough so no onlookers or busybodies could figure out what they were talking about.

Detective Martin lowered her voice to almost a whisper. "So far, so good. I haven't heard from the feds on it, but everything was fine. Your writeup, the contraband, and the one good picture were fine..." She trailed off on the last sentence, and Daniel wondered why she sounded uneasy as she spoke the last sentence.

"Why'd you trail off like that? Did anything happen?" he asked.

"No. Not exactly. It's more that *nothing* has happened. Shawn hasn't been around."

Daniel tensed. "Like he hasn't been to work? Has he called to let anyone know, or did he not show up?"

"He didn't show up. It's only been a day since you left and we set this plan into motion. But it's weird, either way."

"Yeah, that's putting it mildly," Daniel said. "No ideas on his location? Or any of the other bikers?"

"No. But I may do a drive-by of his place later and see if I can see anything from afar. Could be he's just being negligent. Or sick. I'll see what I can find out."

"Thanks." Daniel paused before adding, "Martin?"

"Yeah?"

"Be careful if you do. You don't wanna get outnumbered by those guys."

"I'm not gonna let that happen. Enjoy your trip, Belascoe, and we'll catch up soon."

Daniel heard the click when Detective Martin hung up the receiver. It wasn't the worst news he could've heard, but he didn't like it.

Next, he called the hotel in Charlotte, and neither Tom nor Christina was there, so he left a message with the front desk to let Tom know some vague details about the car trouble and a number to reach him later that night. Finally, he got Big Jim's number off a fridge magnet and called them. More unfortunate news. They wouldn't be able to get out of town until the next day, at least, since the shipment hadn't arrived.

Daniel thanked Dorothy for the sandwiches, which he ate in approximately four seconds before he went upstairs to take a nap. He set the alarm clock on the table for an hour and a half and dozed off curled up next to Rebecca.

CHAPTER NINETEEN

he alarm buzzed at half-past three. Rebecca grumbled when she reached over to hit the snooze button, and Daniel didn't stop her from seizing the opportunity to lie in silence a little longer.

Rebecca wrapped her arms around Daniel and pulled herself closer to him. "Do we have to go to dinner at that deputy's house tonight?"

"You don't. Might get some weird judgment from them. But I'm gonna go. Things got interesting after the hospital when me and Kevin were looking around." Daniel sat up a little on his elbow as he talked.

Rebecca also perked up. "How interesting?"

"So, we went digging around, because he said he smelled sulfur while they were out looking." Daniel filled her in on Kevin's theory before summarizing. "So, Sheriff Sutherland is skeptical, and Kevin thinks it's a demon."

Rebecca chuckled. "I'll believe it when I see it. On the plus side, my interest in attending dinner is higher than it was a few minutes ago. We should get ready."

This time when they took a shower, they navigated the small tub better, despite their statures. Daniel stepped back while Rebecca got under the showerhead and let the water rain on her skin. He lathered up a washcloth and rubbed gentle circles on her back where she couldn't reach on her own. He slowed down more, delaying the words from escaping his lips. "Can I ask you a question and do you promise not to laugh?" he finally asked.

"That's a tall order. I'll do my best. If you keep washing my back like that,

I'll try even harder. I like how delicate your touch is." She ran her hands through her shampooed hair while Daniel scrubbed further down, reaching for her legs.

"Do you believe in ghosts and things like that? Or maybe your friend Nacha?"

Rebecca washed the remaining shampoo out of her hair and stood under the water, crouching to get all the soap off of her. "Switch places." The two of them shuffled in the shower and she started washing Daniel's back. "I've never seen one, personally. But I don't rule it out just because of that. Kevin's story isn't getting to you, is it? I bet if he actually saw a real demon, he'd wanna know the size of its tits."

Daniel laughed before he spoke again. "I agree. But he didn't seem like his usual self. He didn't mention breasts or anything like that. He seemed... earnest, I think, is the right word. Like it really bugged him."

Underneath the water, Rebecca rinsed her hair and face. "Well, maybe it's because he's out of answers and is leaping to the next 'logical' thing. Logical to him, of course, because you don't seem fully convinced, and I don't think anyone else would be either unless they actually witnessed it happen right in front of them and saw it meld right back into hell. Or wherever demons go when they're done demon-ing."

Daniel looked down and chuckled. "Yeah, it does sound pretty ridiculous. But the sulfur smell was real."

"It could've been anything. Did you mention that it might be the water?"

"Yeah, he dismissed it, since nowhere else in town has sulfuric water like that."

"I dunno then. I imagine it'll come out sooner rather than later. Wanna know what I'm *really* looking forward to now?"

Different thoughts raced through Daniel, ranging from mundane to inane and all the way to X-rated, so long as the latter involved Rebecca. "No, what?" he asked, voice dropping low.

"I wanna see this guy's wife. In person. Up close. Where she can talk. I wanna see what makes the two of them click." Rebecca stepped out and grabbed her towel.

"I bet that'll be an absolute treat. I wonder if she's as delightful as he is."

Shortly after, Daniel hauled his massive frame out of the undersized tub and stood in front of the sink. He admired the way Rebecca's body moved in sync with the towel as she dried off. He grabbed his toothbrush and paste and looked up in the mirror.

He stifled a gasp, and his toothbrush clattered against the edge of the sink before it fell to the floor, landing toothpaste side down. Through the condensation on the mirror, John Moore's ghost reflected faintly, tapping his wrist where a watch would normally rest. Daniel turned around to find nothing and faced the mirror again. He wiped off the condensation and looked behind him yet again for good measure.

"Sounds like you're destroying the place more than you're brushing your teeth in there," Rebecca called out from the bedroom.

"I dropped my toothbrush and got the toothpaste on the floor," Daniel replied. He steadied himself and took a few relaxing breaths to abate his momentary fright.

ONCE THEY WERE DRESSED, they headed downstairs and waited while Dorothy and Wayne readied themselves for the evening as well. The four of them hopped into Wayne's car and they drove to the Hall home for supper.

In comparison to the Sutherland house, full of vintage charm, the Hall home was nearly brand new. It had a wooden finish on the outside, dark brown in color, and treated for protection. A brick chimney poked through the roof on their right, and the house itself boasted a plethora of windows to let the natural light in.

Kevin, now out of uniform and in his evening clothes, greeted the four as they walked to the front door. "Thanks for coming by. Wayne, I know you've seen my place before, but Daniel, Rebecca, let me give you the tour."

Even though he was young, Daniel was reasonably sure he knew the general structure and layout of most houses and always hated it when people insisted on giving home tours. Usually, it was less about the house itself and more about the pride people took in it. Or the contents within it. And as Kevin started the tour, it was obvious he was downright giddy with pride.

"Yep," Kevin said, gesturing to the house as they walked beyond the threshold. "I built this house myself. Hired a couple contractors to help out with the things I couldn't do, like the electric, and the plumbing. But the bulk of it is hand built. They don't make 'em like they used to." As he talked about the house, and the intricate process of making the fireplace, the floor, and everything else, Daniel noted that he wasn't talking to anyone in particular. He was just showing off the house to anyone who would listen. Was he nervous about demons? Or was he always like this?

The living room with the fireplace had an extensive collection of portraits contained in it, not unlike the upstairs area at the Sutherland's house. Old family pictures dating back to the mid-nineteenth century. No children of their own adorned the walls, but there were quite a few nieces and nephews on Kevin's side of the family. Daniel was sure they were from Kevin's side of the family since everyone had the same stern jawline Kevin did.

The Sutherlands sat by a wooden bookshelf embossed with vines and Daniel caught a look shared between them as if they were someone else was going on the Hall Home Tour circuit this time.

After the tour of the living room, Kevin led Daniel and Rebecca to the dining room and had them stand in front of an ornate, oaken China cabinet filled with antique plates and bowls. "See this cabinet?" Kevin waved his hands in front of it in triumph. "I made this myself too. In a way, I like it more than the house. The details, the carving, and whatnot. It's more intricate than doing a big project like a house. Plus, it's got a different type of sentimental value to it. The collection of plates and everything, they used to be my grandma's a long time ago. Passed it down to my late mother, and then to me. She was a good woman, my grandma. Meaner than a goddamn wet hen if you pissed her off, but she meant well."

Daniel studied the pieces within the cabinet. They did have an older quality to them and were rough with wear. The cabinet was indeed impressive, too, and Daniel wondered if he was even capable of crafting something in such a meticulous way. "When did you and Amanda meet?" he asked, nodding towards Mrs. Hall in the kitchen.

"Amanda?" Kevin asked. "When did we meet? Oh gosh. I wanna say we met about five years ago. Sometime around Christmas." Kevin scratched his head, thinking. "Honey!" he shouted into the kitchen.

"Yes, dear?" Amanda walked into the dining room, removing her apron and draping it over her arm. She stood next to her husband in front of the oaken cabinet.

"What year was it we met? Eighty-one? Eighty-two?" Kevin asked, as he put his arm around her waist, settling himself closer to her.

"It was Christmas of eighty-one," she said. The rich timbre of her voice was the sound of red maple trees during the peak of autumn; southern and dignified.

"That's it. Eighty-one. She's good at remembering dates and numbers and things. We met in eighty-one at the Middlesboro Gardening Expo."

Rebecca and Daniel looked at each other when Kevin mentioned a gardening expo. "You were at a gardening convention?" Daniel asked him.

"I was. Not for myself," Kevin said, as if it were an anomaly for someone like him to have an interest in gardening. "My grandma liked to garden, so I went for her. Checking out the tools, buying seeds, and stuff like that. What about y'all? How did you two come together?"

Rebecca laughed and looked at Daniel. "He found my dog digging through trash one night, and the rest was history," Rebecca said.

"Yeah," Daniel said, "that about sums it up. Found the dog, called the number on the tag, and that was it."

"Quite a love story there," Kevin said, laughing. "I tell you, I love dogs. Sweet little animals, but they will eat some of the nastiest shit you can find."

After Daniel and Rebecca regaled the Halls with their introduction to each other, a timer went off in the kitchen. Amanda leaned over to Kevin. "Here, come and help me grab the food."

"Sure thing. Let me get them some water real quick." Kevin looked over at Daniel and Rebecca. "Why don't y'all sit down and have a drink of water while we go grab the food? Boss! Mrs. Sutherland! Head to the dining room. Dinner's almost ready."

When Kevin left, Rebecca turned to Daniel. "When you meet my dad, it'll be like this. He's not as cheerful as Kevin, though," she said.

Daniel thought about it for a second, and the prospect of meeting the Church family didn't seem too overwhelming. Not that he wanted to meet them tomorrow or anything. "Well, maybe they can come by this Thanksgiving. Or Christmas," he said, playfully squeezing Rebecca's thigh under the table.

Dorothy sat on the left side of the dining room table facing the kitchen, followed by Wayne, Daniel and Rebecca. Daniel leaned towards Wayne. "They're really into playing host, aren't they?" he asked.

"If they had a family bible, it would be *Better Homes and Gardens*. Kevin used to get it delivered at the station, and he didn't think I knew," Wayne said.

Kevin poked his head through the door from the kitchen. "What can I get everyone to drink?"

"Me and Wayne'll have some sweet tea, please," Dorothy said.

"I'd like a bourbon, neat, too, if you got it," Wayne said.

Kevin nodded to Wayne in acknowledgment.

Rebecca and Daniel opted for a beer, and Kevin made himself and Amanda a martini, with which he garnished the table as he went back to the kitchen. A few minutes later, the aromas of roasted chicken and potatoes wafted in from the kitchen, causing Daniel to salivate in anticipation. Complimenting the chicken and potatoes, were sides of green beans, baby carrots, and creamed corn. Lastly, Amanda brought out bread rolls with butter for everyone to start.

"Nobody else from the search party is coming by tonight?" Daniel asked, as Kevin sat down.

"No, they couldn't make it. I imagine they're all tired, too. It was a long day, and the sun ain't exactly the kindest thing to stand under in the summer."

Daniel reached over for a bread roll, until he felt a hand clamp around his wrist. He turned and Rebecca shook her head, and looked towards Kevin, who was bowing his head for the blessing.

"Everyone, let's join hands," Kevin said. "Heavenly Father, we thank you for this meal before us, and for offering us closure on the case of Max Junior today, as is part of your divine plan. Please continue to watch over us and protect us from evil. Amen." Everyone echoed the close of the prayer and started to eat their bread. This particular meal, along with the meal at the Sutherland's the day before, was something Daniel hadn't experienced in a while. It was different from Mrs. Sutherland's cooking with the lack of fried foods, but it was just as delicious.

After supper, the entire throng of people went into the living room and sat by the empty fireplace, though the aesthetic of it completed the picture in a perfect sort of way. Had there been actual fire coming from it, it would've singed the hair off everyone's arms and there'd be pools of sweat collecting everywhere it could gather. Daniel, Wayne, and Kevin sat with drinks in their hands, and the women sat opposite them chatting about their lives.

"So, did you grow up here?" Rebecca asked Amanda.

"Until I left at sixteen, I did. My parents and I weren't on the best of terms, though," Amanda said, with a forlorn, distant gaze.

Rebecca placed a comforting hand on Amanda's arm. "Might sound crazy, but I know how you feel. Except I read, and kept to my small friend group before I decided to leave."

"In a town like this, it's hard to find people to get close to. Unless you go to the gardening expo, I guess." Amanda took a long drink from her martini.

As they spoke, Dorothy smiled at the two younger women. "I know I'm the old one here, but my parents weren't much different," she said. Amanda and Rebecca turned to her as she went on. "Just keep in mind, things change. This world you're living in ain't your parents' world. Or mine, for that matter. But going off like you did is good for the spirit. Within reason, of course."

Rebecca looked surprised at Dorothy's words. "You mean you had a rebellious streak when you were younger?"

Dorothy's face grew serious, and she leaned in close to them with a conspiratorial look. "Who says I still don't have it still?" she whispered, before turning her lips into a mischievous grin.

The other two joined her.

"When I told my parents I wanted to go to the city, they didn't care for it too much. They hate the city folks and don't trust them as far as they can throw them," Amanda said. "I like it there. It's just busy. And it's hard to fit in."

"Mine were almost the exact opposite. They trusted the city more than anywhere else. They said it was better because you can mind your own business easier. Too many people to waste time getting involved with anything else but their own things."

Amanda laughed and drank some of her tea. "Yeah, and in towns like these, everyone essentially knows everything about everyone."

This time, Dorothy chimed in. "Having that kind of closeness isn't too bad. You always have someone to turn to if you need it." She looked at Rebecca. "Are you planning on a private practice?" Amanda asked.

"It's an option I've considered. Maybe teaching. Maybe both, if I get tired of one or the other. I'm still relatively young, so I got time to think about it."

"Well," Dorothy said, "whatever you choose, I know you'll do great. You and Daniel are troopers for dealing with all of this police business. And from out of town!"

Rebecca leaned back and gave a contented sigh. "There's only a certain level of control we can have over things in our lives. Beyond that, there's not much we can do, except make the best of it, you know? I couldn't predict the car would break down, or that it would break down here when it did. But I couldn't ask for a better place for it to have happened."

Dorothy smiled thoughtfully over Rebecca's kind words. "I hope you still get to make it to Greensboro." She lowered her voice into a whisper and leaned towards Rebecca. "I want you to see Dusty Rhodes knock that son of a bitch Flair out."

Rebecca didn't just laugh. She laughed deeply from her gut that startled Amanda, as well as the men sitting opposite of her. "I hope so too," she said. "Apparently, they're still waiting on the radiator at Big Jim's."

"They're great, over there. They'll do it as quick as they can, if they can."

"Yeah, Mr. Hall said the same thing. Spoke very highly of the mechanics."

Sensing a rise in tension, Daniel turned back to Kevin and Wayne who were discussing the case of the missing children. "Sheriff," Kevin said, staring intently at Wayne.

"Deputy," Wayne returned. Then, he looked at his deputy and gleaned the gravity with which Kevin spoke. "You look like you got something on your mind, son. What's going on?"

Daniel set his drink down before any more liquor could work its way through his system so he could properly listen.

"What do you make of it? You think it's coyotes? Or do you think there's something going on?" Kevin danced around the question he wanted to ask.

Wayne sat back and placed his fingertips together, thinking. "I know for damn sure it ain't no coyote. I know Ed said the coyotes got into the chickens over at his place. But the prints don't look right. And it's not like they were looking for food. You understand?"

The phone rang, cutting Wayne off before he could continue.

Kevin reached over to the table next to him and picked up the receiver. Everyone in the living room could hear the voice from the other end of the receiver, jubilant and triumphant.

"I got the son of a bitch!"

CHAPTER TWENTY

*A*fter Kevin hung up the phone, he leaned over and whispered into Wayne's ear.

"All right, boys," Wayne said, "Max says he got it. Let's go check it out. Y'all, wait here until we get back."

"I think me and the girls will manage," Dorothy said, still in conversation with Amanda and Rebecca. "I think I might have a martini while we wait."

Amanda smiled at Dorothy. "That's a good idea. Rebecca, you want one? Or another beer?"

"Yeah, another beer would be nice," she said.

"Shouldn't be gone too long," Wayne said as the men headed towards the front door. Outside, Daniel grabbed the Mossberg, and Kevin and Wayne grabbed their normal work gear. Daniel and Wayne rode in the same car, with Wayne driving faster than Daniel had seen yet. Daniel had never been on a call for an animal before, and most of the time, the wildlife department took care of these things in the area.

"Did Max say what it was?" Daniel asked.

"No, not really. You ever hear of the Beast of Bladenboro?" Wayne asked Daniel.

"No, I can't say that I have. What's Bladenboro got to do with us?"

"It's a neighboring town, further out than Robinvale, and a little more east. A little over thirty years ago, there were reports of an animal or something like that causing trouble. When we saw the scene the other night, and Ed mentioned his dead chickens, I thought about it. It's why I haven't called the wildlife people or anyone else. I don't want any newspapers writing up ridiculous headlines, making us a laughing stock. Especially not when people are dying."

Daniel looked at Wayne, and perspired, as Kevin's ramblings started appearing increasingly plausible. "Is it like a demon or something? Does Deputy Hall know about this?" Maybe if the two of them were on the same page, even without knowing it, that would be useful for everyone involved.

"Demon? Who knows? Sounds more like a swamp monster or a sasquatch type of thing by my recollection, but who knows what kind of nonsense people get into out there. I wouldn't think it was impossible, although I don't believe in bigfoot or anything like that. Best we see for ourselves."

When they arrived at Max's house, Kevin and Wayne's cruisers flew up the driveway and skidded to a stop. Daniel got out of the car last, shaking with the mounting adrenaline and overriding the desire to get the hell away from some unknown foe. The three of them armed themselves with their guns and their authority as Max ran out to the porch to greet them.

"I nailed it. I knew I'd find it. The damn thing came back to finish the job, but I was ready!" Max said, ecstatic.

Wayne, doing his best to calm the mood and be rational, looked at him. "All right, Max. Take us to him." As good of a job as he did maintaining his composure, his voice couldn't hide the few cracks within it, betraying his apprehension. He looked at Daniel and Deputy Hall before adding, "Be careful and be ready, you two."

Max led them to the backyard towards the tree line in a hurry, the same one from Ed's house the night before where they found the other missing child. As they edged closer to the woods, they heard a rustling. Specifically, a rustling mixed with whimpering. Daniel wiped his hands on his pants as they drew nearer, guns drawn, and ignored his increasing heart rate in favor of doing the job. They crept through the thick of the trees, and suddenly it was right in front of them. Wounded, but very much alive.

Daniel looked at the figure. A bear trap that looked like it was a century old, or more, clamped down tight on the animal's hind leg, nearly severing it at the bone. Although, it seemed to Daniel that the strength of the leg itself had to have prevented it from happening. Immobile, but apparently fine, otherwise.

The rise and fall of the creature's breathing quickened as Daniel stepped closer to it. The animal looked the result of a cougar and wolf mating. It had feline-like eyes and ears, the tail of a wolf, and canine looking legs.

It had the telltale nose of a dog, with the slits on the side to keep the airflow going to allow for better olfaction, and it looked pissed. Pissed that it got caught and that it was hurt. Its ears were flat against its skull and its teeth, which were almost three times the size of any you'd find on a German shepherd, were bared. Strangely, it made no move to go after Daniel or anyone else. It just lay there.

Morbid curiosity mixed with Daniel's fear. He kept the Mossberg ready and moved around the back of the animal as Kevin and Wayne kept their weapons trained on the front. Max explained to them about how he trapped it. Despite the animal lying prone, the three officers kept their guards up. As Daniel got closer, that distinct smell from earlier crept into his nose. The smell of sulfur. He raised up and joined the other men in their conversation.

"I figured if something was out here scooping up kids, it had to be some sorta animal. I laid that iron bear trap and figured there couldn't be any harm in it. Either I catch something, or I don't." Max's excitement was still evident as he spoke. "And the hospital people said Junior can come back tomorrow. They released him from the coma now that the swelling in his head went down. He recognized me, knew his alphabet and birthday and everything else."

Daniel sighed in relief at Max's mention of the good news. "Max, I'm glad to hear your boy is coming back. That's great news."

"Well, I couldn't have done it without the three of you. Any idea what in the hell this thing is?" he said.

Daniel and Kevin shared a look before Kevin spoke. "Sheriff, what do you suppose we do now?"

Sheriff Sutherland looked towards the animal and back at the other three. "Well, my first instinct is to put a bullet right between its eyes, to be honest with you. But let's take a look at it one more time before we do. It looks pissed off, but it's not acting pissed off."

The creature panted as it lay with its leg trapped. They lowered their weapons cautiously except for Daniel, who crouched with his gun ready, looking at its paws. "Do these look like what we saw in the woods?"

"As far as I can tell, they do," Wayne said. "What the hell is that rotten egg smell?" Wayne sniffed around, with a slight focus towards the creature in the trap. "To hell with it. Let's get this over with. You two, clear out, I'm gonna take care of this." He stepped right in front of the animal while Daniel and Kevin moved to the side and drew his revolver from his holster. He leveled the weapon right at it and pulled the hammer back, before delivering a bullet directly into its brain.

The animal ceased breathing as thick, black ichor oozed from the hole in its head as the four of them examined it further. "Max, you wanna open this trap so we can remove it?" Wayne motioned to Daniel and Kevin as Max opened the trap. "Now, we can call the wildlife people and let them sort it out."

The closer they got to the animal, the worse the sulfur smell grew, peaking when they touched the short, rough-textured fur. They carried the carcass out of the woods, its heavy weight surprising Daniel, though they didn't struggle much. They dropped it about twenty feet into Max's backyard.

With the open sky above them, and the lights shining from the house, they got a better view of the animal. Its body was covered with golden brown and black fur. The larger-than-average teeth belied an entirely misshapen skull altogether, along with its other limbs, as if someone took random bones and stuck them together in the shape of a quadruped.

As they finished up their business, the animal's chest moved, rising and falling in rhythm as the black goo stopped oozing. The wound from Wayne's bullet appeared to heal itself, at which point Kevin let out a high-pitched shriek and cut the stunned silence.

Kevin was scared shitless, Wayne too stupefied to aim his gun, and Max too furious to do anything but curse the sky. So, Daniel took a shot with the Mossberg and completely missed the resurrected animal as it ran right towards him. It started running on four legs, and made its way up to two legs, and despite being shot at twice already, the only attention it paid to the four of them was to shove Daniel out of the way, knocking him flat on his back as it bounded off into the night.

CHAPTER TWENTY-ONE

"What the hell just happened?" Without waiting, Daniel sat up, stunned, as he watched the creature speed off into the night. "You shot it in the head, right?"

"I sure as hell thought I did," Wayne said, frowning and raising his eyebrows as he looked back at his gun as if it betrayed him.

"I knew it was a damn demon. How else do you explain that? Things just don't get up after a thirty-eight round to the head," Kevin said as he stared off in the direction the beast ran to.

"Daniel, get up. Let's go after it." Wayne pulled Daniel up before he ran to the car, frantic to catch the escaped creature.

Kevin and Daniel looked at each other and ran after him. "Are you sure you wanna go after this thing? It already didn't die once when you shot it. What makes you think we can get it this time?"

"I don't know," Wayne said, quickening his pace more with Daniel and Kevin nervously trailing him. "But I ain't gonna let that son of a bitch get away on my watch."

They rushed into Wayne's police cruiser, and Wayne floored it out of Max's yard. As they drove across the open field in pursuit of the creature, all they had were footprints and headlights to guide them through the dank and humid night. Daniel bounced around in the back seat, holding the shotgun, as Wayne drove with precision over the unpaved terrain.

"Be on the lookout, the both of you. If you see it, shoot it. Maybe you can cripple its leg, like the trap did." At that directive, Daniel planted his feet on the floor and stuck his head out of the window with the Mossberg ready, and up front, Kevin grabbed the handle above the window, with nearly half of his body hanging outside. Wayne drove through the overgrown grass, making good time before they pulled up to the edge of the infinite woods around Middlesboro. Wayne left his door open as he grabbed a flashlight along with his weapon and ran into the woods.

Daniel and Kevin followed closely. The entrance that the creature chose wasn't hard to miss with all the branches askew, broken, and shoved out of the way, along with the dirt it had disturbed on its run. Based on the stride length, Daniel came to two conclusions. Not only was this creature enormous, it covered a lot of ground in a short amount of time.

Guided by Wayne's flashlight and the waning gibbous moon above the canopy of trees, they sprinted further into the woods, breathing in the humidity, and mosquitoes as the brush grew denser, further hindering their path, even with the small trail the creature made before them. Daniel occasionally sniffed for the sulfuric odor the creature leaves behind. Finally, after a half an hour of looking for the monster at a grueling pace, they stopped.

Daniel placed his hands on his knees and bent over, catching his breath. "Why didn't that thing go after us? We were right there." Daniel stood up and looked directly at Wayne.

"Might be that it was scared and wanted to escape," Wayne mused, as his breathing relaxed back to normal.

"Even though it didn't die, it was scared?"

"Dammit, son, I know just as much as you," Wayne said through gritted teeth. "It's hard working on barely any information, much less information that doesn't make any damn sense."

"Well," Kevin said, a calm voice between the others, "it attacked two kids. Killed one of them. Left the other when it was near a church. We got the brimstone smell. And apparently, it's immortal. That's what we know, and it confirms the demon idea. Or it comes close."

Wayne turned to Kevin with his hands on his hips. "You want us to get an army of preachers to go after this wolf thing or whatever it is?"

"I dunno about an army of preachers. I don't know if we can find any. Ray might be a good choice, though," Daniel offered. "And if the creature doesn't have any interest in killing us, it might not kill Ray, either."

"I second the idea of getting Ray and at least talking to him," Kevin said.

"Dammit, Hall. For one, we don't know if it's a demon. And I doubt it is, since we've never seen one before. Second, if it is a demon, we can't walk around like Barney Fife out here," Wayne's voice rose, and he started pacing back and forth.

"What do you suppose we do then, Sheriff?" Kevin looked at Wayne.

Wayne looked down a moment before his eyes followed each stride the creature made. "We find him now. It's fast, sure. But we can tell where he went with the way he bolted away from us like that. Let's be quick." Wayne continued down the trail and the others followed.

Daniel hoped that every good meal he ate didn't come with the price of running after weird animals right after it. He and the rest of them ran deeper into the woods, with only the night sky shining through the fog to accompany their weapons.

As they kept their search on, Daniel looked for anything useful. Like the smell of sulfur. He wouldn't admit it out loud, but he kept an eye out for any new bodies, as well. They kept going, plowing through the brush, with the occasional thorns slicing their clothes and hands. After another hour of going back and forth around the woods, Daniel came upon something interesting.

He gave a long sniff of the air, but his olfactory senses only met the scent of earth, pine, and wet leaves. Amidst all the disturbed greenery, he came to a spot where the leaves were less dense on the woodland floor. Here, instead of leaves and small, broken twigs, he found what looked to be like a fence enclosing a circle, made of some of the thicker logs from the dead trees in the area.

Daniel looked at his companions, beckoning them to help investigate the foreign construction site. They stood a few yards away from the makeshift building.

"I know it didn't go after us before, but do you think it will now?" Daniel whispered.

"We don't wanna take that chance. Make sure the Mossberg is ready," Wayne said. "Deputy, are you feeling up to it?"

Kevin had a serious look about him, mixed with trepidation and determination, as if he was ready to charge to his own death. "No, I don't think I am, but that's no reason to stop now. If it's even in there. Could be a campsite."

"No fires. And the path of destruction seems to point here." Daniel looked around at the thrashed woods around him. "More or less anyway."

"We'll go over and look at it together and get it done with," Wayne said as he slowly crept forward towards the log-built enclosure.

They all were as silent as the ground allowed. Daniel held his breath and sweat dripped from him. He wiped his hands on his pants to get a better grip on the Mossberg. Even Wayne looked frightened at what might be ahead, though he soldiered on anyway. Kevin breathed heavily and deliberately, exhaling in and out in a slow tempo.

They couldn't see over the enclosure when they reached it, although Daniel was closest to the top of the walls.

"Deputy, why don't you hold your hands out and take a step for me? Sheriff, you too, so I have better balance."

With Kevin on his left, and Wayne on his right, Daniel stepped his feet into their waiting, cupped hands as they lifted him the few extra inches it took to see inside. He checked the circumference of the area, and near the center he saw what they'd been looking for. It looked at Daniel with grotesque eyes as big as saucers as dark as the night around them.

The creature made no motion to strike out at Daniel from where it lay, nor did it show any manner of hostility; it simply sat there, as if resting. It didn't seem tired in the slightest. When Daniel looked at the correct angle, the moonlight sank in the darkness of its eyes, instead of reflecting it back the way a dog's eyes did when it caught light. Daniel saw none of its earlier wounds as he scanned the creature's body.

Daniel and the creature stared at each other. Such destruction it caused, though at the moment, it looked at Daniel, sated. Daniel moved a free hand around to attract its attention elsewhere, but the beast made minimal movement. Finally, Daniel's curiosity got the best of him.

"Lift me a little higher, if you can," he called down to Wayne and Kevin. The two of them hoisted him up a little higher, at which point he grabbed one piece of wood on the large enclosure before lifting his left leg up to rest. With one fluid motion, he completed his entry into the heart of where the beast lay, taking the Mossberg with him. His heart pounded like a drum from a distant marching band and sweat beaded all over his forehead. He could feel it collecting in his shirt.

Daniel took a stand, planting both feet into the ground, and held the shotgun ready. The monster glanced at Daniel and quickly lost interest in the human before it. Resting without sleeping. After three deep breaths to steel himself, Daniel took a step closer towards the creature.

The creature offered nothing in return.

Outside the enclosure, Kevin and Wayne protested repeatedly, remarking about how this was the craziest act they'd seen a sane man engage in. Daniel thought they both might scramble to find a way in themselves without ripping the enclosure apart.

"Guys, I don't think this is as big of a deal as you're making it out to be. This thing isn't even doing anything. If you hear me scream, you'll know this didn't go well." He took another set of deep breaths before taking another step. "And if the worst happens, don't spare Rebecca any of the details. Let her know I died being an idiot." Daniel didn't want any false memories should a disaster befall him and thought it better that Rebecca knew the truth.

As the monster rested, Daniel didn't. Even the weight of the Mossberg and the company of his companions offered little comfort. Was the creature toying with him? Or did the creature simply not care that this wooden enclosure had a visitor, a human, not unlike the people it had taken out or tried to take out in the previous days? The lack of eyes on him had Daniel think it was the former and that he was relatively safe.

"Yeah, we'll tell her," Kevin called back. "But how the hell are you gonna get back over?"

Shit. Daniel hadn't thought that far ahead. "We'll climb that wall when we come to it, I guess," he called back.

"Damn kid is gonna get himself killed," Wayne said to the air and anyone who would listen.

When there were no more steps to take to bridge the gap between monster and man, Daniel bent his knee and stared at the monster right in the dark chasm of its eyes.

Still, it didn't acknowledge him.

Daniel examined its head. The mixture of canine and feline qualities, the misshapen and ragged teeth, and the soulless eyes almost gave the appearance of a mythic creature—not fully alive, but real. Against his better judgment, Daniel reached a hand toward it, drifting the beast's head.

Daniel knew the monster was aware of him. The creature's head didn't move, but its eyes moved around in the sockets, seeing everything going on around it. Daniel looked at his hand, hoping it wouldn't be the last time he saw it attached to him.

He closed the gap and stroked the head of the enclosed beast, petting it as if it were Rebecca's dog, or any other cat he'd come across in his life.

"What the hell is going on in there?" Kevin yelled.

Daniel stayed quiet for a moment as he reached his hand further down, petting the fur between the monster's gargantuan shoulder blades. From this close, he could examine the body more accurately. The monster didn't need an opening in the enclosure to escape. It could simply jump in and out at will. Daniel looked at the strength of the sinew of the creature's hind legs and the size of its paws, in awe of the beast in front of him. Powerful, majestic, and despite that, not caring that an armed human occupied its space.

"Daniel!" Wayne shouted. "What's going on in there? It's a little too quiet."

Daniel felt warmth from the creature radiating into his hand as it rested on the area between its scapulae. Within seconds, the warmth spread into Daniel, and he started dreaming. He knew he wasn't really dreaming, since he still felt the physical sensation of being awake, but he couldn't will himself to move as he held his hand on top of the creature. Daniel looked around him, and the enclosure was gone, as were the voices from outside.

Everything was different, and more abstract, now. Slowly, shapes formed, and theory assembled themselves into what appeared to be the real world he lived in. He was running faster than he could as a human. He bounded over blurred shapes and jumped higher than he ever had before. As he kept traveling this way, it occurred to him to look at his surroundings to abate his fear. When he did, he got an aerial view of the events. He saw the creature doing the very things he felt himself doing. Running through the woods that now formed, and out into the open. He looked on from the monster's point of view, running farther and longer than he'd ever witnessed anything run before.

He peered into the sky before looking to his left and right and took a long sniff of the air before continuing on with his trek. He passed Ed's house as he made his way into the nearby woods. When he kept going, Daniel heard two voices. The first voice gave a command. It sounded like neither man nor woman, falsified by something, and unnaturally deep, mixed with higher tones, like a recording of harmonic singing. The command was simple. "Get him and eliminate him," the voice said.

The other voice was laughter. A child's laughter. He went through the woods quite a way before he stopped his pace and crept with more deliberation and stealth, stalking upon four legs, making his way towards Representative Johnson's son. He stalked from behind the bushes as the child played in the thickets of the woods, throwing sticks and kicking leaves around him. The child couldn't discern anything as he darted to the side, with his eyes trained on the target.

Once he got behind the child and the child went back to what he was doing, he stood on his two back legs, casting a malignant shadow within the sun shielded woods, and grabbed the child by the waist like a cheap rag doll.

Daniel fell back with what seemed like a metaphysical push on his chest. He was back in his own body, staring at the beast in front of him. Shock rippled through him at the realization of what he'd seen and the insight it gave him into their investigation.

Still, the creature never moved.

Before he lost his wits, Daniel grabbed the Mossberg and scooted backwards on the ground toward one edge of the enclosure. "Okay, get me out of here. Quickly!"

The two men rustled around on the other side of the enclosure, and Daniel assumed they were trying to find a way to lift him over the top of it again. His assumption was erroneous as one post of the enclosure started to move. The two men on the other side strained as they moved the post back and forth, until at last it came free from the ground, and Wayne and Kevin tossed it aside.

Daniel tried to squirm through the first opening but could only reach a part of his arm through. By now, the creature hadn't moved around much, so he wasn't scared of it. But the images he saw moments ago while touching it frightened him even more. He pushed his fright aside for the moment as he helped the other two remove more of the posts, and finally freeing himself after the third post was taken away.

"You all right, son?" Wayne put a hand on Daniel's shoulder. "You look like you seen a ghost or something."

"I think I might have," Daniel said.

Kevin's eyes brightened a little, with worry and vindication. "So, do we think it's a demon yet?"

Daniel looked at Kevin before he shifted his focus to Wayne, worrying about how the latter would react to what he would tell them. "I don't know if it's the Beast of Bladenboro or if it's a demon."

The other two looked at him and waited for him to continue. "But it isn't a normal animal."

"Then what the hell is it?" Wayne asked, looking more concerned than he had been in the day since Daniel met him.

CHAPTER TWENTY-TWO

On the way back to the cruiser, Daniel explained to Wayne and Kevin the weird vision he saw when he touched the monster. The effort he expended on talking exhausted him more than it should have. Now that he thought about it, walking wasn't so easy, either. More than once, his legs almost gave out from beneath him, so much so that Wayne and Kevin grabbed his arms and put them around their necks to help assist.

When they got back to the cruiser, they helped him get in the backseat to rest. The men looked at Daniel, and then at each other.

"Should we get the preacher man now?" Kevin asked.

Wayne seemed at a loss before coming to a decision. "No," he said, after pausing for a moment to think. "Let's get him back to the station."

The three of them rode back to the empty moonlit police station where Daniel was relieved to discover that he could walk on his own again.

"How ya feeling?" Wayne asked, his hands out, ready to catch Daniel if he should falter.

"Better. I think," he said, stepping gingerly.

Once they got in the station, Daniel went to the break area and poured himself a glass of water as Wayne and Kevin stood in the main lobby. Wayne was on the phone speaking swift and direct instructions into the receiver, and after a minute, he hung up.

Daniel heard Wayne's footsteps coming to the room. "That's gotta be one of the strangest experiences in my life."

"Hopefully it doesn't get much stranger," Wayne said. "I called the doctor, and he's gonna come by and check on you to see if anything's wrong. I called Amanda, too. She and the others are coming by with food."

Daniel protested. "We really don't need to get the doctor involved in this. I'm fine. I can walk on my own. My head's clearer."

"Well, maybe you are. But a second opinion from a doctor won't hurt anyone."

Daniel looked at Wayne, biting back a reply.

"What is it?" Wayne asked. "You look like you wanna say something. Either you don't know what it is, or you'll think I'll have you committed. Just tell me, it won't get any stranger at this point."

"I think we should call Ray." Daniel said it with no hint of derision or skepticism this time.

"Why's that?"

"Well," Daniel said as he scratched his head and paced the room, "what if it is a demon? Or this Beast of Bladenboro?"

"What makes you think it is?" Wayne asked.

"What makes you think it's not?" Daniel asked in return.

Wayne sat down and thought. "It might be. I don't know. But we can't go bringing more people in on this, when they're untrained, and they might die. I already got you here, but at least you have some experience." Wayne looked at Daniel. "Not a lot of experience, but you're not a novice at any rate."

"Why don't we think of it as a consultation? We know where the creature is, and we know it doesn't attack us directly. We can just ask Ray some questions, get some advice. If it fails, we can go back to the drawing board."

"He's also not from the town. It would take a while to round him up," Wayne replied.

"Or we can sit here and do nothing, wait for the doctor and everyone else while the questions go unanswered, and the thing still lives."

Wayne leaned back in his chair and ran his hands through his hair as he looked up at the ceiling. "Fine. We'll consult Ray on the matter. But you have to make the call."

"You want me to invite him down here?" Daniel asked.

"You're making the call. You make the choice."

Daniel knew Wayne had good points for not bringing anyone else involved. The potential loss of life was the most important one, and one Daniel took seriously. On the other hand, an extra capable person to talk to, share ideas with, and maybe get physical with the thing wouldn't be bad either. Even worse than one new person dying, Daniel could die, or anyone else with him at this point. And if they didn't get to the bottom of it, where would that leave the rest of the innocent people in town?

As Daniel sat and pondered, the door to the police station opened, and Dr. Burton walked back into the breakroom. Daniel leaned against the counter near the sink, while Wayne sat in the chair at the table, and looked toward the doctor when he walked in.

"What's the trouble, here? You get your head knocked? Shot?" Dr. Burton asked, plopping his medical bag down on the table and pulling out the light to shine on Daniel's eyes.

Daniel laughed a little. "No, nothing like that." He offered the doctor a truncated version of the strange vision he had and the subsequent fatigue it left him with after the fact.

"Psychic vision, huh? You wouldn't be the first person to experience anything like that." Dr. Burton looked unsurprised, as if you went up to him to tell him that the sun would rise in the morning and set in the evening.

"I wouldn't?" Daniel was more confused now than he was before.

"Not at all. When you've been around as long as I have, in a place like this, you run into many weird things. Now, whether it's exhaustion and you have a second wind, or it's a legitimate psychic vision the way others describe it, that's not up to me, I'm no theologian or spiritual guide or what have you."

The doctor looked at Daniel's pupil dilation, asked him a series of questions to make sure his cognitive abilities were where they should be, and made sure his eyes still moved correctly.

"What do you think? Am I normal?" Daniel asked him.

"You're a bit taller than most, and have a hefty frame, but your eyes are working. You know who and where you are, and you can think straight. Seems all right to me," he said as he started packing up his medical bag.

If he seemed all right now, his next question might make the doctor think otherwise. Still, it was worth a shot, since Daniel didn't have medical training. "You ever see an animal take a bullet to the head and shrug it off like nothing happened?" Daniel asked the doctor.

"Not unless it had a skull made of a few bricks. But I've never seen that, either."

"Dr. Burton," Wayne said from the chair, "you ever hear of the Beast of Bladenboro?"

Dr. Burton paused and looked at Wayne, surprised. "I have," he said. "I've not heard the name in…" he looked to the ceiling as he counted the years on his fingers, "maybe thirty or so years. But I remember."

"What do you remember about him?" Wayne asked.

"I remember it happened in Bladenboro, not far from here, in the fifties. The thing killed some animals, if I recall."

"And they said the witness reports looked like wildcat or something, right?" Wayne asked.

"If I remember correctly. You don't think that's what this is, do you?" Dr. Burton looked at Wayne as if it was a preposterous idea.

"Not sure at the moment. The beast did target animals, and as of now, no reports that it killed any humans back in the fifties. But if you saw this thing, you'd see where the idea comes from."

Daniel spoke up this time. "The thing we saw, the one that killed Matt Johnson and knocked out Max Junior, sort of looked like a cat. Like a mixture of a cat and a dog, with the fur, and almost pointed ears. Gnarly teeth and it smelled like sulfur. It's also huge."

"How huge?" The doctor asked.

"Taller than I am if it stood on its hind legs. Maybe a foot or two taller, if I had to guess. I don't know that I would wanna see it stand up that high in front of me. I likely wouldn't live long to tell you about it if I did," Daniel said.

"Well, I dunno if it's the beast or not, but that doesn't sound like no animal I ever heard of," the doctor said. He thought for a moment before speaking to Daniel again. "Have you considered seeing a psychiatrist when you get back to Savannah?"

As the doctor finished his sentence, the door from the lobby opened and several sets of feet clomped on the wood floor of the police station, making their way to the break room. Rebecca, Dorothy, and Amanda strolled in and made themselves comfortable as Daniel and the doctor wrapped up. Daniel looked at the him, knowing he meant well, but somehow still feeling the sting of an insult given what he saw. "I will. She actually just walked in."

Wayne shook Dr. Burton's hand. "Sorry to call on you so soon. Just wanted to make sure he's on the up and up since I'm responsible for him here."

"No problem at all, Sheriff. I hope you take care of whatever is going on. Nasty business. Have a good night." The doctor shook his head and walked out the door.

Rebecca walked over to Daniel, cupped his face with both hands, and peered into his eyes. "Hey. You all right?"

"Yeah, mostly. Wanna go outside and chat while I have a cigarette?" Daniel asked.

"Sure, let's do it."

The two of them went outside the police station, standing in the humid coating of the Carolinas. The moonlight cast the occasional shadow, mixing with the occasional but dimly lit street lamps.

"What'd you really wanna come out here for?" Rebecca asked him.

Daniel lit a cigarette. "I really did want to come out and smoke. And talk to you."

"No shit? You made it seem, obviously, I might add, that there was more to it."

He lowered his head, searching for how to begin. "I was that obvious? Well, it's been quite a night, and the story is getting stranger by the minute." He considered how much to tell her before deciding to dive in. "The thing that got the kids doesn't die. It lives in a circle surrounded by wooden logs keeping it in, and it seems to ignore all of us when we're around. Kevin thinks it's a demon, and the Sheriff thinks it's some Beast of Bladenboro, which apparently is a cat that killed some animals."

"Like mice? Cats usually kill mice," Rebecca said, trying to understand him.

"No," he said, blowing out some smoke, "not a house cat, but like a cougar or something bigger. And cougars and coyotes don't go around mauling kids and leaving carnage and dead bodies in their wake. On top of that, Kevin thinks the church might have scared it off, which is why Max's kid is alive. Power of God type of thing." Daniel spoke quicker than normal despite not having any coffee in a long time.

Rebecca stared at him. "I need you to do me a favor." She kept her eyes on him, waiting for an acknowledgment.

"What's that?" Daniel asked.

"Take a few deep breaths."

Daniel took several deep, diaphragmatic breaths.

"Now, I want you to take a moment and think."

"What am I thinking about?" he asked.

"You've told me what the deputy and the sheriff think. But you haven't told me about what you think. So," she sighed, "what do you think?"

Daniel got up and started pacing, piecing together his thoughts as he inhaled the smoke from the noxious weed in his hand. "Good question. I think," he went on, "that the smell of sulfur is important. Deputy says it's a sign of a demon. And he would know about the sulfur water more than I would, so I doubt he'd make a mistake like that. I dunno if it's actually hellfire and brimstone, like he thinks or not. But the sulfur does seem to be around the animal, and in places where it's been."

"So, you have the sulfur, an undying creature, and it may or may not be repelled by the sight of hallowed buildings or people, right?"

"Yeah, I think so," Daniel answered.

"And it doesn't die. And *both* of them know that it doesn't die, right?" she asked.

"The sheriff was the one who put the first bullet in its head before it got up and knocked me on my ass."

"That's a long fall too," Rebecca said with a lighthearted smirk.

"It'd be even longer for you, you know," Daniel said, laughing back.

"So, what does it mean?" Rebecca asked him.

"What do you mean?"

"Things usually die when they're shot in the head. This thing didn't," she stated.

"It means the only logical conclusion is that this thing isn't natural," Daniel said.

"Right. And what similarities do these things have with our world?"

"Besides living in our world? Or hanging around in our world? I have no idea." Daniel blew out his cigarette smoke and then stomped the cigarette into the dirt.

"This is why you need to watch more movies," Rebecca said. "It means they have rules, too. We have natural laws. They're here on earth, from wherever they come from, and they have rules too. They have to follow them."

"But then there's the vision. That's the weirdest part of it all. It's like I was seeing its...thoughts, I guess?"

"So, it was like a psychic vision. You saw what it saw."

Daniel lowered his head, sadness inflicting him. "Yeah. I saw it go after the Johnson boy."

Rebecca pulled him in for a hug and the two of them stood in the dank, humid moonlight of North Carolina, embracing each other. "I'm sorry, honey. Nobody should have to see that."

"And the parents have to live with the grief, now. Living with grief is a life-long event," Daniel said, as tears started rolling down his cheeks.

Rebecca pulled his head to her shoulder and held it. "It's gonna be all right."

"I know. Part of it's the sadness, but there's a huge part that's pissed off that I can't figure out what's going on and take care of it and give the people some closure around here."

"This isn't gonna be easy to hear, but it's not your job to give anyone closure. They have to find that themselves. The problem is, it's never what people think it is. Sometimes, not knowing, or even having a shitty outcome, is closure itself."

"You're right," Daniel said, looking up at her. "You're pretty damn smart, you know." He kissed her deeply before he pulled back to go inside.

"Thanks, the smarts cost quite a bit, but sometimes it feels worth it. Hey, don't go back in just yet," she called after him.

"Why not?" he asked.

"I wanna have a few minutes with you. We've been around people since we got here, nonstop. Searching, eating, socializing, and all that. Plus, I can tell you about what we did after you all left."

"What'd you guys do?"

"Well, we sat around a few minutes, but then Amanda had another drink and invited us to go look at the garden in the backyard."

"Weirdly, the deputy didn't mention it when he was talking about how he'd built the house and everything in it," Daniel said.

"Probably because it was her idea and her work," Rebecca said, laughing. "Plus, it's pretty new. I think she said she started it this year. Planting Brussels sprouts, beans, and some other stuff, too. The fertilizer, which she made herself, stunk to high heaven."

"Did she make you get your hands dirty?" Daniel smiled at her.

"She asked if we wanted to help, but I think Mrs. Sutherland didn't wanna do much after dinner. She was feeling great, too. I know I didn't. Plus, the smell. Smelled like rotten eggs," Rebecca said.

Daniel tilted his head to the side and looked at her. "Say the last part again."

Rebecca looked at him, confused. "It smelled like rotten eggs."

"And rotten eggs smell like sulfur." Daniel's eyes gleamed as he stood up. "Let's head back in." He pulled Rebecca up by the hand and hurried back inside with her not far behind.

CHAPTER TWENTY-THREE

$\mathcal{W}$ hen they got back inside, Daniel grabbed a legal pad and sat at a table with Rebecca, away from the main purview of everyone else, but in a position where he could survey everyone in the room. As he started putting his puzzle pieces together, he focused on Kevin and Amanda in particular. Kevin was older than he was, at least by a decade. Amanda seemed somewhere in between his and Rebecca's age. And she was attractive, in ways relevant to Kevin's lustful pursuits.

The more Daniel ruminated, the more questions he had. Why those two children? He grabbed a case file from Wayne and studied it intently, as he marked up his legal pad with notes.

"Do you think you'll actually be able to read any of that later?" Rebecca asked. "Your writing looks like a grade schooler's."

"I think I'll manage," Daniel said, working out the equations in his head.

After scribbling, more scribbling, and flipping through the page notes on the pad, he went back to Wayne's desk. He leaned towards the sheriff and whispered something in his ear, and noted the look of realization on Wayne's face after he did so.

Daniel went back to join Rebecca as he watched Wayne dial a number on the phone. Less than a minute later, he hung the receiver back up and walked over towards Daniel.

"You fancy meeting the preacher for a cup of coffee?"

Daniel nodded his head. "Just us three?"

"Yeah. I'll go deal with everyone else," Wayne said, starting towards Kevin and Amanda.

"You think you can make it? Being around them any longer?" Daniel looked at Rebecca and squeezed her hand.

"I think I can manage. Dorothy is far more delightful than I imagined. I could listen to her talk all day," she said.

"Good. Hopefully, we can figure this out soon, and get to Greensboro," Daniel said with more notes of fatigue settling in his voice. He stood up and kissed her forehead before he met Wayne to head over to the diner.

Wayne and Daniel hopped in the cruiser and headed to the same Waffle House Daniel and Kevin had met to discuss the deputy's demon revelation. Along the short drive, they remained quiet, and though he never said as much, Daniel was sure that Wayne was coming around to the idea of the monster being otherworldly.

When they arrived, Reverend Ray was sitting in a booth with two extra coffees, waiting for the newcomers. "Good evening, officers." The pastor stood up and shook their hands before they all sat themselves.

"How's it going, Reverend? What can you tell us about demons?" Daniel asked.

"Well, what do you wanna know about demons?" he asked. "A lot of people think the demons out there are the devil. Well, more specifically, the devil's minions. Helpers, kind of like."

"I think what Daniel wants to know," Wayne began, "is what, if any, experience you have with them. I realize it's a strange question, but I have never seen anything in my life take a bullet to the head and survive. And then heal itself soon after."

"Yes," Ray said, "that is strange. And you saw it get shot?"

"Course I did. I was the one who shot it."

Reverend Ray studied Wayne for a moment before he leaned forward and continued. "Usually, when people come talking about this stuff, they get the details wrong. Not on purpose, they just misremember. They're so surprised, and filled with awe, it makes it easy to do. In my humble opinion, we wouldn't have theology and everything that comes along with it without these experiences." This time he focused on Daniel. "And to be clear, you also saw the thing take the bullet?"

"I did," Daniel said. "And then it jumped up, knocked me on my ass, and ran out into the woods before we found it again."

"When you shot the thing," Ray started, looking back at the sheriff, "what was going on? I assume no creature, predator, prey, afraid or not, would just stand there and let it happen. Except maybe if it trusted you already." Ray took a sip of his coffee and looked at both Daniel and Wayne. "And I don't think this creature was in a position to trust you, given that you were out looking for him."

"Well, when I shot it, it was trapped in one of the resident's bear traps. I shot it in the head, and when we pulled it out of the trap, that's when he made a break for it," Wayne explained.

The pastor ruminated and drank his coffee. "You opened the trap, and that's when it finally made a move? Did it struggle while it was in the trap?"

"It just kind of laid there. Like it was waiting," Daniel explained.

"You got any idea what the bear trap was made of?" Ray asked, looking at either of them.

"Some kind of metal, I guess," Daniel said.

"It was an older trap, so I think it would be mostly iron," Wayne said. "What's that got to do with anything?"

"Well," Ray took another sip of his coffee before continuing, "there's some legends that spirits don't take too kindly to things made of iron. It's a good way to keep them away from you. That's partly why people believe horseshoes to be lucky. It ain't the shape itself, it's the material."

"So, if we assumed that to be true, then the iron of the bear trap kept the thing docile, allowing me to shoot it?" Wayne asked incredulously. "What made it stay alive?"

"That, I don't know," Ray said, shrugging his shoulders. "But, in my opinion, it sounds like it is something otherworldly. Demon or not, I can't really say, but it doesn't sound like anything of this world." He focused his gaze on Daniel. "What else happened? You said you came close to it, right?"

"Yeah, I was face-to-face with it. It didn't even care that I was so close." Daniel explained the vision he had, and the voice he heard from within that vision.

After Daniel's story, Ray rested his chin on his hands and thought for a moment. "Based on what I know, that ain't a demon. A demon can essentially do whatever it wants. It wouldn't stand there and let you shoot it or avoid you entirely when you creep into his space. They have agency. They just use it for a different purpose than you or I would do."

Daniel thought about the vision and the sulfur smell. "So, is it possible for someone to…possess…an animal? Or something like an animal?" he asked.

"Keep in mind," Ray said, "I've never seen anything like that happen in my life. But you don't grow up down here, with this kind of history, without hearing about some crazy things over the years," he said. "So, I wouldn't rule it out."

Wayne and Daniel looked at each other and back at Ray.

"How do we stop something like that?" Wayne asked him.

"The easy way would be to find out who's controlling it and make them stop."

Daniel and Wayne shared another look before thanking Ray for his time and apologizing for the interruption of his night. Shortly after, Pastor Ray departed, leaving Daniel and Wayne by themselves.

"I know what you're thinking, son." Wayne ordered a refill of his coffee. "But you know we can't just arrest anyone right now, not without enough evidence. It would destroy the two-man department if we botched it. I would lose what reputation I have as a lawman, especially because of outside influence. No offense."

"None taken," Daniel said, his thoughts harmonizing with the sounds of spatulas clinking and eggs cracking, all culminating in the scent of sizzled butter and pork fat. "What's the connection? What does she have to do with Max, Representative Johnson, and their death and disappearance?"

"That's not something I'm entirely sure of myself," Wayne said.

Both men paused for a while, looking at the cosmic swirl of the ripples in their coffee. Daniel disrupted the microcosm when he snapped his head up with a thought. "When we were talking over dinner. She mentioned being away from Middlesboro, off in Atlanta. Do we know what she was doing during that time? Does Deputy Hall?" Daniel asked, the frustration in his voice rising.

"No, she hasn't spoken much about it. Well, not in any great specific detail, at any rate," Wayne said.

Daniel pulled out the legal pad he took notes on back at the police station. He scanned over several of the lines and stopped, pointed at one, and spoke again. "What happened to Max's wife?"

"She passed away," Wayne said.

"How did she pass?" Daniel grabbed a pen and was ready to write again.

Wayne scratched his chin and looked up. "Pneumonia, if memory serves. What're you thinking?"

"I'm not sure yet," Daniel said, as he started scribbling more notes on the legal pad. He bit the cap of his pen and looked up as he kept piecing the puzzle slowly in his head. "And Johnson is still married?"

"He is. Do you think we've missed something the entire time?"

Daniel sighed and scratched his head as he turned the pages of the legal pad back and forth, studying each one, over and over, to no end. "Maybe. No idea what it could be."

"It's about time to get back, I reckon," Wayne said, rising from the table.

Daniel followed him out to the cruiser, and they made their way back to the Middlesboro Police Station.

CHAPTER TWENTY-FOUR

*B*ack at the station, the Sheriff parked behind the other cars on the dirt lot. Daniel pulled out the case file and walked up the steps into the office, while Wayne trailed behind. As he opened the door, Daniel bumped into someone, the force of it knocking him back a few steps. Everything spilled out of the case file onto the ground. He stooped down to grab various papers and yellow carbon copies of forms with various signatures tabulating the bureaucratic process.

Two photos stood out from the pile. The first is a picture of Representative Johnson's son, Steve, and the other is a picture of Max Junior. Daniel placed the two pictures on top of the stacks of paper and glanced up at the person he collided with Amanda.

He looked at the picture of Max Junior, and back at Amanda. After a moment of scrutiny, he said, "Careful, you might give me a concussion next time."

"Sorry about that," she said. "Have everything?"

"Yeah, thanks." Daniel headed toward Wayne's desk to reorganize the contents of the case file.

"You know you don't have to do that at my desk, right?" Wayne asked, laughing.

Daniel, his face serious as his eyes bore holes through the pictures, glanced up at him. "Do you see it?" He nodded towards the photo and refocused on it.

Wayne followed Daniel's gaze. He turned his head back towards the door.

The sheriff frowned at the pictures looking back at him. "Yeah. I think I do. We need to go to talk to the doctor. Again."

"I imagine he's gonna be pretty pissed off with us bothering him again today," Daniel said.

"Well, he can worry about it tomorrow. His feelings don't mean nothing to me when we got one death to get to the bottom of and another serious injury to account for," Wayne said, raising his voice.

As they spoke, Kevin walked up to them. "You guys find out anything?"

"Not as much as we need, but we got more than nothing," Wayne said.

"Yeah. Turns out, you weren't far off," Daniel said. "At least according to the pastor."

Daniel filled Kevin in on the rest of the conversation with the Reverend before he asked him his last question. "Where'd your wife run off to so quickly? She didn't say much after we bumped into her."

"She had to get back home. She was getting tired and wanted to clean up the house before she went to bed," Kevin said.

Daniel, about to say something, was interrupted by Wayne. "Why don't you go along and help her out?"

"What for? Don't we have work to do?" Kevin asked. His voice rose in inflection and he spoke faster, giddy with the possibility of being correct about the demon, along with solving the mystery. Daniel had a small hope that Kevin would hold onto that excitement for as long as he could.

"We do," Wayne said. "It ain't going anywhere tomorrow, and it's getting late." Then, he leaned towards Kevin's ear and whispered, "And, with the children dying and almost dying, some women get...sensitive about that kinda thing. Hysterical, I mean, so it's best to be with them when they get like that."

"Well, you have a point. I know she'd be worse, too, if it happened to one of our own." Kevin looked around and thought some more. "Yeah, I think I'll do that. Thanks, Sheriff. I'll see y'all tomorrow." With that, Kevin walked out of the station, leaving Daniel, Wayne, Dorothy, and Rebecca there alone.

Daniel smiled to himself. "Nice work with him."

"They ain't gonna teach you this at the academy, or anywhere else. Well, maybe if you get to be a federal agent, but this job, and many others, it's all about knowing people. You know people well enough, you can use it to your advantage."

"Isn't that kind of unethical?" Daniel asked.

"It depends. But think about it like this: would you wanna lay an accusation like we have against someone, and have someone they care about right there beside them? Especially if they're also supposed to be looking for the answers to the same questions you have?"

Daniel thought about it for a moment. "No, I don't think that'd be a good idea."

"And you've seen how he can get about some issues and the way he views women. Truth is, he does need to be with his wife now. We don't know what the future holds."

Daniel nodded his head, understanding.

"You just can't go abusing it. That's unethical, and it makes you an asshole," Wayne said. "Let's get the doctor and Johnson over here."

"You wanna bring them *here*?" Daniel asked.

"Absolutely. They'll know it's serious, and it places me, and you, in our place of authority. Context matters. You can go off duty and be friendly all you want. And you should, it's part of the community. And people might give you answers they didn't know they were giving you, sometimes. But when they see you, the lawman, in the building of the law, in uniform, it changes things."

Daniel realized there was more to Wayne Sutherland than he could fathom, after knowing him for such a brief amount of time. Untold wisdom gleaned by simply being kind more often than not, and doing his job to the best of his abilities when it was absolutely necessary.

* * *

AN HOUR LATER, Representative Johnson and Dr. Burton arrived at the police station at roughly the same time. The pair of them stood beyond the threshold, dressed casually after a long day of whatever their work entailed. Daniel hoped they wouldn't be here long.

"Excuse us gentlemen, let Daniel and me talk a minute more. We'll be right with you. Go help yourself to some drinks in the breakroom." Wayne smiled at the two as he gestured towards the break room. "Let Dorothy regale you with some stories if we take too long."

"Where's the deputy tonight?" the Representative asked.

"Well, he and his wife headed out a little earlier than expected. All the news of the past few days was catching up to her and they took the night to be together." Wayne laid on the stern southern charm, playing to the crowd of two in front of him.

Daniel had only seen him do a lot of physical work at this point, as it related to the job. Other times, Wayne had entrusted Daniel with the interpersonal side of things, and now he knew why. It was a masterpiece of theatrics mixed in with genuine care and concern for the surrounding people.

When the two guests went to the break room, Daniel and Wayne conferred with each other one last time and made their plan.

"Remember, we have the advantage," Wayne said. "We know things they don't think we do. I'll talk to the doctor; he and I have a good rapport, but when it comes down to it, I'll get what we need out of him. You have the task of talking to Representative Johnson. Remember, titles mean everything to him. Typical politician with an even bigger ego, somehow. You remember what to do?"

"I do," Daniel said. Adrenaline coursed through him and rubbed his sweaty palms on his pants as Wayne went back to the breakroom to round the two of them up.

When the sheriff walked out of the breakroom, he motioned towards Daniel, beckoning him further down a hallway just before they got to the final area that housed a holding cell. Just before the cell on each side of the hall was a door, and Daniel and Representative Johnson went into the one on the right, as Wayne and the doctor went to the one on the opposite side.

The room was largely bare. The table in the center of the room beneath a hanging excuse for a spotlight had a color like mud, caked in and unable to be removed. The light shone over every bump, recess, and imperfection in the table, highlighting it against the few unsullied sections surrounding them. Daniel went to a filing cabinet in the corner immediately to his right and reached inside to pull out a tape recorder. "You can go ahead and sit down," he said to Rep. Johnson.

The representative scraped the chair a little along the floor and sat down, his hands resting on top of each other. The legs of the chair didn't align perfectly, and Johnson leaned askew to keep it from wobbling.

As Daniel pulled out the tape recorder, he rummaged around the drawer of the cabinet a little longer, delaying what he knew was to come. He did, however, pull out an ashtray before he sat down opposite Rep. Johnson.

"Officer? I'm sorry, what was your name again?" Johnson asked.

"Belascoe. Daniel Belascoe, with the Savannah Police Department, deputized in the town of Middlesboro by Sheriff Wayne Sutherland to assist him as an extra deputy over these past few days." Daniel studied the man in front of him. By his estimation, and according to the constitution of the United States, he placed Rep. Johnson at thirty-seven years of age.

"So, what's going on here? Am I under arrest for something I don't know about?

Daniel chuckled and lit a cigarette. "No," Daniel said, "legally, you've done nothing wrong. Hopefully, working in politics doesn't change that." Daniel shifted in his seat and looked at Rep Johnson straight on. "Ethically, I'm not so sure." The smoke trailed upward, filling the room, and taking the form of the cone of light coming from above.

Johnson's face contorted to one of confusion. "What do my ethics have to do with my dead son?"

"We don't think it was an animal attack that killed him," Daniel said. "Which means someone was out to get you as well as Max. I've got my suspicions, but if you lie, it won't help us, and it won't help you."

Johnson huffed and ran his hands through his hair. "All right, let's get on with it then. What about my ethics are under investigation here?"

"Rep. Johnson," Daniel said, "you remember JFK, right?"

"Yeah, of course I do," Johnson snapped, his annoyance increasing.

Now that Daniel had found a way to rile him up, he figured he could get to the answers he needed rather quickly. "Of course you do. You would've been alive for his presidency. I was born a year after he died. Almost a year, actually, so I don't have my 'where were you when Kennedy got shot' story like I imagine you and a bunch of my other colleagues on the force do."

Johnson sighed again and rapidly tapped his thumb on the table.

"Refresh my memory. What was Kennedy known for when he was in office?"

Johnson looked down at the table, thinking for a minute. "I think one of the big things would be the Bay of Pigs Invasion in Cuba, and he was about to gear up for some big civil rights legislation, too. And possibly his deals with the mob. Why? What's this got to do with me, or my goddamn dead son?"

"What else was he known for during his presidency?" Daniel asked, keeping his demeanor calm.

"I mean, those are the big ones. There was also the Peace Corps, and the Space Race, among other things."

"I suppose I should just come right out and say it then," Daniel said. "He was known for having lots of affairs. The high-profile one was Marilyn Monroe if I remember correctly. And depending on the circles you travel in, the CIA might have had a hand in her death because of that affair." Daniel wiped his forehead with the back of his hand and stubbed out his cigarette in the ashtray. "But that isn't relevant right now, Marilyn dying."

"So, what *is* relevant right now?" Johnson asked.

"The affairs. Not *his* affairs. But it's a common thing with politicians, right? I imagine it's not just a presidential thing." Daniel paused and watched the realization crawl over Johnson's face. "You know, you guys go to Washington or wherever you go, leave your families behind, and everything. A man's got needs, right?"

"Yeah, some guys run around on their wives, so what?"

"Well, that's where the ethics matter more than the legality," Daniel said. "I imagine a young, up-and-comer like you, was in no unique position compared to some of these other guys. You ever, uh, get your needs met? While you were out there on your political travels?"

Johnson's mouth was clamped shut and Daniel watched with satisfaction as a vein rose and throbbed on his forehead. He said nothing.

Daniel took a breath and leaned back in his seat as he looked at the politician. "Come on, Ken, you can be honest with me. Remember, you can't go to jail for it. I'm sure as hell not gonna tell Mrs. Johnson anything. This town is already out of my jurisdiction as it is. It wouldn't do me any good to rat on you." When Daniel said that, he leaned forward and whispered conspiratorially. "Besides, we're men, and we gotta look out for each other. So, talk to me man to man. You ever satisfied those needs while you were out politicking?"

Over the years, Daniel never really cared for eye contact. Most of the time maintaining eye contact took a physical toll on him, but growing up, every male authority figure in his life emphasized that people look each other in the eyes as a measure of character. As inane as Daniel thought it was, he didn't want to let his father down. Or anyone else in his life.

Like anyone else, Daniel faked it as often as he could. At first, he would talk to people and look at the space directly in between their eyes where the bridge of the nose flattened into the forehead. Over time, he developed the skill of direct eye contact, and since it had never been natural to him, he overcorrected himself and often made others uncomfortable by how often and how intense his gaze could be. That was the position Johnson found himself in right now. The room was silent, cut by the rhythm of a ticking clock on the wall and the combined breaths each man took.

After the silence became too much, Johnson broke. "Of course I have. Do you have any idea how much pressure there is out there with the people you work with to play the role? To be one of the guys?"

Daniel knew. "I hear that," he said. "But as men, we also have to be true to our word. At least, that's how I grew up. So, when the preacher says, 'Death do you part,' it seems like a big promise to make. But like I said. Your secret's safe with me."

Johnson let out a sigh of relief and relaxed.

"But that's only the first part of what I hope my final question to you is. Answer this last one, and you can go. Are you ready?"

"I guess I don't have much of a choice, do I?" Johnson said, with dread painting his face.

"You do, but like I said before, it'll be a lot easier if you just tell the truth." Daniel lit another cigarette and continued. "You ran around on your wife. I know this isn't a big town. If I remember, the sign said the population was somewhere around a few thousand. Less than ten, I remember that much. It's not a big place. With so few choices, I suspect we all know the person you cheated with. Even me, and I've only been here for just over a day. Wanna tell me who she was?"

Johnson sat in his defeat in a situation he had no way of getting out of. "You already know, god dammit," he spat.

"I might, but I wanna check my work."

"Fine," Johnson said, muttering under his breath. "It was Amanda. The Deputy's wife."

"I didn't know it before, but I had my suspicions," Daniel said. "And now, one last question."

"You said that was the last one!" Johnson hit his fist on the table, rattling the ashtray and knocking Daniel's cigarette from it onto the table.

Daniel grabbed the cigarette and puffed on it before returning it to its resting place. "I did, but I misspoke. But I suppose the doctor can answer it for me if I really need it. He could be answering that question right now, maybe."

Another wave of realization backhanded Johnson. "What is it?"

"If I go and pull some records, like say medical records, would I find out anything worthwhile? Maybe prenatal medical care, an abortion, or anything of that nature as the result of your affair with Amanda?"

Johnson's face grew pale, and Daniel knew he got his answer.

"No," Johnson said.

"No? So, there wouldn't be any sort of medical records that would disclose the result of your affair with Mrs. Hall?"

"No, there wouldn't. The abortion was off the books, and I gave Dr. Burton money to keep it that way."

"Smart thinking, you wouldn't want that sort of thing to become public knowledge. Not down here, that's for sure. And, now, since you've been so cooperative, indulge me. This isn't relevant to anything, but I just wanna make sense of it. You paid the doctor off so that he would perform an abortion for Mrs. Hall. And he did, and now the evidence is gone. At least as far as the records go, now a few more people know that secret, at any rate." Daniel thought some more before he continued. "You pay Burton off. He performs the abortion. Why not go to a different doctor, out of state? Or in Atlanta or Savannah?"

"I'm not a fucking monster," Johnson said. "I wanted her to live through the procedure and I trust Doctor Burton."

Daniel tilted his head as he looked at Johnson. "That's very...noble...of you," he said with no sincerity. "We're done, feel free to go."

Johnson immediately fled the room while Daniel looked through the haze of smoke. He thought about the events from the moment he and Rebecca came to Middlesboro, and now he finally had a part of a motive. Hopefully, he could corroborate it.

CHAPTER TWENTY-FIVE

*D*aniel knocked on the door to the other office, interrupting Sheriff Sutherland's interrogation. He motioned for the sheriff.

"Pardon me a moment," Wayne said, scooting the chair out and walking towards Daniel to confer with him at the threshold.

"He told us everything we needed," Daniel said, loud enough so not only Wayne could hear, but the doctor could, too. As Daniel looked at Dr. Burton, he saw him slump in his seat ever so slightly and let out a breath. Daniel put his mouth up close to Wayne's ear and mentioned some of the pertinent highlights of Johnson's taped confession.

"And you got it on tape?" Wayne said to the room before he leaned in closer and lowered his voice to keep the doctor from hearing. "Remember what we do next."

Daniel walked in and took a seat at the table next to Wayne, who continued the line of questioning.

"Look, we already know Representative Johnson paid for the abortion and paid you to keep quiet. You got the payoff, and the job is done. Honestly, I think it's good that you did it. She was better off with you, on account of your credentials, expertise, and skill level. Nobody's calling into question any of that, and the secret's still safe." Wayne shrugged his shoulders at the doctor. "Plus, he's a powerful man, being in politics like that. You did what you thought was reasonable."

The doctor sat in the chair opposite him and started bawling, wiping tears and snot on the sleeve of his shirt. "I never meant for anyone to end up like this," he said, his voice thick with mucus. "I just wanted to do the right thing."

"Well, now," Wayne said, "in a way, you did do the right thing. You kept her safe and didn't allow any harm to come to her. That's the Hippocratic oath, right?"

Dr. Burton nodded his head.

"And these guys, these politicians," he said, pointing his thumb near the door Johnson walked by moments ago, "you know how they are. With that power, they can put the pressure on. If anything, you made the right choice, given the circumstances they presented you with. In situations like that, it's the best thing we can do. It's just..." Wayne stopped his sentence and leaned back in his chair before he eyed the doctor and continued. "It's just we feel like there's a little more to it. You're in a heap of it now, so we need the answers so we can get to the bottom of it. That's all we're asking of you."

Daniel kept his eyes glued to the doctor the entire time, so much so that Dr. Burton glanced nervously at Daniel every few seconds, with the moments in between getting far narrower as time went on.

"Just tell us what you know, doctor. It can't be any worse than what you've already told us, and what Johnson told him," he said, gesturing to Daniel.

The doctor broke down further. Tears dripped on the table in front of him, and he frantically moved to clean them off with his other shirt sleeve. He sat up in the chair, wiped his eyes clean and kept talking. "Fine, I'll tell you *everything*. Max and his wife, they couldn't have any children of their own. So, when Amanda got pregnant again, she didn't wanna get the abortion. Frankly, I don't know if I was willing to do that and go through it all again." The doctor sniffled and wiped his nose. "So, Max and Justine were more than willing to take on a child they could adopt."

Wayne shook his head in that I'm-not-mad-just-disappointed way all fathers do when they're reprimanding their child. "So, instead of a medical procedure, you committed some fraud on the documentation. Amanda gives birth to Max Junior, and you alter the birth certificate to read Max and Justine as the parents, let them raise him as their own, hoping nobody will be the wiser. Have I got that right?"

The doctor finally stopped crying and sat there in the chair, crestfallen. "Yeah. That about sums it up."

Wayne looked at Daniel. "You got any questions for the doctor?"

Daniel shook his head and tapped his finger on the edge of the table.

"Dr. Burton, thanks for your time. You're free to go." Wayne reached his hand out, and the doctor feebly returned the handshake. Wayne and Daniel sat in the room thick with the silence after Dr. Burton walked out.

"So, do we have to get Max involved, too?" Daniel asked.

Wayne stood up and paced around the room. "I'd rather we not. Poor man's had enough of it these past few days, and he loves the boy like it was his own. I can't fault him for that. Can't fault Justine, either, rest her soul. She loved Max Junior, too." Wayne looked through the glass pane on the door and thought it over some more. "No, I think we can leave him out of it. We have almost everything we need."

"That means we have to confront her. What are we gonna do about Kevin?" Daniel asked, rising to stand near Wayne.

"That's gonna be tough. He might have his issues, especially where women are concerned, but he's also fiercely protective of his own, and he is committed to right and wrong. But I've never seen how that commitment holds up when it's on his doorstep, holding the proverbial gun to his face. We'll head back and I'll talk to them both."

"What do you want me to do?" Daniel asked.

"No idea," Wayne said. "This whole situation is pretty unbelievable except to those of us involved."

Daniel looked at Wayne for a moment as he thought about the steps he needed to take when Wayne confronted the Halls.

"Let's head back over."

* * *

Daniel and Wayne rode with their significant others to the Sutherland house on a silent and tense drive. Dorothy and Wayne walked ahead, and Daniel grabbed Rebecca's hand and slowed his pace to get a moment of solitude with her before the two men made their way back to Kevin's place.

"You're tense," Rebecca said, looking sideways at Daniel.

"What makes you say that?"

"Nothing, other than you holding my hand in a death grip," she chuckled.

He relaxed his grip and stopped walking. Daniel pulled her close to him and wrapped his free arm around Rebecca's waist. "I am tense," he said. "And scared. If Amanda confirms everything we think we know, I don't know what's gonna happen."

"It's not gonna be dangerous, is it?" Rebecca squeezed his hand a little tighter and inched forward so their bodies touched.

"No," Daniel said. I don't think it'll be that bad. Just emotionally heavy for the Halls."

"Good. Tell me everything when you make it back later," Rebecca said, smiling.

"Count on it."

Rebecca pushed the back of Daniel's head towards her and kissed him. When she pulled away, she said, "I'll see you soon." She turned and walked towards the door as Wayne exited, and the two exchanged a brief goodbye.

When they got to Kevin's place, the house was a little quieter than it had been earlier, and the only indication that anyone was home, aside from the cars populating the driveway, was the light on in the living room.

Wayne rapped his knuckles on the door. Not long after, Kevin answered the door, having not changed his clothes since the last time they'd all seen each other.

"Hey, Sheriff. What's going on?" Kevin asked, standing with the door open, looking out at Daniel and Wayne.

"We found out some more interesting news, and I think it's about time we told you. Is Amanda still up, too?" Wayne's voice this time was flat and stern, with no hint of humor or mirth at all. The look on Kevin's face after he spoke understood it was something serious.

"Let me go check." Kevin turned to walk back but hesitated and turned around again. "If she's sleeping, you want me to wake her up?"

"Yes," Wayne said. "Please."

Kevin left the men on the threshold and went towards the bedroom they shared.

"Whatever you intend to do, think of it now. I'm gonna get the two of them together and talk about what we learned."

Daniel turned to Wayne before entering the house. "Do you think it's gonna go well?"

"Hell no. I think it will go any way but well. But it has to be done, and if we all behaved based on how we thought a situation would turn out, nobody would do anything worth a damn in this world."

Daniel returned Wayne's hard gaze, and stuffed his tense, shaking hands in his pockets.

Wayne clapped him on the shoulder and nodded to him. Daniel relaxed with that small, wordless vote of confidence. It had been a short amount of time since they'd met, but from what he gathered, moments like these had happened to Wayne often enough to give him the ability to handle them in the way that he did, though they'd likely been far less frequent over the years. He looked at the old man beside him with admiration.

Amanda came out in a nightgown, followed by Kevin close behind. "Hey, Sheriff. What's going on?"

"What do you say we go to the kitchen and put some coffee on? Daniel, are you in the mood for coffee, too?"

"Uh, no sir, I'll pass. I'm gonna stay out here while you three talk." Kevin gave Daniel a skeptical look before leading Amanda and Wayne to the kitchen. With his jaw tense, and beads of sweat pooling on his upper lip and temples, Daniel watched the three of them disappear into the kitchen.

When he heard chairs slide along the floor, Daniel wandered into the living room and took a seat in front of the fireplace, to silence his beating heart and steady his breathing. He scrutinized the room from his chair, his eyes resting from one point, and moving to various other fixtures as if he were dotting them to connect later. The living room fireplace, and the mantle above it. The picture on the mantle of Kevin and Amanda embracing each other, smiling. From there, he turned to a bookshelf nearby. Daniel's eyes lingered on it for minutes while he sat.

After the sweat dried and his heart calmed, Daniel got up and started perusing the spines, looking at the titles. The top row was filled with fiction books, and when he made it to the non-fiction books, he saw a few on gardening. He scanned the rows of gardening books and decided upon one that caught his eye; *We Must Tend our own Garden: How to Get the Best From Your Brussels Sprouts Crop This Summer.*

He read Amanda's notations as he leafed through the pages, most of which noted rain patterns, homemade irrigations systems, or diagrams in the margins. Other notes she made detailed her personal preferences on how to sow and reap the crops.

Further in, Daniel saw instructions for making the soil as rich as possible for the vegetables to thrive, the key ingredient being sulfur. He stopped, remembering the smell. He took his time in that section, hoping it would help him learn something, but he found nothing of interest beyond the fact that fertilizing soil can sometimes involve sulfur.

He sighed, and snapped the book shut before sliding it back in place. There was nothing to be found, and Daniel questioned whether he and the sheriff were incorrect about their assertion. Then again, a forced abortion, an asshole father, and another out-of-wedlock child living right under her nose was a motive that nobody could ignore. But how? What was he even looking for? Would the secret to possessing a weird animal that shouldn't rightly exist be in a series of gardening books?

He plundered his way some more and grabbed a book on crop rotation for higher yields every harvest season. Much like before, he found a whole lot of nothing, and now he knew that sulfur was not uncommon for someone to own if they were a gardener. He clenched his teeth and huffed in frustration before he put the crop rotation book back in its place amongst the rest and scanned the shelves some more, this time moving to a section other than gardening.

Daniel browsed through a couple of non-fiction books and settled upon a history book about the Pacific Theater during the Second World War. He skimmed through that one, and nothing of interest turned up, aside from an entire section of the war that he didn't remember going over in school.

He paused, listening to the sounds from the kitchen. He hadn't been looking long, but they only had so much time. Wayne couldn't keep them there all night.

He quickened his pace. His anxiety over finding anything caused him to move almost carelessly, until he stumbled across the last book that caught his eye: a volume on the South in the Antebellum period and how slave trade influenced the local economies.

When he opened the book, the first hundred or so pages were exactly what they appeared to be: words written on paper. By the end of that first hundred page section, he came across a thick block of pages that appeared to be glued together.

Upon close inspection, he saw a thin circle cut within the middle of the block of pages, and a small tab of the paper that screamed for him to pull on it. As excited as Daniel was, he took care to slow down so he wouldn't botch anything. He took a seat in front of the fireplace again and deftly pulled the covering off the hidden compartment nestled within the book.

He glanced in the direction of the kitchen and shifted his gaze to his left and right, like a thief in the middle of shoplifting.

In the hollowed out block of pages was a small drawstring bag with a Crown Royal logo on it. Daniel felt the fabric but couldn't recognize any of the objects inside, though he could tell there were at least three different items inside. He grabbed the bag, closed the book on his lap, and let it sit there as if it were a small, makeshift table before he carefully dumped the contents on top of it.

Daniel's lips turned down, and he narrowed his eyes on the items. What he saw didn't make a lot of sense to him. A piece of thick, purple chalk, a small toy that resembled some sort of generic quadruped, and a thick sheet of note-book paper folded over itself several times. The chalk and the figurine were what they appeared to be, the latter made of pewter or some sort of metal.

Carefully, Daniel unfolded the sheet of paper in his hand, flattening it out over the face of the book. He stared at it, like he was waiting for it to speak to him and simply tell him what it was.

It looked like complete nonsense. A circle with odd but distinct symbols marked around the circumference intersecting the circle itself in various spots. Above and below the circle were more strange symbols, as well as letters from the alphabet. Despite his literacy giving him the understanding of the letters he could read, he still wasn't sure what to make of the contents of the hidden compartment, but he knew it could lead to something. Although he wasn't sure what.

CHAPTER TWENTY-SIX

*A*fter gathering the contents of the book, he walked over to the kitchen where Wayne sat opposite of the Halls at the kitchen table. Daniel took a seat next to Wayne and studied Amanda and Kevin as the silence hung in the air like a soiled shroud before him. He steeled his nerves and placed the chalk, the figurine, and the paper with the strange symbols down before him delicately.

Amanda watched him set the items, one by one, with a small, theatrical pause, on the table.

Each pause between the revelation of the objects held space for the small and vanishing hope that he and Wayne weren't about to upend this woman's life. Each object lain crushed those hopes, one by one. Daniel focused his peripheral vision on her waiting for any kind of reaction, though she didn't make a motion or act in any special way.

Wayne looked at Daniel, surprised by the interruption, but he said nothing at first, as he let Daniel get to work with whatever he had planned.

Daniel straightened himself and turned his downcast face at Kevin.

Kevin looked at the items and back at Daniel, confused. "Dan, you wanna tell me what the hell I'm looking at here?" The inflected confusion ended closer to anger.

Daniel looked at Kevin, then Amanda, and sighed. Before he spoke, he glanced at Wayne. "I was sitting in the living room and decided to look at the book collection on that shelf you made. Imagine my surprise when I picked up *The Economics of the Antebellum Slave Trade*, and I found a hidden compartment inside of it." Daniel threw in a forced chuckle. "Just like you'd read about or see in a movie." He started fingering the paper in front of him. "And when I looked into the compartment, I found these. A little piece of purple chalk. Strange symbols and writing on this otherwise plain piece of notebook paper. And this." He held up the figurine of the quadruped. He breathed in and looked at Amanda and straightened his face. "I think you might know what these are. Why don't you tell your husband and the Sheriff?"

Amanda sat, and as the moments trickled by, the cloak she hid under slipped away and she sunk her shoulders down, nearly slouching in the seat. She remained silent.

"Amanda," Wayne said, "the best thing you can do right now is to cooperate with us. You're digging yourself into a hole the more you don't."

She looked up at Wayne and Daniel and then at her husband and sniffled. "You wouldn't understand." When she spoke, her voice came out just a few decibels above a whisper.

"It isn't that hard to understand," Daniel said. "You were pregnant. Johnson talked you into getting an abortion, solely to keep his political career and his marriage looking good for the public. Then, you got pregnant again, but this time you stuck to your convictions, and had the kid. You struck a deal with the Reavills and gave them the one thing they couldn't have. You gave them a child."

Daniel paused to collect himself, careful not to rush the words he was eager to be done with. "Dr. Burton was in on it, too, and helped you all out by sliding everything under the radar, so that if anyone cared a little bit, things would look fine. You went out for revenge, but you couldn't bring yourself to have your own living child murdered. Maybe it was a clever play, or maybe it was the love you still have for Max Junior. But you didn't prepare for people caring so much about it." When he got to the end his voice lowered as the gravity of it all, spoken into reality, weighed upon them all.

Amanda started sobbing, snot and tears decorating her face while she nodded in agreement with him. She took a few minutes to compose herself before she looked at Daniel straight on. "It's true," she said, this time speaking a little louder.

Kevin looked down at the table as he rested his head on his hands before turning back to Amanda.

Daniel said, "So, why don't you tell us about these items I found in your book? It's not like we can arrest you for playing with ghosts or anything. It would never hold up, you'd never serve any time, and nobody would believe it."

Amanda's sobs continued, but then she composed herself, scooting the chair away from the table and stood before the men in the room. "It's easier if I show you," she said.

Daniel raised an eyebrow to Wayne who shrugged before he got up and went to Kevin's side to help him up.

She led them all into the living room, in front of the fireplace. She moved the pokers and other accoutrements aside then removed the carpet covering the area before the fireplace, exposing a small edge made of brick, and sat upon it. Beneath the rug, on the hardwood floor, there was a circle about four feet in diameter in front of them, made with the purple piece of chalk. The symbols surrounding the circle matched perfectly to the circle and symbols on the piece of notebook paper Daniel found in the book.

"What in the hell is this?" Kevin asked, raising his voice. "Are you conjuring goddamn demons in my house?" He moved closer to her, seething.

"Deputy Hall," Wayne bellowed, moving to stand within reach of Kevin, "I think you'd better stand down."

"Damn it, Sheriff," Kevin said, as he got cut off.

"Deputy Hall," Wayne said again, emphasizing the words, "Stand down!"

Daniel, distracted by the commotion of the two men and remembering how precarious their hierarchy was, missed the moment Amanda decided to lunge for him. She snatched the figurine from Daniel's hand and placed it within the circle. When Daniel tried to enter the circle to grab it, he struck himself dumb on an invisible barrier that barred entry and fell back to the chair. The Amanda now standing before him in the circle starkly contrasted the crying, bereaved mother in the kitchen minutes ago. Daniel froze with inaction.

After seeing Daniel fall back into the chair after striking the invisible wall, the other two men looked at him strangely and then turned to Amanda in the circle. They both tried to follow his lead and penetrate the circle, but that force that stopped Daniel stopped them, too.

In the center of the circle, Amanda kneeled, muttering strange phrases in a low, guttural, and seemingly otherworldly voice. As the chanting continued, the men pounded on the barrier that enclosed Amanda and kept everyone else out.

Before long, Kevin gave up and pleaded with his wife. "Amanda, please! Stop and let's talk."

Wayne backed up from the circle. "Mrs. Hall, listen to your husband, for the love of God," he said, trying his damnedest to maintain a modicum of composure.

Still, she chanted.

The sound of muffled stomping from outside the front door crescendoed. Kevin and Wayne stopped in their tracks, and while Daniel's brain didn't fully process what was going on, he did recognize the danger lurking closely. Within the circle, the still-kneeling Amanda held her left hand palm upward, with the metallic figurine resting upon it.

The noise of the stomping reached its peak, adorned when the front door splintered off its hinges. Standing before the three men was the creature. The same one they'd seen before, except now it was full of life. Amanda's eyes rolled to the back of her skull, and she swayed as she kneeled. The monster stared at them from the threshold of the Hall household.

Daniel, Kevin, and Wayne cringed at the smell. Every breath the beast exhaled reeked of sulfur mixed in with the shit-smelling aura of a petting zoo. The men looked at each other, stupefied. Unlike before, the creature salivated. It took a thunderous step forward, ready to spring. The beast looked at Daniel who took a step back and gulped as he returned its stare.

The report of a gun sounded, and Daniel saw the recoil of Wayne's revolver just as he sent another bullet right into the eye of the unflinching monster. The shot to the eye did nothing as the creature started with its quick stride across the room. Kevin looked back to his wife in the circle and then to the beast as Wayne fired off a third shot into its head.

Daniel searched frantically for something to help even the fight as the creature reared back, spun around, and planted its two hind legs right into the sheriff's stomach, knocking him up against the wall before it turned around and headed towards him.

Daniel swung his head, desperate to find anything to help, until finally, his eyes landed on the living room chair next to him. He grabbed it with both hands and with the legs pointed at the monster like a lion battling with a tamer. The beast smacked the chair out of his hands, and Daniel quickly jumped to the side. More gunfire clued Daniel in that Kevin was now in the fight.

Kevin fired a round off into the monster, and immediately another, followed by a third. Amanda swayed within her circle and guided the monster to her husband after his three gunshots. The monster charged towards him, as he frantically fired off another round into the heart of the monster, although it did nothing to stop the creature. The monster raised his unnatural claws to swipe at Kevin, but the deputy sidestepped it, firing another round into it.

Dread buried itself into Daniel's heart as he realized any option available seemed useless. Even if he had the Mossberg, the monster would shrug it off. Worse, Amanda was protected by the circle and her own husband couldn't reason with her. The beast had knocked Wayne against the wall, and he only just started to stir. If the creature went to him, he wouldn't live.

Daniel froze again, but not because his current reality didn't mesh with reality as he had experienced it thus far, but because he was out of options. The beast cornered Kevin, so Daniel did what seemed sensible. He threw things at it. First, another chair. It hit the monster who all but ignored it. He ran to the fireplace and grabbed the picture from the mantle and flung it at the creature. He grabbed a partially burnt log from the fireplace itself and chucked it at the creature.

Now, the beast turned to Daniel, and behind it, Kevin scurried over to Wayne, who lightly smacked his face.

Daniel backed up further and stopped when there was no open space available to him, then shuffled to his right, knocking the fireplace tools to the floor. Daniel looked at them, hoping one of them might be useful as a weapon. The small broom was out of the question. And the shovel for ashes. His eyes lit up when he saw one other tool. Reverend Ray's voice echoed in his head. *There're some legends that spirits don't take too kindly to things made of iron.* Then he thought about the first time they all saw the monster, trapped in the iron jaws of the bear trap. The *iron* bear trap in Ed's yard.

The fear wasn't fully gone, but there was something mixed in with it, now. There was, maybe, a chance. Daniel grabbed the poker. He wasn't a metallurgist, but he was at least aware that this tool, like the trap, was made from iron. He hooked his finger onto the curved end close to the point, launched it upward, and grabbed the handle.

Behind the beast, Wayne pulled Kevin towards him and said something to his deputy, and immediately Kevin ran towards Daniel, gathering the monster's attention with another gunshot and bringing the creature closer to the both of them.

Daniel held the poker at his side, and as the monster closed in on the two men, he raised his right hand, the poker jutting from it, and plunged it upward, directly into the monster's eye. When the tip pierced the creature's eye, it let out a horrifying wail, something mixed between the sound of hounds baying, a cat caterwauling, and something altogether otherworldly. The rotten egg smell coated the room and Daniel grabbed the poker with his other hand, and with the added strength, pressed further, walking the wailing creature back towards the wall, until the poker plunged from the other side of the creature's skull. Now stuck to the wall behind it, the monster was impaled and lifeless. From within the protective circle, Amanda shrieked when she saw what happened to the creature.

Daniel turned to her, and then back to the monster. He motioned toward the circle and Kevin went to see his wife while Daniel went to the creature to make sure it was actually lifeless. As Amanda's shrieks subsided, Daniel confirmed the monster wasn't alive. Or at least whatever "alive" meant to something like that. No blood flowed, and no breath came from its lungs while the iron tool held the beast to the wall behind it.

When Daniel turned back toward the circle, Amanda was no longer inside of it. She'd dashed over to Wayne, grabbed his gun, and hit him in the head with the stock, and his body slumped over and lay prone.

She trained the gun on Daniel and Kevin, alternating between the two as she backed into a corner, panting.

Daniel looked at her, armed with nothing, while Kevin held his weapon at his side.

"Amanda, put the gun down," Kevin said, his voice breaking away from the mostly professional and occasionally crass tone he always had. With his free hand, he wiped his eyes clear. "Put it down, and we can leave this behind us."

Amanda's hands shook as she pointed the gun at her husband. She said nothing, but her aim faltered.

"Listen," Daniel said, "you don't wanna shoot anyone."

"You don't know that!" she screamed beyond her sobs. "I have nothing! And you both made sure of that." Her finger crept around the trigger as she pointed it towards her husband.

Daniel looked over at Kevin who seemed lost in his pain. "You still have a chance at living, at least," Daniel said. "Kevin, your husband, is still here, too. He cares about you." Daniel's voice cracked when he spoke.

"What the fuck good is living gonna do?" she asked, as her sobbing abated.

Kevin straightened up and wiped his eyes again. "Baby, you're still young. You can still have a life. We can still have a life. It doesn't have to be this way," Kevin said.

Daniel stood by, watching Kevin's sincerity. Amanda kept the gun trained on him, then pulled the hammer back on Wayne's revolver. "For you, maybe!" she seethed. "I won't ever have anything normal to go back to."

"Put the gun down," he pleaded. "Please." He holstered his weapon and held his hands up in surrender.

Daniel looked at the husband and wife, separated by a few feet of distance. She had to know there was still hope left. Her own husband did. But they both had gone through a very different set of circumstances to end up where they were.

Amid the standoff, Daniel looked at Amanda to help bring her down to earth. His eyes landed on her in time to see her plant the barrel of the revolver into her chin and pull the trigger, letting a shot ring out, cutting the silence and the tension in the room.

Surprised, Daniel closed his eyes for a moment, as the smell of gunpowder and blood permeated the living room. He opened his eyes again, focused on Amanda's body in front of a backdrop of blood, brains, and chunks of her skull, all of which stuck to the wall behind her. Whatever didn't stick to the walls slid downwards in a trail of brain matter and tissue.

Kevin fell to his knees and looked at the floor as tears started dripping into a puddle. His body went limp while he knelt and wept. He wiped his eyes as he bawled on the floor of his house. The dead monster behind him surveyed the scene, impaled on the iron, a stark reminder of it all. Daniel put a hand on Kevin's shoulder, but the deputy brushed it away as he went to where his wife lay among the pieces of her shattered skull and brain matter.

Daniel finally moved, walking over to Kevin and looking on at a broken man and his dead wife. He sat there for a moment processing everything they'd seen. Finally, after some time had passed, he let Kevin do the same.

Kevin stayed exactly where he was while Daniel went to the kitchen for a glass of cold water. He brought it out with him and kneeled down to Wayne's body. The sheriff was moving but needed a boost. Faintly, he felt the pulsating of the sheriff's heart, and to wake him up, he dumped the glass of water directly on Wayne's head.

The older man opened his eyes and spit some of the water away from him and slowly sat up. "That son of a bitch nearly did me in," he muttered. "What the hell happened?"

Daniel looked to his right where Amanda's body rested while Kevin still knelt there looking at her.

Wayne followed his gaze, and his face drooped into melancholy. The sheriff sighed and stood up, surveying the scene before walking over to his deputy.

Kevin, grief stricken, glanced up at Wayne with eyes rubbed raw from the tears. When the sheriff extended his hand to help him up, he took it. The three men stood in silence as they let the scene wash over them. Kevin finally broke the silence. "What now?" he asked.

CHAPTER TWENTY-SEVEN

Nobody said anything. Daniel didn't have to assume or guess what they all felt, especially when it came to Kevin. Nausea gripped Daniel's insides. He didn't pull the trigger. But he didn't do a good enough job in talking her out of it, either, and it might have been equally as bad. Her own husband couldn't. Wayne was largely out of action during the part that mattered most. He had the look of a man who wasn't comfortable with nor accustomed to failure all too often. By comparison, getting rid of the monster was easy.

"Damned if I know, right now," Wayne said. He looked at Kevin, concerned.

Daniel was at a loss for words and wondered how anyone got past the weight of failure and loss.

Kevin's face was raw with anguish and tears. He managed a smile and rubbed his eyes again. "We were gonna go for a long drive and see the red maple trees this September. I was gonna help her with the garden for the first time."

Wayne patted Kevin's back and said, "Let's get out of this room. Catch some air outside."

They walked out to the porch, and Daniel sat on the steps, smoking, while the other two talked amongst themselves. Daniel didn't make it a point to listen in on their conversation, but what he caught was mostly words of comfort, with each man doubtlessly putting it all on their own shoulders.

Daniel did so, too. They'll probably talk of how they'll write the report up so they maintain their credibility to the outside world, and things of that nature. Despite his personal failure, deep down, Daniel knew it was so much more than the failure of an outsider and two law men. Everything that happened was the result of people doing their best to maintain the status quo.

Wayne walked up to Daniel and put a hand on his shoulder. "Take him back to my place. Go grab him some clean clothes and a few other things."

Daniel finished his cigarette and stood up. "All right. How long until you get there?"

"Couldn't tell you. I'll get back as soon as I can. I have a lot of work ahead of me." Wayne sighed and rubbed his temples.

"I didn't wanna pry, but I heard a few things. What exactly are you gonna say for the writeup?"

Wayne took a deep breath and let it out. "Do you know the problem with this job? Well, one of them anyway."

Daniel shook his head, wondering where this line of thought would lead.

"Everyone, and make no mistake, I mean *everyone*, will eventually bend the rules for one reason or another. Some do it to make themselves look good. Others do it to hide their wickedness and corruption. Rarely does anyone do it to make themselves look good enough to not get hauled off to an asylum for talking about ghosts and demons and a vengeful wife. The system is flawed, son, you already know that. Kevin, Amanda, and definitely Matt Johnson didn't deserve this." He looked up to the sky and rubbed his chin before settling his gaze back on Daniel. "So, I think it behooves me to use these flaws to at least try to make something good happen."

Daniel looked at him for a minute, organizing the thoughts in his head. "Is it the right thing to do, though?"

"No," Wayne said. "Not by the letter of the law, anyway. But to keep the people from panicking and to get them some sort of closure?" He shrugged his shoulders. "I think it's a better idea to bend the rules than to not. Plus, this wasn't your fight, and I dragged you into this," he said.

Daniel cut in, "But I said I would. I could've said no." He looked down to the ground and muttered, "I could've done a better job at talking her down."

Wayne shook his head. "Son, none of us could. Not even her husband. But the official stuff? You won't have to worry yourself."

"What do you mean?" Daniel asked.

"You're young," Wayne said. "You got a whole life ahead of you. You don't need to get wrapped up in this mess beyond what you and Rebecca already have. Just wait until tomorrow. You'll see. I'll see you then."

With that, Wayne stood on the porch as Daniel took Kevin back inside to grab some essentials before they left for the Sutherland house. The only noise as they drove was the sound of the wind rushing by and the never ceasing cicadas and other insects making music within the woods of North Carolina that night. Kevin looked aimlessly out the window the whole ride there.

After they arrived at the Sutherland home, Daniel stepped out and opened Kevin's door and let him out.

Kevin stood next to the car door, looking at Daniel for a long time, until he finally spoke. "Thank you," he said before he paused. "For helping us out. For finding out everything you did. And everything else."

"It's no problem. I hope you're gonna be okay," he said.

The deputy looked down and cried again. "I just wonder what I could've done different," he said through the pain.

Daniel pulled Kevin in for a hug and let him cry on his shoulder for a while under the black, star-dotted southern sky. When Kevin composed himself, he sniffed, wiped his eyes and nose, and straightened his shirt before they walked inside.

Rebecca and Dorothy came up to the door upon seeing the condition Kevin was in, and Daniel held up a hand and motioned them away as he led Kevin upstairs.

"Let's get you cleaned up real quick," Daniel said.

"Thanks," Kevin said, as they made their way to the bathroom. "I can handle it from here. I'll be back down shortly."

When Daniel went back downstairs, he joined Dorothy and Rebecca in the living room and sat with them in silence for a few moments.

Rebecca looked at Daniel sitting there in the most haggard state she'd seen him in. "So, what happened?" she finally asked.

He looked at Rebecca and then at Dorothy, wondering how he would explain what happened to the both of them. "Kevin's wife died." He searched for what to say next. Ultimately, he knew that Wayne would tell Dorothy everything in a matter of time, and he would do the same for Rebecca. "And we found out a lot of stuff about the missing kids and everything else that's been going on here the past couple of days. The sheriff is back at the scene handling it. He'll be able to give you a better recap of everything."

"Why don't y'all go on up to bed?" Dorothy asked. "I suspect Kevin might wanna be alone right now. Either way, I can talk to him. You two need to be with each other right now."

Rebecca and Daniel nodded to Dorothy and made their way up to the guest room.

* * *

LATER IN THE NIGHT, Daniel lay next to Rebecca as moonlight shone through the window of their guest room. Neither one of them slept yet, so they stared at the ceiling above them, chatting. During the quiet peace of that summer night, Daniel shared all the details with Rebecca.

"Is this the type of life that I have to look forward to in the coming years?" Rebecca asked him.

"You've already been thinking about our potential future?" Daniel shifted, turning towards Rebecca, and propping himself up on his elbow as he spoke to her.

"Of course I have," she said. She paused and smiled at him. "Judging by the sound of your voice, you don't sound unhappy about it, either."

He let out a contented sigh. "I'm anything but unhappy about that idea. The adventure, however, I can take or leave." He grabbed her hand, weaving his fingers in with hers, and held tightly. "I just wanted to go see the wrestling match."

"God, me too. Well, hopefully, we can at least make it to Greensboro in time for the Flair and Rhodes match, if nothing else."

"And maybe go on a double date with Tom and Christina. He'll be sore he missed out on all the excitement, I think."

"Excitement?" she chortled. "A dead kid, an actual witch with a vendetta, and a mess to clean up like this is exciting?" Her face quickly sobered. "I do feel bad for Amanda, though."

Daniel grew serious when she mentioned that. He replayed her death in his head ever since he left Deputy Hall's place. "Yeah," he said. "I do too. Why do you think she did it?" Maybe the therapist-to-be would offer some comfort.

Rebecca turned on her side and faced Daniel. "It's hard to say why, exactly, she did it. Mostly because there's likely not one reason that led to it."

"What do you mean?" Daniel asked.

"Remember when you grilled Johnson about the abortion and everything? You may or may not have known it at the time, but you spoke to a lot of insecurities and worries people face. Particularly women."

"It just made sense though," he said.

"That doesn't make the things you said any less true. Pregnancy itself is dangerous. It's not glamorous. It's not easy. And it's painful," she said, rubbing a hand over her stomach.

"How bad is it?"

"Well, there's the morning sickness that happens later on. The weight gain, the heartburn, the back pain, the hormones going haywire, for starters."

Daniel nodded, as she kept speaking.

"Not to mention, in the worst cases, having a husband who doesn't care or seem to understand. Or, in some poor areas of the country, they might not even have a father around to help take care of them at all, leaving a woman alone to fend for herself, all while dealing with the bullshit they carry from the relationship once it's over. Sometimes the bullshit they carry is a fetus."

Daniel put some more of the pieces together in his head. "And then, if a place isn't exactly in favor of abortion, a mother might have to resort to risky procedures to stay alive." He didn't ask Rebecca this, but he concluded it. "Have you ever been pregnant?" he asked her.

"I have. I didn't go all the way through with it, so I didn't get the worst of the pregnancy symptoms."

Daniel looked at her for a long while after she said that, wondering if he should ask his next question. He did it anyway. "And you aborted it?"

In a matter-of-fact way, Rebecca answered. "Hell yeah I did."

"Is there...uh...well, do you regret it all?" he trod carefully over his words. The subject wasn't one he ever spoke about with anyone he knew, much less anyone he knew on a personal and deep level.

"Good question," Rebecca said. She shifted to lie on her back again, and looked up at the ceiling, lost in thought. "No. Not 'regret' but more like wondering 'what if?' if that makes sense. Like, if I went through with it and had a kid, what would have happened?"

Realization crept within Daniel. "Right. You have school and you're passionate about it. And a parent wants to provide the best they can for their child."

"Exactly," she said. "Could I have been a good mother while doing grad school? Would I be able to afford both? If I sacrificed school and the potential for a good career, what kind of life would I have been able to give a baby? Or, who knows, it could have all worked out for the better. I could have had a baby, been a mom, a student, and been fine. There's a girl I was in a class with a while back who seemed to do fine as a mother in grad school."

"Wow," Daniel said. He hesitated again before talking more. "What happened to the father?"

Rebecca chuckled. "He was a coward. I told him I was pregnant, and he refused to believe it was his and accused me of cheating on him."

"Did you?" Daniel asked, before quickly adding. "No judgment if you did. I'm just curious. And I don't think—"

"It's fine. You don't have to over qualify your questions. But, no. I didn't. Even if I wanted to, practically, I wouldn't have had the time. School, work, him, and something resembling a social life."

"Yeah, that makes sense. So he just didn't wanna face it?" Daniel asked.

"Exactly. And can you believe that hypocrite? He was 'pro-life' as well."

Daniel mulled that over for a moment. "He was pro-life but abandoned you." Daniel considered the other implications. "That doesn't make sense."

"No, it doesn't make any ounce of sense. That's why I can laugh about it now. In psychology, we learned about this concept called cognitive dissonance. Basically, it's when you have two conflicting thoughts that clash with your beliefs and values."

"Like being pro-life but also fully willing to abandon lives when it suits you," Daniel chimed in.

"Yep," Rebecca said, "that's pretty much it. And, as terrible as he was, it's not his fault. We all have cognitive dissonances. When we realize them, that's when crises of faith happen. Or existential crises, if you're godless, like me."

"I never understood that about those types. It's none of their goddamn business, and it doesn't affect them at all."

"It's political. You've witnessed it firsthand," Rebecca said.

Daniel nodded his head in agreement and brought Rebecca's hand closer to him. "Whatever happens, I support your decision."

"Thank you," she said, squeezing his hand. "Just try not to come in my hair too much. It's a pain in the ass to get out."

Daniel laughed, and once it subsided, they fell asleep holding each other.

CHAPTER TWENTY-EIGHT

*E*arly in the morning, Daniel woke up to the sound of three quiet but sharp knocks on his door. He rubbed his eyes and looked over at Rebecca. The knocks hadn't disturbed her at all. She lay on her stomach, softly snoring as Daniel slid out of the bed to let her sleep some more.

Daniel crept to the door and opened it a crack.

"Put some clothes on and fix your hair up a bit. It's time for a photo op," Wayne whispered through the opening.

Daniel tilted his head, confused. "Huh?"

"You'll see when you get down here," Wayne said.

Daniel went to the bathroom to splash water on his face and brush his teeth. He ran a comb through his hair. As he looked in the mirror, he dragged his hand along the stubble bedecking his face but decided against shaving it. Not only did he not want to waste time, he sort of liked the look and figured he would keep it for a while longer, until he had to return to work. He grabbed his jeans and a white tee and made his way downstairs, finding Dorothy and Kevin in the kitchen sipping coffee at the table.

"Coffee's ready for you," Dorothy said, gesturing to the percolator on the counter.

Daniel thanked her, but otherwise didn't say much as he readied his coffee. He kept an eye on Kevin. Despite the passing of night, he looked slightly better than the miserable state he was in last night, as far as Daniel could tell.

But he didn't sleep much, and it showed. Once his coffee was ready, he finished it in under a minute.

"What's going on?" he asked everyone in the room.

"We got those tabloid people out there," Kevin said. "They wanna get a photo of the people who took down The Beast of Bladenboro." He didn't look anywhere in particular when he spoke, but he wasn't as out of it the way he was the night before. Daniel hoped it was the first step to a long road of grief.

"Tabloids?" Now Daniel was even more confused. He looked at Dorothy, who only offered a shrug as a response.

"All right, I guess," Daniel said. He looked at Kevin for a moment. "You doing all right?"

"About as much as I can, you know?"

Daniel nodded. "Well, let's head out and get this over with, then," he said.

Kevin stood up and pushed his chair in before he collected his and Daniel's coffee mugs and washed them out in the sink.

"You set those mugs down and let me take care of it," Dorothy said, heading over to the sink to oust Kevin from the position.

"I wouldn't dream of it, Mrs. Sutherland. Hospitality goes both ways, and I like to be a polite guest." He continued washing the mugs and rinsed them before he and Daniel set foot outside.

Wayne stood off to the side on his porch talking to a reporter with a notepad. Next to them, another with a camera looked on.

"Thanks, Sheriff Sutherland. We really appreciate you calling us and letting us know. Any chance you can show us the scene of the incidents, too?" he asked.

"Yeah, maybe, if I got the time later," he said, a little rushed.

Daniel expected more people, but after looking around, he realized they were the only two people there, besides Kevin, Wayne, and himself.

"All right," the reporter said, "let's get you all out in the yard for the photo."

By now, Daniel thought he had a sense of what was happening. If Wayne didn't want anyone to panic, he needed to tell the story properly. He and Kevin made their way down the few steps on the porch, and Wayne followed closely behind. The reporter and photographer stayed behind and talked for a moment, as they pointed to various spots in the yard, deciding where to get the best angle based on the sun's position. Eventually, they settled on having their backs to the sun, and the three men stood in front of them, with the barren road looming in the distance behind them.

The reporters posed them and took several snapshots of the trio before parting ways, leaving the three men standing on the front lawn of the Sutherland home.

"What was that all about?" Daniel asked, hoping to confirm his suspicion that Wayne set up a subterfuge to keep Amanda, and to an extent, Kevin protected, and keep their credibility intact.

"I'm sure you figured it out by now, but I suppose some of the finer details wouldn't hurt," Wayne said. "Deputy Hall, you know already, so I understand if you wanna go back in so as to avoid digging it all up again while it's so fresh."

Kevin waved the sheriff off. "I think I'll be okay."

"The way I figure it," Wayne began, "is that we'd get the weird portions of the story with the people who specialize in that type of thing. Let them continue on being crackpots with crazy theories. Nobody takes them seriously, and they don't have the readership to arouse any suspicion, anyway." Wayne started pacing back and forth during his monologue. "And that damn Johnson ain't gonna want any of this getting out, either. Same with Max Reavill, and while he's not the nature of a son of a bitch that Johnson is, the man needs his privacy. So does Max Junior, for that matter."

Daniel spoke up at the pause in Wayne's story. "Speaking of Max's son, how is he?"

"Oh, he's doing great. As great as anyone can after something like that. Max's gonna pick him up from the hospital either today or tomorrow. They gotta watch him for a while, but the doctors over there expect him to recover fully, they said." When Wayne spoke the good news, his lips curled into a small smile.

"Good," Daniel said. "What's the official story, then?"

"The official story in the books is that you helped us figure out what happened with the kids and surmised that it was an animal attack. And that animal got spooked, and we then found it and took care of it. Last night was a separate, but unfortunate, incident involving a couple falling out of love and not dealing with it in the best way." When Wayne mentioned that part, his face grew sullen, and he looked at Kevin. "Kevin, I'm sorry for your loss. As your boss, I'm telling you to take some time off. Go on a fishing trip. Maybe go on up to Lake Lure. Or Asheville. Something to clear your head."

Kevin scratched his head and looked up, thinking about it. "Yeah, I think that's a good idea," he said. "Hell, I might do it today."

Daniel could see inside of Kevin by now. Maybe leaving for a time would be nice so that he didn't have to start reassembling his entire life so soon.

"Good," Wayne said, before turning his attention to Daniel. "Son, you picked a hell of a time to get stranded here, but I can't thank you enough for the help." He shook hands with Daniel.

"Yeah, likewise," Kevin said, reaching his hand out to do the same. "You're a good man, and you got a good career ahead of you, too."

"Thanks. Both of you. For the hospitality, and everything else."

Kevin started shuffling the dirt and grass with his foot before he looked back at Wayne. "Boss, if it's all the same, I think I am gonna take off unless you need me for anything else."

"Consider it the start of your vacation. You'll find your house clean when you go back to pack."

"Thanks again, Daniel," Kevin said before he got in his car and drove away.

"You must have had a long night," Daniel said to Wayne after Kevin left.

"It was. Could've been longer, but it's amazing what people's guilt can do to them when they're part of a big mess like this," Wayne said.

"I take it you got the doctor to help?"

"Indeed, I did," Wayne said. "Lisa, from over at Big Jim's called, too. Car'll be ready around lunchtime, she said. In the meantime, you can go back to sleep for a couple hours. We'll feed you before we drop you off, too."

"I can use the sleep. We'll see you again shortly." Daniel went back upstairs and crawled into bed next to Rebecca, who hadn't moved since he left.

* * *

Two hours later, Rebecca stirred next to Daniel, waking him up. He didn't fall into a deep sleep because of the excitement of being able to make it to the wrestling match despite the past couple of days they had.

"You were snoring this morning. Did you sleep well?" he asked Rebecca.

"I did not!" she said before her mouth opened into a massive yawn. "And yes, I did."

"Did too. Also, Lisa the mechanic called, and the car should be ready around lunchtime," he said. "And the Sutherland's offered to feed us before we left, and I think we should take them up on it."

"You think I would turn down *any* of their food? It's so good," she said.

"Great minds think alike. And we'll get to make it to the wrestling match. I was getting a little worried," he said.

"I imagine this place being so out of the way, things come in late all the time," Rebecca said. She turned towards the door and sniffed. "I think they're starting lunch. We should go check it out."

They went downstairs and, as they got closer to the dining room, the overwhelming aroma of bacon and maple syrup wafted their way. In the dining room, the table was set, and the Sutherland's started bringing out dishes with the bacon, scrambled eggs, and pancakes with syrup on the side to go along with it.

Daniel grabbed two of the pancakes along with some heaping spoonfuls of eggs and a few slices of bacon and looked on in awe when Rebecca grabbed at least twice as many pancakes as he did, along with gratuitous eggs and some slices of bacon. She ate all of it, as did Daniel.

During their late breakfast, the excitement and adrenaline had worn off, and nobody said much. Then again, they didn't really need to. They all witnessed parts, if not all, of the preceding days' events. When breakfast was over, Daniel and Rebecca went back upstairs, packed their bags and showered, and the Sutherlands took them back to Jim's Gas and Go to pick up their car.

CHAPTER TWENTY-NINE

*L*isa and Little Jim greeted everyone as they all got out of the car.

"Sheriff Sutherland," Little Jim said, shaking the elder man's hand. "Mrs. Sutherland, good to see you again," and the two of them gave each other a light hug.

"Lisa," Wayne said, "I haven't seen you in a while. How are you?"

"I'm doing great," she said, "but you know how you can fix that?"

"How's that?" Wayne asked.

"Just damage your car more often and we'll be here to fix it," Lisa said, laughing.

Wayne joined in the laughter before he spoke again. "How's school going?" he asked her.

"It's going pretty great. My grades are good, and I'm just moving right along. Should be out of there next year," she said.

"You still planning to go to law school after that?" Dorothy asked.

"Yes, ma'am. And all the teachers say I'm on the right track for it. Some of them even said I got potential to be an excellent lawyer," Lisa said, smiling with pride.

"I can see it," Wayne said. "Don't let them tell you to stop talking with the southern accent, though."

"Why's that?" she asked. "They said it'll make them take me seriously. And think I'm smart."

Wayne waved his hand dismissively. "To hell with that. Let those city lawyers think what they want and blindside 'em with justice. It'll knock them down a peg, and you'll win all your cases."

"I like that. Thanks, Sheriff." She turned and looked at Rebecca. "Ma'am, your car's all set. It was taking seven forevers and a day to get a radiator shipped out this way, so Little Jim and I went over to the next town and found a junkyard. So, it's used. I hope that's okay."

Rebecca thought for a minute. "Is it in good condition, at least?"

"Oh yeah, it should last you a while. Doesn't look like it's seen much wear and tear. Of course, we're gonna knock off a decent amount on the price on account of it being used and everything. We just wanted to make sure we got you out on the road in time so you didn't wind up stuck here."

"Well," Daniel said, "I imagine there are worse places to be stuck," he said as he looked at the great company he and Rebecca had the past couple of days.

"Yeah, the Sheriff is all right in my book," Little Jim said. "Let's get you inside where it's cooler, and get this all settled, and y'all can be on your way."

Everyone made their way to the office where Lisa went in and printed out a receipt for the services rendered on the Oldsmobile. "And if it gives you any problems, let us know. We'll replace it for you."

"Thank you," Rebecca said, shaking Lisa's hand.

Daniel nodded his thanks at the mechanics and turned to head back to the Oldsmobile.

"Little Jim, Lisa," Wayne called back, "we'll head back in and catch up with you here in a bit, Dorothy and I are gonna walk them out to the car."

When they all got to the Oldsmobile, Daniel loaded their bags into the trunk and stood next to Rebecca, facing the Sutherlands, waiting for the words to form. "Well, son," Wayne said. "I guess this is it. Don't be a stranger." He turned to Rebecca. "Make sure y'all invite us to the wedding, too."

When he said that, Rebecca's cheeks reddened, and Daniel let out a small laugh.

"Before you go, I wanna give you something," Wayne said. "Wait here just a second." He turned and went to his car, leaving Dorothy with the young couple.

"And it goes without saying, you're welcome back anytime," Dorothy said.

"Thank you," Daniel said. "It's worth it for your cooking alone."

She beamed at the compliment. "It's just one of those things that gets better over time."

Wayne walked back to the car, with a rectangular box over three feet long and a foot and a half wide. "I want you to take this. As a gift for the hard work you didn't have to do, and because I think it suits you." He handed it to Daniel.

Daniel set it on the trunk of the Oldsmobile and opened the case. Inside was the Mossberg 500 Wayne had him carrying throughout his stay. "Wow," Daniel exclaimed. "Thank you."

"And you don't wanna leave without some of these, either." Wayne extended two twenty-five boxes of shotgun shells towards him, which he grabbed.

"You sure you wanna give me a gun this nice?" Daniel asked.

"Well, I already did, didn't I?" Wayne asked, chuckling. "It's yours. I hope it serves you well." He grabbed Daniel's hand, and pulled him in for a hug, and the two men embraced. "Y'all take care out there."

Dorothy hugged Daniel, and Rebecca joined in the goodbyes, until the Sutherlands headed back to their car and left for their home. Shortly after, Daniel and Rebecca left Middlesboro for Greensboro.

CHAPTER THIRTY

$\mathcal{T}$hree hours later, Daniel and Rebecca arrived in Greensboro, several days later than planned, but still in time for The Great American Bash, and the championship match between Ric Flair and Dusty Rhodes. They pulled into the parking lot of Tom and Christina's hotel and made their way up to the room, hoping to surprise them.

Daniel rapped on the door twice and raised the pitch and timbre of his voice. "Room service," he said.

"Did you order room service?" Tom asked, his voice muffled by the closed door.

"Babe," Christina replied, equally muffled, "This is a Best Western. They don't have room service."

Daniel knocked again.

"Hold on!" Tom called.

From inside, Daniel heard rustling fabric and the clink of a belt closing, followed by steps coming closer to him.

"What is it?" The door opened, and Tom looked out and saw Daniel and Rebecca standing there, and his frown morphed into an enormous grin. "Glad you can finally make it." Tom closed the door a bit and looked back in. "Put some clothes on. Our friends are here." A few minutes later, Tom led Daniel and Rebecca inside.

Inside, Daniel set their things on the floor and looked around at the decent sized room with its two beds. "I can't believe you thought this place would have room service," Daniel said.

"Yeah, well, maybe that fake voice of yours fooled me for half a minute," Tom said. "Now that you're here, we can finally grab something to eat before we head out to the arena later."

"Yeah, that's not a bad idea. But I have a better one," Daniel said.

"What's that?" Tom asked.

"Why don't the four of us head over to a bar and chat for a bit and work up an appetite before we eat?" he asked. "Rebecca and I had a hearty meal before we left Middlesboro." Daniel paused for a moment. "By the way, Rebecca, this is Tom and Christina. Tom and Christina, Rebecca Church, PhD candidate and soon to be Dr. Church."

"It's nice to meet you," Tom said, shaking Rebecca's hand. "I think we can do that. Chris, you on board with that idea?" Tom then leaned over to Daniel and whispered, albeit loudly, "We worked up an appetite while you two were driving here."

Daniel, with no qualms about keeping his voice the same volume as it had been, said, "Ah, you two have been doing it, I take it."

"Yes, smartass," Tom said, lightly punching his friend on the shoulder.

* * *

HALF AN HOUR LATER, they'd arrived on foot at a nearby dive bar and ordered drinks they took to a booth to get some privacy in their conversation.

"What in the hell happened down there that kept you so long?" Tom asked.

"First, this one," Daniel said, pointing his thumb at Rebecca, "insisted that we take her Oldsmobile instead of the heavy Chevy, and it started off a series of chain reactions that led us getting stuck in a pretty small town right off the highway."

"I *suggested* it because of the leg room," Rebecca said. "That truck can barely fit you. How would it fit the both of us?"

Tom and Christina laughed at her reply. Christina looked at Rebecca and Daniel. "She has a point, Daniel. You both are like redwood trees. Tom and I are more like a fern."

"So, she says it's the leg room, and that's fine. You just know how I am about driving. I trust the Chevy. It'll be a classic someday. A legacy vehicle, *if you will*," Daniel said, inflecting his last sentence the same way Dusty Rhodes did in his interviews.

"Yeah, a legacy at the junkyard," Tom said.

"Anyways, we decided to take the Oldsmobile, and we get a couple hours away, and I start to smell the smoke. Damn thing overheats, cracks the radiator." Daniel went on, regaling them with the details of the car repair, and meeting Sheriff Sutherland and Deputy Hall.

"You mean a real life small-town sheriff? You got to meet one? What was it like?" Tom asked. "Was it like in the movies?"

"Kind of. He kind of *is* the law, and it's a small town, so they really only need the two of them for everything. It's a lot different than it is in Savannah, that's for sure." Daniel paused and looked at the table and tapped his finger on the shiny wooden top. "There was more, too."

"What do you mean by that?" Tom asked. "You sound a little hesitant to mention it."

Daniel glanced at Rebecca and then back to Tom, deciding whether to mention the entire truth behind the missing kids, or keep it with Wayne's "official" report. His credibility and the world's incredulity won, so he touched on Amanda's death and left out the involvement of demons as he told the rest of the story to his companions.

When he finished, Rebecca side eyed him, and changed the subject. "Christina, do you compete?"

"Not yet," she said, "but I'm planning on doing some bodybuilding shows."

"I can tell. You have amazing quads," Rebecca said.

"Thanks. You look like you lift yourself. Don't think I didn't see those shoulders peaking at us," Christina said.

"I do, sometimes. Not like at your level, or anything, but I like to go when I can."

"I'm always up for a gym buddy. Especially if it means we get to show these dudes a thing or two," Christina said, prompting Rebecca into laughter.

"Consider it done," Rebecca said.

"All right, y'all ready to eat, now?" Tom asked.

Daniel searched Rebecca's face, guessing what she might want to do, then turned to Tom. "You all right with us going back to the room while you go to eat? The beer made me tired, and I could use a nap. Rebecca, would you be opposed to that?"

"Not at all," she said. "I wanna be fresh for the bash."

"How about Tom and I go off for a bit, and we just come and get you when it's time to get to the arena?" Christina asked.

"Works for me," Daniel said.

. . .

BACK IN THE HOTEL ROOM, Daniel and Rebecca curled up on the comically undersized bed in the hotel room and held each other as they enjoyed a respite from everything.

"Sometimes, I wish I was pint-sized like Tom. Must be nice to lie out wherever you please and still have room to spare," Daniel said.

"Yeah, tell me about it. It's bad enough buying women's clothes, but at this height, it's a downright pain in the ass." She turned and looked at Daniel. "But you know what?"

"What?"

"At least you can reach the cookie jar for him."

Daniel smiled and kissed her.

"You didn't tell him about the demon monster," Rebecca said.

"I was scared," he said.

"Scared? Of what? You and I lived it. *That* is scary."

"What if he didn't believe it and started distancing himself from me and didn't wanna be my friend anymore?" Daniel asked.

"I doubt that would happen," Rebecca said, squeezing his hand. "He might think you're a little weird, but we all do anyway. I think he'd hear you out."

"Maybe." He thought about it some more. "I'll tell him eventually, I think."

The two of them napped until showtime.

CHAPTER THIRTY-ONE

$\mathcal{W}$ hen twilight fell, Daniel and Rebecca woke up to the sound of the room door opening. Daniel rubbed his eyes as Tom and Christina walked in and sat on their bed.

"Good morning, sleepyheads," Tom said. "Ready to head to the match?"

"You're damn right I am," Daniel said.

He and Rebecca readied themselves quickly, and they all piled into the Oldsmobile since it had room enough for the four of them. They hadn't been driving for any significant length of time when they stopped. The air conditioner in the Oldsmobile did little to remedy the heat piercing its way into the car, but nobody cared.

The palpable energy inside the car mingled with everyone else on the way to the arena. People cheered at each other on the road. Others bellowed the Ric Flair "woo" from out their windows and from the beds of their pickup trucks. More of them drank beers while they drove and passed cold cans from the coolers to other motorists. Cars on the highway headed towards the arena were backed up for miles; everyone wanted to see Ric Flair defend his title against Dusty Rhodes.

After over an hour of slogging through the Greensboro traffic, the quartet finally found their seats amongst the fifteen thousand other patrons in attendance. Luckily, they came in about halfway through the show. The collective presence and energy of the crowd, along with dozens of gallons of alcohol, cheap food, and collective cheering overpowered Daniel, and he couldn't help smiling the whole time, like a child in awe at a carnival.

Match by match and wrestler by wrestler, the ring in the center of the arena showed visible signs of the night's wear and tear, as blood, sweat, and the occasional cup of beer decorated the canvas mat. Each match grew in intensity, spectacle, and aptitude of the wrestlers, culminating in the penultimate match of the night. The crew of workers set up the chain link steel cage over the ring for the next one and the fans that didn't take a trip to the concession stand or the restroom stayed behind cheering.

"You look a million times better than you did earlier today," Tom said, cupping a hand over Daniel's ear to drown out the peripheral crowd noise.

"I feel better, too," Daniel said.

Tom took a half step back and pointed at Daniel's shirt with a confused look. "What's that?" he asked.

Daniel looked down at his shirt and saw nothing. When he lifted his head again, Tom slapped him in the chest with a deafening smack followed by a loud taunt in imitation of Ric Flair. Since he towered over Tom, it didn't take Daniel long to close the distance and lift his friend up onto his back and form the human version of the letter T. After he hoisted Tom, he caught Christina and Rebecca rolling their eyes.

"Boys, right?" Christina said to Rebecca, who shook her head with a smile.

Daniel promptly set Tom back down on his feet, as the empty seats began to fill again, and the collective buzz grew even louder. When the ring announcer came out and announced the next match, the audience, as if on cue, booed when the tag team champions, the bad guys known as the Midnight Express, came out and their manager introduced them individually. The jeering increased in volume when the announcer mentioned their manager, Jim Cornette, would be a tag team partner in the match. In the ring, Cornette played to the crowd and made them hate him.

In a mood reversal, the crowd roared ecstatically when he announced the challengers, the Road Warriors, decked out in spikes and leather along with their face paint, and their guest tag team partner for the night, Baby Doll.

Once he introduced them, Cornette whipped the crowd up again by taking the microphone, addressing Baby Doll as a fat pig, and challenging her to wrestle right away. The chorus of booing nearly drowned out the manager's harsh words wrapped in a Southern accent.

During the match, the forces of good and evil battled, each one struggling for the upper hand until Jim Cornette tried to make his escape. Baby Doll grabbed him from the cage as he climbed, pulling him down into the ring, and when he stood, she socked him in the face, drawing a large round of cheering from the crowd, including Christina and Rebecca, cheering right in Daniel's ear. Baby Doll pinned Cornette for the win.

The cage stayed assembled for the final match, the match that pit Ric Flair against Dusty Rhodes, for the world championship title. The crowd fell into their roles, as good faced evil again for the victory and golden prize at the end. They booed when Flair acted the coward and cheated, and cheered when Rhodes nailed him with his patented bionic elbow. Daniel sighed and smiled wistfully, knowing that after this weekend, concepts like good and evil were far more nebulous than they had been days before.

"Yunnastand, baby, big Dusty gonna win that title tonight," Tom said in Daniel's ear in his best Dusty Rhodes impression.

Immediately after he said that, Flair jammed Rhodes's head into the steel cage. After showboating, Flair grabbed Rhodes and did it again, drawing a chorale of boos from the crowd along with blood on Rhodes's face.

"I wouldn't be too sure," Daniel said, "Flair's killing him right now."

"It ain't ova, baby," Tom said again in his Dusty voice.

And it wasn't. Flair chopped Rhodes in the chest, the impact heard throughout the arena and had him against the ropes. In a stunning reversal, Rhodes bounded from the ropes and knocked Flair to the ground, but just escaped winning the match by missing the three count when he pinned Flair. In his quest for vengeance, Rhodes paid Flair back and grabbed a lock of the blond hair and rubbed it into the cage, drawing blood on Ric Flair's once clear face.

Not long after, Rhodes took Flair's finishing move and trapped him in it, leading to an escape, followed by Rhodes delivering a barrage of chops to Ric Flair's chest.

Beleaguered, Flair slowly stepped away from the corner of the ring and face-planted onto the ground.

In the culmination of this match, the entire arena gasped when Ric Flair went to body slam Dusty Rhodes, only to have Dusty reverse the slam into a pinfall and win the championship belt. The resultant roar of the crowd shook the arena, and Daniel, Tom, Rebecca, and Christina, all cheered along with them.

Following that, all the "good guys" came out to congratulate Dusty on his win, and help the new champion celebrate, leaving Ric Flair in the corner of the ring, alone and dejected. The four of them made a quick exit from the arena during the celebration and piled back into the Oldsmobile afterwards and sat amidst the quiet for a few minutes as the energy from the spectacle dissipated.

"Sort of reminds me of how last year, all the bad guys came and congratulated Flair for winning," Rebecca said from the passenger seat.

"You went last year?" Tom asked, surprised.

"Of course I did. It was in Flair's hometown. You know it had to be good."

"Danny said you were a fan, all right. This was our first time," Tom said.

"How'd you like it?" Daniel asked.

"I wanna go back and see another one," Christina said.

"Me, too," Tom echoed.

"All right," Rebecca said, "you ready to head back?"

Everyone agreed they were ready to head back to the hotel room, so after waiting a few more minutes for the cars and traffic to dissipate, the four of them pulled out of the parking lot on the way back to the Best Western. Rebecca steered the Oldsmobile onto the highway, and after a few miles of driving, pulled off and found their way to the hotel parking lot.

Daniel was the first to step out of the car. He went to the driver's side and opened Rebecca's door for her, and the two of them waited for Tom and Christina. Once they closed the doors to the Oldsmobile, something sounded in the distance. It started as a low rumble, and the noise crescendoed, drawing closer to them by the second.

"What the hell is that noise?" Rebecca asked.

Daniel's stomach churned, his palms perspiring as it dawned on him. "Motorcycles." Not a moment after he said that, dotted headlights greeted him.

CHAPTER THIRTY-TWO

*D*aniel looked on in slack-jawed amazement as the bikes pulled into the parking lot of the hotel followed by a memorable shit-brown colored 1980 Pontiac at the tail of the caravan. The Pontiac pulled in last and immediately blocked the exit of the parking lot when it turned sharply to the right, in the worst parking job anyone had ever seen.

"Daniel," Rebecca whispered, trembling as she grabbed his arm. "What the hell is going on?"

Her voice snapped him out of his momentary trance. "My partner's here with a biker gang and he's pissed. Put your keys in my back pocket and get ready to run."

Rebecca inched closer to him, and slid the Oldsmobile keys into Daniel's back pocket, as Tom and Christina moved forward to join them, all eyes on the bikers and the Pontiac.

"Daniel, please tell me you're armed," Tom said in a low voice.

"Twelve gauge in the trunk. You?" Daniel spoke but kept his gaze forward.

"Forty-five," Tom said. "In the car."

Daniel moved only his eyes towards Tom's Nova at the end of the parking lot, knowing if either of them made a break for it, they would be dead in seconds. He scanned the area and saw no way out. "God dammit," he said under his breath.

Everyone on their vehicles shut off their motors, and from the Pontiac emerged Shawn, in his paunchy glory. He casually sauntered over to Daniel and his companions with a victorious smile on his face that somehow looked even more out of place the closer he got to Daniel.

Daniel moved forward, away from Rebecca, to meet him face to face. He took note that the bikers hadn't pulled their shotguns from their holsters as of yet, but once they did, any ensuing fight would be far from fair.

"Well, you two-faced piece of shit, here I am. This is your chance to get rid of me," Shawn said, spreading his arms out to the side. "You can blame your friend, by the way. He was so excited for his Greensboro trip he told everyone in his precinct about it and practically did all the legwork for me."

Daniel readied himself to throw a right cross at Shawn, but Shawn held a finger up as he did, and the bikers all drew their guns the moment they had the signal. In addition to the visible shotguns, they had handguns that he hadn't noticed. Daniel stayed still as Shawn slowly drew out his revolver and pointed it at Daniel's heart.

To everyone's surprise, Christina walked forward, her hands up. "Uncle Al?" she asked, looking at the biker at the forefront. "Uncle Al, what the hell are you doing here?"

The bikers glanced at Christina as they kept their weapons trained on Daniel.

"Babe, don't," Tom whispered, "you're gonna get us killed."

"No wonder the family never liked you," she said to Uncle Al. "No wonder your wife left you. Probably the smartest thing she ever did."

Uncle Al tilted his head, like a confused dog towards his niece. "You might wanna think about leaving," he said, "this don't concern you." After a pause, he lifted his lips into a grim smile. "Be a shame to have to tell everyone how you died snooping around instead of minding your fucking business."

As the two family members spoke, Daniel felt a hand reach into his back pocket, removing the set of keys there.

"Enough!" Shawn screamed. "Al, why didn't you tell me your family would be here, too?"

"How the fuck was I supposed to know?" Allan answered.

"Nobody told me my derelict uncle would be here, either. But here we are," Christina said, eying her uncle.

Uncle Al's smile dropped, and he lowered his weapon a bit. "Seriously, kid, get the hell out of here."

"No, I think everyone needs to stay where they are," Shawn yelled over the low rumble of American steel and exhaust. He looked over towards the bikers one more time before he addressed Daniel. "You—"

Daniel smacked the revolver out of Shawn's hand, letting it fall to the asphalt of the parking lot, allowing Daniel to slide it behind him with his foot. Once Shawn's weapon was gone, Daniel yanked on the right arm, spinning Shawn around, and pulled his partner close to him with a forearm wrapped around his neck nearly at the point where it would cut off his circulation.

"This is your chance to go," Daniel said to the bikers. He kept his head close to Shawn in the event any of the others wanted to take a chance and shoot him in the head.

The bikers laughed at him, and in the chorus of laughter, two shots rang out. After the second one, Daniel felt cold and a searing pain all in his highly exposed left leg. He fell to the ground more shots rang out, pelting cars, gravel, and who knows what. Daniel looked to where he thought Shawn's gun fell but couldn't see it. Even if he did, the sudden weight on top of him wouldn't let him get to it.

After the first fist to his face, Daniel rolled onto his back, despite Shawn's weight bearing down on him. He put his hands up to protect himself, as the fists crashed into them. By the time he covered his face, his forearms were bruised from the blunt force hitting them. It was then he felt a constant and repetitive stabbing in the newly minted bullet wounds in his thigh. He looked, and Shawn was pressing his thumb into the wound, and every increase of pressure sent a sharp, searing pain throughout Daniel's body.

In his periphery, he saw the trunk of the Oldsmobile open, amidst the gunfire, and heard the report of a round fired off close to him. He could only hope his companions knew what they were doing. And that Rebecca would live. Through all that, doors opened, and people nearby added to the cacophony with their gasps and murmurs, and various demands that someone call the police. Meanwhile, Daniel curled up into a ball to protect himself as Shawn rained down the blows.

"You cost me my job, you son of a bitch," Shawn spat into Daniel's ear before landing a punch to his ribs. "And my retirement plan," he said, followed by a punch to an open spot on his face.

Another bullet fired next to Daniel.

More shots rang out from the biker side. Daniel couldn't keep track of their ammo. They'd have to run out eventually, right?

Shawn pummeled Daniel, and throughout it, he tried to buck his partner off of him to gain some sort of advantage. Every increased ounce of pressure he put on his left leg ripped through his body with blinding pain as he lay, trapped. Every time he moved, pain stopped him, leaving him only able to feebly push himself away.

As Daniel grew colder, time slowed down, and he saw what was going on.

Two bikers on the ground and the other two looking around behind and beneath the cars in the lot, Christina and Rebecca were nowhere to be seen. Or Tom, for that matter.

Daniel spit out a mouthful of blood into Shawn's face in a pathetic attempt to blind him but failed. Shawn wiped some of Daniel's blood off and used the same hand to slap him in the face, painting Daniel with his own blood. In the distance, someone shouted "Fire!" from a hotel room, and Daniel felt the heat as the flames erupted within the interior of the shitty Pontiac.

Confusion filled him when he looked to the left. John Moore's ghost stood next to him, looking down on Daniel's carnage. A blast of cold swept over Daniel. Shawn finally noticed the ghost, and the color fled from his face.

"What?" Shawn said, dumbfounded.

John Moore's ghost smiled at Daniel before it evaporated, leaving both Daniel and Shawn stunned. Daniel couldn't push himself anymore and closed his eyes in the hopes he'd have a reprieve. In that moment, the familiar sound of the Mossberg cracked, and half of Shawn's head, rendered in chunks of brain, blood, and bone, flew to his left, splattering the asphalt next to them. Shawn's headless corpse slumped unceremoniously on top of Daniel.

When he looked up for the last time that day, he saw Rebecca covered in sweat, a few scrapes on her arm, and her hair looking like several bird's nests entangled holding the Mossberg and pointing it at the area where Shawn's head once occupied. He saw the smoke from the barrel, smelled the gunpowder, and rested his head before everything else stopped and faded to black.

CHAPTER THIRTY-THREE

Beep. When Daniel opened his eyes, the light above him blinded him. *Beep.* The surface on which his back rested was softer and more forgiving than the asphalt of the parking lot he last remembered. *Beep.* Frightened, he looked to his left and right, and saw the lines of the heart monitor as it beeped again.

Shortly after, Rebecca, Tom, and Christina walked into the room.

"Danny, you look like hell, man," Tom said. "Your face, especially."

Daniel smiled, and the bruising and swelling on his face pained him as he did so. "It's nice to see you, too," he said. "What the fuck happened? How did I get here? Was there a fire?"

"You bet there was," Tom said. "I figured you could get Shawn out of the way if I distracted everyone else, so when his gun fell, I grabbed it. It was a six shooter, so I had to be careful, but I got two of those assholes right where they stood."

"I went to the car and grabbed Tom's forty-five," Christina said. "Got one of the others in the knee, and the genius over here somehow managed to light your partner's car on fire."

"I guess he got tired of the shit color. He had a thing of paint samples and an owner's manual. Set those on fire, and the car went up with it. I asked the fire crew why cars don't explode. He told me I watch too many movies, because apparently that doesn't happen."

"And I knew you wouldn't get to the trunk soon, so I got my keys back and waited to grab that and took care of that asshole on top of you," Rebecca said.

Tom didn't let any silence linger for too long. "Witnesses were talking about another guy disappearing. Like not running away but vanishing. Thin air, and all that."

Daniel flashed back to the image of John Moore's ghost next to him as he lay on that asphalt. The gust of icy wind, the smile, and the departure. He had set it up and Rebecca took the shot. "Can I talk to Rebecca for a minute?"

"Oh, yeah," Tom said, "the doctor said you need to rest anyway and I'm going off a mile a minute here. We'll check back in with you soon."

Tom and Christina cleared the room, leaving Rebecca looking over Daniel.

"That was a ghost, wasn't it?" It was a question, but her tone indicated she already knew the answer.

Daniel nodded his head. "Are you okay?"

"Full of adrenaline, and I got some scrapes. Other than that, yeah. They were after you more than anything else."

"You killed a man for me," Daniel said. "Thank you."

"You would have done the same for me. We could've all been dead." She reached over and stroked his hair. "I'll probably need therapy because of the trauma," she said.

"I'm glad you all made it," Daniel said. He tried to raise his arms to hug her, but the pain was too much. Instead, she leaned over and kissed him on the forehead.

"Get some rest. The doctor said you should be free to go tomorrow."

"How bad was I hit?" he asked.

"One was a clean shot that went right through. The other wasn't bad, but the bullet lodged into your thigh. Christina got the bullet out while we waited for medics."

"She's a lifesaver," Daniel said.

"I'm gonna let you rest, but I'll be back for you tomorrow," Rebecca said.

"Make sure you get some rest, too," he said.

"I will. I think Tom will get the best sleep of us all since the hotel offered to comp the room." Rebecca smiled at him.

Daniel laughed, despite the pain that ebbed and flowed as he shook with the movement. "Sounds like him, all right. Sleep tight." He admired Rebecca as she walked out of the room, thankful that she was in his life. Somehow, she wanted to stick around, despite all the action of the previous days.

"That was a close one," a voice nearby said.

Daniel looked at a chair to his right, and sitting in it was John Moore's ghost. "I think you helped my odds," he told the ghost.

"Your former partner was an asshole," John's ghost said. "I did the world a favor."

"But we never did any for you," Daniel said. "Why?"

"Time works differently when you die. When you're wherever I am. There's no past, really, and no future. It's all lumped together. I can tell you, with certainty, yours is interesting. You can do a lot of good. It won't seem," the ghost paused, searching for words. "It won't seem meaningful, but doing something can make a big deal. And when I needed help, guess which of the two of you cared?"

Daniel looked at John Moore's ghost for a while, perplexed.

"Goodbye, Daniel. For good, this time." Instead of disappearing like he did before, the specter walked through the door of the room, and Daniel never saw him again.

* * *

THE NEXT DAY, Rebecca drove Daniel back to his place in Savannah, with Tom and Christina following. He could stand on his own but walked with a cane while his injuries healed. Captain Wilcox suspended him with pay because of everything that went on, though Daniel thought he seemed impressed with his accomplishments. He later found out that Sheriff Wayne Sutherland had a hand in that since he sent Captain Wilcox a glowing letter of commendation for Daniel's strategy and bravery in the line of duty as an authorized deputy in Middlesboro. It was likely that letter that cleared Daniel of any wrongdoing throughout his brief visit to North Carolina after Internal Affairs looked into it.

On Thursday evening following the incident, Daniel lay on the floor in the living room, doing some light physical therapy for his leg, when a knock interrupted him. He braced himself with the coffee table and pulled himself up, with far less pain than he had in the previous days. He grabbed his cane and limped to the door.

"Belascoe, I heard you limping to the door. Open up."

Daniel smiled and opened the door to see Detective Martin and Sofía standing there. "What are you guys doing here?" he asked.

Sofía moved into his full view, holding a box of half a dozen doughnuts from Daniel's favorite place, with a cup of coffee perched on top of it. "Holly says you could use some of these. There're only five doughnuts left, though. We split one on the way over."

Daniel looked over at Detective Martin, who only offered a shrug, and he motioned for them to come in.

"Christ, Belascoe, you're healing up nicely," Detective Martin said as she sat down next to Sofía on Daniel's couch. "Apparently, you did some good police work, too. All without getting paid."

"Yeah," Daniel grunted as he limped towards the arm opposite of his two guests and sat upon it. "I was the one who paid."

Detective Martin sighed. "We all do. One way or another." She grabbed Sofía's hand. "That little bit you and I did help the feds, so if you see a newspaper headline about a bust and the Savannah Swamp Demons going down, you know why. Apparently, after Ryerson arrested Andrew, he made a deal with him. Sort of like having his own personal informant and mule, and they used it to take out the competition."

Daniel thought back to the night when he broke into the crime scene only for Shawn to find his way in not long after. Finally, his suspicions were confirmed. "Thanks, Detective. What's it like back at the station?" he asked.

"Business as usual, mostly. Some people are pissed at you, though."

"What for? I did them a favor." Daniel scoffed indignantly.

"You went after one of your own. Some don't look too highly on that. I'll keep a lookout for anything suspicious in the meantime. For now, get your rest, and I'll see you in no time back at the station."

"Thanks, Detective."

Daniel saw them to the door but stopped them just before they left.

"Can you do me a favor?" he asked. "Can you grab my mail before you go? I would do it..." he said, holding up the cane and pointing at it.

"Yeah, I can get your mail." She went to the mailbox and back and handed him a thick stack of envelopes. "Take care, Belascoe."

"You too," Daniel said before he shut the door. He went to his couch to sort through it all. There wasn't anything of interest, save a manilla envelope with a Middlesboro return address. As he opened it, his phone rang, interrupting him. "Dammit," he said, getting off the couch.

On the fourth ring, he made it to the phone and picked it up.

"Hello?" he said.

"Hey," Rebecca said from the other end. "How ya feeling?"

"Not bad, all things considered. Better, now that I'm talking to you."

Rebecca giggled on the other end. "Nacha invited us to dinner later on in August. Some archeological thing."

"So, we eat food and look at clay pots?" Daniel asked.

"Something like that. She said there's a book there she wants to see called *The Book of Enoch*. Really old, and supposedly this copy is one of the oldest ones in existence. I dunno, it might be fun. We can even dress up."

"Yeah, that should be fun. And it doesn't sound overly exciting, which is good news for me," Daniel said.

"I thought so too. If you're up for it, do you want some company tonight? This weekend I need to finish my thesis so I can prepare to defend it, so I wanted to get some time with you while we *both* have the time."

Daniel smiled. "I would love that. Bring Bentley, too."

"See you soon," she said, before adding, "I love you."

Stunned, he replied, "I love you, too." And he meant it.

When he finally sat back to read his mail, he grabbed the manila envelope and opened it. He pulled out a letter addressed to him from Wayne. Along with it, a newspaper from a cheaply made news rag called *The Middlesboro Gazette*. The headline read "Bladenboro Beast is Beat!" The sub-header said, "Off-Duty Officer and Hero Solves One of North Carolina's Biggest Mysteries." Daniel shook his head with a smile and tossed the paper on his coffee table before reading Wayne's letter while he waited for Rebecca.

ACKNOWLEDGMENTS

Here we are again. The end of the road. Or, this road, rather, since I don't see the well drying anytime soon for Bethany, Daniel, or their friends, lovers, and associates. Part of that is your fault. You read Rain City Gothic, and you liked it. That said, I hope you told your friends, and I hope that you all left reviews on Goodreads, and anywhere else you can. Believe it or not, those things matter, and I want the world to read about these characters. You love them, make it happen. Thanks in advance.

I started writing this in 2020, and things in the United States were…different. Things the characters said back then suddenly became more prescient in the middle of 2022. If you look at the laws restricting abortion in the south, you'll notice a few things, a few of which I'll share with you. Where overall poverty is high, child poverty is high. Not only that, abortion access is low. Quality of sex education varies in the United States, but in those states where poverty is high and abortion access is low, there's a noticeable lack of good sex education. And that's in the south. In states like Georgia, Louisiana, or my home state of Florida. Besides the lack of resources, accessibility of abortion not only refers to the lack of physical places to go but also the barbarous and dictatorial nature of the laws themselves. So, be a pal. Donate to the National Network of Abortion Funds at abortionfunds.org.

Once again, my eternal gratitude goes to Kelsey, one of my editors. She knows Bethany and Daniel better than I do. Not only that, but Emmie Hamilton, the other editor who made this book readable and who kept me from using the same words ad nauseam.

Early readers, Maddi and Fern. You both are great, and the early feedback helped me make something worth sending off to Kelsey. Not to mention all three of you are uniquely gifted and adept in your own writings. Having said that, hurry up and publish something (said with love).

In a category of her own, author Gillian Dowell. She's a fellow indie author, and has done nothing specific to garner my thanks, aside from writing some of the most brilliant prose I've read in a while. That alone is inspiration to keep going and to continue honing the writing skill.

Over the years that the Belascoe's have existed, there were other people who helped them come alive during the halcyon days of tabletop gaming. As adults leave their twenties, things happen. Families form. Some of them end. Still, some of them change shape and context, and where you once fit, you no longer do. And when those circles break and meet their end, it's sometimes bittersweet. Sometimes it's acrimonious. For those once longtime connections that fall into the latter category and helped bring Bethany and Daniel to life, you have my thanks, too. We might never find our way back to each other, and that's okay. With love, I fondly remember the best of our time together. Come whatever may, I hope to see all of you here again.

COMING ATTRACTIONS

Bethany, Meghan, and Caroline will return in book three.

ALSO BY PETER D. BAKER

Rain City Gothic

Printed in the USA
CPSIA information can be obtained
at www.ICGtesting.com
LVHW090831271023
762280LV00010B/219

9 798985 661958